Reviewing Robert T. Chambers'

"Kimberly"

"It's Outstanding: an insightful look into a Naval Career"

Major General William P. Bowden, USAF retired, Oklahoma City

"Kimberly illustrates triumph over tragedy through resilience, perseverance and tenacity. A gentle reminder that overcoming adversity is possible."

Tammy Goerger, teacher, Wahpeton, ND Public Schools

"Kimberly" is an enjoyable, absorbing read. I found myself caring about the welfare of the main character, Kimberly, and I really appreciate that the book contains a lot of interesting US Navy and historical information. I recommend giving it a read.

Scott Thorsteinson, Chief of Police, Wahpeton, ND

"Kimberly knew from the first attack what she needed to do in life to help her country. She is a true hero. Kimberly is the type of person I would want on my side! Great Book, I enjoyed it!

Rick Fiedler, Sheriff, Wilkin County, MN

"Dr. Chambers' second military heroine novel is a fast-moving, compelling story of a smart, independent, strong woman who sets her sights high and gets what she goes after. The characters are presented in a way that they quickly become authentic to the reader, and every scene is very visible in the mind's eye. He has outdone his first novel, "Hidden Wounds," which was also a thriller, and his readers will anxiously await his next work!"

Dr. Robert Zarrett, retired trauma surgeon. Bemidji, MN

"The story of Kimberly, the female warrior, reminds me of the many women who fought for our freedoms such as those who built the Liberty ships during WW II. My mother was one of them. I highly recommend this book!"

Ed Warner, CEO Nelson Williams Linings, Inc., Mountain Iron, MN

KIMBERLY

Robert T. Chambers

Ed,
Thanks for your help
with This.
Robert T. Chambers.

Connelly Publishing

Connelly Publishing
1952 300th Street
Breckenridge, MN
USA

Acknowledgments

SEAL Team 5 member IS3 Shaun Page, discharged due to injury, was an invaluable help in getting specifically the SEAL and, more generally, the U.S. Navy information correct. Thanks also to Grand Master Eric Greenquist of the Greenquist Academy for his help with the martial arts. Menah Khodair was a great help with the Arabic language and culture.

This manuscript was written before "Hidden Wounds" but had multiple problems in the early chapters. Beta-reader Susie Palmer rescued it by suggesting moving the timeline up. Aside from all her other detailed editing, structure and content editor Barbara Leclerc convinced me to get rid of chapters 2 through 5. I had no clue what to do with that backstory until, while on a bus one evening near Lucerne, Switzerland, it occurred me to condense it into a conversation on a destroyer. Beth Althoff, very much a detail person, was great assistance as the copy editor. Tammy Goerger was to read a pre-release copy for comment. Her teacher persona arrived, thus, she did a lot of editing and commented which is immensely appreciated. The cover was created by artist, designer, illustrator, and graphic designer Julie Rettig (www.julierettig.com).

Paperback   ISBN: 978-1-7348073-0-1

e-edition   ISBN: 978-1-7348073-1-8

Attribution for cover photograph of the LCS USS Freedom: United States Navy photograph by Mass Communication Specialist 1st Class James R. Evans.

Also by Robert T. Chambers and available on Amazon:

Hidden Wounds

"Kimberly" is a work of fiction. None of the characters or incidents are real, nor are they even loosely based on actual events.

Author e-mail: rtchambersauthor@gmail.com

Author Facebook page:

www.fb.com/roberttchambersauthor

Kimberly

Chapter One: It All Starts

Kimberly, Allison, and Layla were to eat lunch together. Allison joined Kimberly in their favorite spot, a small alcove near the back of Augusta, Maine's Madison Junior High cafeteria.

"Where's Layla?" Allison asked.

"She's coming," Kimberly replied as Allison sat down.

"That Tommy James wasn't nice to me this morning," Allison told her friend.

"Tommy's an idiot and a bully. I can't stand him," Kimberly said, flipping her long black hair.

"The problem is he's going to high school with us next year, and we're going to have to put up with him for another four years," complained Allison.

"Just avoid him. He's not going to change," Kimberly told her friend. "How's your mother doing with the Katy Perry concert tickets, because I may have a problem?

"Not good, we need to talk. Last night she said she hasn't been able to get tickets yet. We may not be going."

"I wonder when our parents will allow us to go alone?" Kimberly mused.

"Like never if my parents have their way. I don't even think my mother's working all that hard to get the tickets."

"Yeah, my parents are the same way. But I've got a big taekwondo competition that weekend, so I can't go anyway."

Facing the central part of the cafeteria, Kimberly could see Layla coming toward them from a corridor on the opposite side. There was a boy she didn't recognize a few feet behind Layla. Something was not right. He had on a heavy jacket, which was weird this early in the fall. Instinctively she started to get up to find a teacher. Before her eyes, the boy disappeared in a cloud of fire, black and debris. As she ducked under the table, she saw Layla flying to their right. The explosion was sufficiently violent that the glass behind Kimberly and Allison blew out. Kimberly immediately got to her feet and began running toward the blast zone.

"Wait, Kim, don't go there," Allison yelled after her, "we've got to get out."

Kimberly could hardly hear her but yelled, "Come on, people will need help."

The people, kids, and teachers near them, were on their feet or sitting stunned. With Allison following, Kimberly ran to where she had seen Layla. In front of them, there was a black void where nothing was moving. Around the periphery, kids, and adults, were screaming, many people were down.

Layla was down, her body sprawled grotesquely, not moving; Kimberly squatted and felt for a pulse. There was none. Layla's head was loosely, grotesquely, positioned on her body.

"Oh my God, she's dead, isn't she," cried Allison.

"Yes," replied Kimberly. She had never seen a dead person before, but there was no way Layla was alive. Kimberly shook her head and swallowed as she tried to process what she was seeing. Allison was sitting crying.

"Come on, Allison, we're Girl Scouts and know first aid. We can't help Layla, but others need us."

Allison stared at her. Putting her hand out, Kimberly pulled her friend to her feet and got in her face. "Come on; we need to be useful."

The crying girl nodded and followed as Kimberly turned to look for living victims who needed help. Within a few steps, she almost tripped over somebody.

Tommy James was wiggling about and trying to get a hold of his neck where blood was pumping out. Instinctively Kimberly tore off her blouse and padded it up as she knelt beside Tommy.

"Try to be still. I'm going to put pressure on your neck. It may hurt." She pushed down with the blouse pad until the pumping blood stopped. "Can you still breath?"

Tommy was coughing, but it was coming from his neck and not his mouth. He tried to speak, but there was no sound. The gushing blood stopped.

"Okay, I think this is under control. Lie still; help will be here soon."

"Oh my God, oh my God." Allison was standing, looking in horror at the scene.

Kimberly still could not hear well. "Damn it, Ally, move," she barked at her friend. "do something, help someone. We didn't learn first aid in Girl Scouts for nothing,"

Allison stared at Kimberly's face, then at where Kimberly held the pad to Tommy's neck. Allison shook her head, then tried to focus on moving forward to find a victim needing aid.

Kimberly spotted Mrs. West, the social studies teacher wandering close by, aimlessly. She yelled, "Mrs. West, snap out of it; people need help."

The woman looked blankly at Kimberly then spoke sharply. "Put your clothes on, girl. You can't come to school like that."

The woman was not going to be much help, and Kimberly saw nothing wrong with wearing only a bra on her top. The bikini bra she wore at the beach was more revealing. The woman continued to drift aimlessly.

Kimberly saw that Allison had also removed her blouse and was pushing on someone's groin. She could hear sirens; help was coming.

The initial first responder to come down the hall was a police officer, his weapon drawn. His eyes surveyed the scene then settled on Kimberly. "What the hell happened here?"

Kimberly barely heard the officer. "Explosion, probably a bomb on a kid; doesn't seem to be anything more. Get lots of help and ambulances," Kimberly told him.

"God, yes," the officer said before putting his weapon away and calling on his radio for more help. He continued talking on his radio as he moved forward, surveying and telling dispatch of the damage. More officers and firefighters arrived.

"What's the problem?" A firefighter kneeling by Kimberly asked.

"Blood was pumping out of his neck, and he can't talk. There is a huge cut on his neck. I think it got the big artery in the neck and probably his windpipe. He's breathing through his neck."

The firefighter frowned as he looked at all the blood around Tommy's head. "Don't take the pressure off," he told Kimberly. She had no intention of letting go. The firefighter reached for his radio and then spotted some emergency medical services people coming through the door.

"Hey EMS, over here, we need a paramedic now," he hollered at the EMS people.

In more detail, Kimberly repeated what she had seen to the female paramedic.

"You okay?" the paramedic asked Kimberly. "Hell yeah, it's Tommy who needs help."

The paramedic grinned at Kimberly. "Good, keep the pressure on. We'll need to get an airway in him, and an IV started, then we'll get him to the hospital. Here, without letting the pressure off, work this pad between your fingers and your blouse. Your blouse is getting very wet." Kimberly did as told.

The paramedic sucked the blood out of Tommy's throat. "I'm going to try to get a tube in this way. If I can't, we'll intubate him through the wound to control his airway. Don't take the pressure off, but I may need you to push things around a bit. Okay, I see the cords." Kimberly could feel the tube slip under her fingers and past the wound. "There, now when I inflate the little balloon, we'll have the airway secure." After suctioning out more blood, she had the EMS technician attach a bag connected to oxygen. By squeezing the bag, he could breathe for Tommy.

Tommy's veins had collapsed, but the paramedic was able to get a line by going under Tommy's collarbone. Tommy was very pale, and out of it, moaning. The EMS technician put dressing and tape all over the site where the line went under Tommy's collarbone as the paramedic listened to his chest and checked his pulse.

"Okay, we're going to move him onto the gurney," the paramedic said. "What's your name? Move with us and keep that pressure on his neck. If need be, you can put more pressure on as the airway is secure."

"Kimberly Callahan, and yes, I understand."

The paramedic with two EMS people and the firefighter moved Tommy to the gurney. "Okay, keep the pressure on, we're going to bring the gurney up and roll out to the ambulance," the paramedic told her.

Kimberly did as told and was able to glance toward Allison, who was with EMS personnel working on the victim, where she had controlled bleeding in the groin. Slowly the gurney with Tommy on it moved down the hall, outside, and to an ambulance. There were police lines set up, but the chaos outside was almost as bad as inside.

"Keep the pressure on as we put the gurney in the ambulance, and even once it's in place."

Soon the ambulance rear doors were closed, the technician went to drive. Kimberly heard the sirens start and the reflections of the flashing lights. The area was jammed with emergency vehicles. There was a way out and almost no traffic on the route to the hospital. Kimberly saw that squad cars were blocking the side roads. The paramedic took Tommy's vital signs and radioed his status to the emergency department, asking for a vascular surgeon to be standing by.

"You saved this guy's life, good work," the paramedic told her as she checked Tommy.

"Instinct," Kimberly told her, "and Girl Scout training."

"I suspect you want to stick with him, but once we get to the hospital, someone will take over for you to get him to an operating room. I'll have this scrub top for you once your hands are free. Do you have a cell phone with you?

"Yes."

"Call home; your people will be worried."

"I will. You're going back to school. Can I go back and help you?"

The paramedic gave Kimberly a long look. "I don't think so. For one thing, you need a shower. You're covered with blood. What happened?"

"I think a bomb strapped to a kid. Allison and I sat down to eat lunch, and suddenly there was a loud explosion."

The paramedic nodded as the ambulance pulled into the bay at the hospital. "Were you unconscious even for a moment?"

"No, we were in an alcove. The blast went past us. I still can't hear very well."

Just inside the emergency department door, a nurse took over from Kimberly as the paramedic gave a report. Tommy was going directly to an operating room.

"Let me look at your ears." With an instrument, the paramedic looked in each of Kimberly's ears. "Okay, both drums are intact. Might be middle ear problems, but I don't see bleeding. Likely your hearing will improve, but I'd get your ears checked in a couple of weeks. Here, go to a washroom and try to remove some of the blood, then put this on." The woman handed her the scrub top.

In the washroom, Kim saw what a mess she was. Wet paper towels removed only a bit of the blood. Kim slipped on the scrub top.

Back in the emergency department lobby, Kimberly called her Dad's mobile.

"Hey, Dad, it's Kim."

"Oh my God, we were so worried. Where are you? Are you okay?"

"I'm okay; I wasn't injured. Layla is dead, Allison is okay. I helped bring Tommy James to Mercy Hospital. Oh my God, he's a patient, so you can't repeat any of that. Can you come get me?"

"I don't think so, they've cordoned off the school, Mercy and a couple of other hospitals. Let me figure something out. I'll call you back."

Kimberly thought she should try to contact Tommy's parents. Girl Scouts had emphasized that they could not talk about victims, but Kimberly did not believe that extended to parents. She wondered about calling Layla's parents. That would be up to the police or somebody.

Everyone was busy, but at a clerk's station, Kimberly found a phone book. Fortunately, the James' still had a landline. A woman answered the phone.

"Mrs. James?" Kimberly asked.

"Yes," the tone was suspicious.

"I'm Kimberly Callahan, a classmate of Tommy's. There was an explosion at the school. Tommy's alive and at Mercy Hospital. The big blood vessel in his neck and his windpipe were cut, must have been flying glass or something. They've already taken him to the operating room."

"There was an explosion?"

"Yes, Tommy's going to be okay." Kimberly dearly hoped the latter part was correct. The woman said she would call her husband.

"Hey, you need a lift to beyond the police lines?" It was the paramedic who brought Tommy in with her.

"Yeah," Kimberly told her, relieved. "If I can get somewhere that my Dad can get to, I'll call him again."

Once again, the paramedic told her shower when she got home and that she was not going back to the school with them. Her Dad picked her up on a corner two blocks east of the main route between the school and the hospital.

"Oh, God, you're hurt!"

"No, a wall protected Allison and me, and we were on the other side of the cafeteria. It's Tommy James' blood. He's in the operating room. Layla is dead, but don't tell anyone until the police can."

Her father stared at her. "What happened?"

"Big explosion, I think a kid was wearing a bomb."

Initially, the media had all sorts of unhelpful conjecture. The police investigation included a review of the Madison Junior High's security cameras that clearly showed a boy walking into the cafeteria wearing a bulky jacket. The FBI learned that the boy's uncle was a radicalized terrorist. The uncle had made the bomb. His nephew had set it off in the middle of a crowded cafeteria.

.

Chapter Two: Sea Duty

Kimberly was off watch, leaning against a rail staring out to sea. She loved the sea, perhaps due to growing up in Maine. The sea was calm, the air warm. She was aboard an Arleigh-Burke class destroyer on her first sea duty as an Ensign.

"Hey." Billie Jo Dufrene, another Ensign, and Academy classmate interrupted her musing. They were something of a Mutt-and-Jeff team as Billy Joe was five foot six and Kimberly five-ten.

"Hey, how're you doing?" Kimberly asked.

"My mother is likely bull-shit, but I love the engine room. "

"Why, bull-shit?"

"Oh God, don't start me, I'm supposed to be a proper young lady."

"As opposed to a naval officer?"

"Yeah, she doesn't distinguish ranks, and even becoming a mechanical engineer was heresy. How's your family doing?"

Billie Jo did not know much of Kimberly's story. Even with both in the mechanical engineering cohort, they had only been acquaintances at the Naval Academy. Now they were roommates. Billie Jo's focus was propulsion. Kimberly did not get SEALs and was learning Surface Warfare. Kimberly wondered how much to say. "Why did you go Navy?"

"It was easy. Both my grandpa and my pa were enlisted Navy. For me, it was a way to get an education and serve the country. Grandpa is proud of me, Dad is too, but grumbles about having to salute his officer daughter."

Kimberly laughed, "Career?"

"For sure."

"I'm going to have to kill you if you tell anyone this."

"Why?"

"Don't know, superstitious, I guess. I got blown up in junior high."

"What?"

"Well, not me, a friend. Allison and I were in an alcove, so the blast went past us when a kid walked in with a bomb jacket on and blew up the cafeteria one noon. Our friend Layla was killed. Since then, I've wanted to get the terrorists, so Navy and I had hoped, still hope, SEALs. You can't talk about that. My family understood and was proud when we graduated from the Academy but worry. Likely they would prefer I had an onshore civilian job, but that can be dangerous too, so what the hell? I haven't told them I want SEALs."

"Yeah," Billie Joe said, "I tried the 'civilian life is dangerous' logic with my family. Even with all the gang violence around us, my mother couldn't see it. So, SEALs is why all the running and stuff?"

"Yeah, in high school, I spent a lot of time in the weight room, track, or the gym climbing rope and stuff. They regarded me as weird, and it didn't help that I was allegedly a brainiac."

"Oh, God, tell me about it. In my neighborhood, I had that reputation. Jeez, the guys were afraid to date me."

"I turned that around. Brad Watson was cognitively challenged, but the quarterback, so that got me into a crowd that I no longer see as cool. He was a loser, failing out of engineering school and then engineering technology. Guess I shouldn't have done his homework for him."

Billie Jo laughed. They both stared at the sea. Kimberly did not bother to add that in addition to having academic problems, he was a lousy lover. It had been all about him.

"What happened to your friend that was with you in the cafeteria?" Billie Jo asked.

Kimberly paused. "She hasn't done well. Allison always was a bit of a tender soul inclined to music and art. We were both Girl Scouts, and that day I pushed her into using our first aid training when she wanted to run. The whole terrorist thing kind of drove her underground. Last I heard she's teaching music."

"What about you?"

"What do you mean?"

"You didn't get SEALs."

"Yeah, I will."

Billie Jo let it go, but Kimberly knew what she was asking. Staring out over the ocean, she recalled an episode early in her plebe summer when she thought she was being dropped.

"Callahan, report to room two-four-oh."

Kimberly recalled feeling the panic start. The order meant she was going to have a one-on-one interview with a psychologist. Questions on your psychological profile test precipitated those interviews, and an interview frequently resulted in the plebe leaving.

"You did very well on your psychological profile; do you have any idea why we think you did too well?" was the psychologist's opening.

None of the admission paperwork asked about catastrophic incidents, but Kimberly guessed they knew. "The terrorist attack at my Junior High?" Breath normal, Kimberly told herself.

"I have the police summary here. A lot of kids died."

"And teachers, cafeteria workers, and custodians."

"Yes. Where were you?"

"In an alcove with a friend."

The psychologist frowned and nodded. "A friend died?"

"Yes, Layla Mattan."

"You saw her dead?"

"Yes."

"You remained in the cafeteria?"

"I had Girl Scout first aid training; I thought it might help."

More damn nods from the shrink. "You saved a boy's life."

"My friend Allison and others also helped."

"You were grieving over Layla?"

"At first, I didn't have time to think about it, but yes, at her funeral."

"That's difficult for anyone, let alone a thirteen-year-old." It was a statement; Kimberly did not reply. The psychologist was watching her. "Losing a friend is hard." Another statement, but he was pushing her.

"Yeah, but we had worse. In high school, three of the kids died in a car wreck. The fourth kid in the car was hurt, not critically, but pinned under her dead friend. That would have been awful."

"How is she doing?"

"The girl pinned under her dead friend, not well, but she was kind of a flake anyway."

"You're tough?"

Kimberly thought about that. She had grieved over Layla but realized that there was nothing she could do about her friend's death. That was not true; she had focused on the problem, terrorism. "More pragmatic."

"Tell me about your nightmares."

"I don't have any."

"That you had after the incident."

"I didn't have any."

The psychologist stared at her. His mother never taught him that staring was not polite. Kimberly looked back. "How do you feel about the incident?" he asked.

"People I knew died, including a good friend. The terrorist incident was the fault of no one at the school but of the broader mess of the world. It happened, I needed to move on, and likely it is what drove me toward the Navy to help defend this country."

"How much do you drink?"

"I don't drink. I tried a beer at a party once and didn't like it, plus I'm underage."

He was back to nodding and shuffling papers. He looked up and met Kimberly's eyes. "Callahan, you come off as one cool customer. We couldn't believe that your profile was so good, given what you've been through. The Academy can beat a person down, get help early if things start to fall apart. Back to your unit, I'm passing on you psychologically."

Looking back now, Kimberly was less sure that they should have passed her. Maybe questions around that incident were what had kept her out of the SEALs.

"Earth to Kimberly," Billie Jo interrupted her thoughts, "it's getting cool. Let's go in."

Once in their quarters, Billie Jo decided to continue the conversation. "What happens when you appear at home in uniform?"

"Yeah, I don't. You know the Navy doesn't like us traveling in uniform unless we're on duty, and frankly, I prefer to wear civilian, as there're fewer questions. When I'm traveling, and some male gets nosy, they usually shut up when I tell them I'm a mechanical engineer. I've just never worn my uniform at home. My mother was bullshit when I cut my hair."

"They don't know what to do with me," Billie Jo allowed.

"Who don't, family?"

"My high school friends. Most never got to college, so the gap is huge now,"

"Yeah, me too," Kimberly replied. "Typically, I just listen or go off on my own. I like my bike for that."

"I saw you ashore with that, what is it?"

"A 2015 Harley-Davidson Softail Classic. My Dad got it for me as a graduation gift. He'd been saving money to help me in college and didn't need to spend it when I went to the Academy."

"You look so effing cool on it. They're dangerous."

"Life is dangerous. I had a good trainer. You thought the DI's plebe summer were tough? Rocky Lachance is a demanding little prick, but you're a good driver when he gets finished with you. If you ever get a bike, you're coming to Augusta so he can train you." From Billie Jo's expression that was not out of the question.

Aboard any warship, it behooves an Ensign to shut up and pay attention. That had been Kimberly's mantra all through the Academy. Aboard, she learned how much she enjoyed the sea. She could feel the excitement, even more, when the seawater spray hit her face. While becoming highly proficient at the various jobs aboard, she had preferences. Although she was good at it, driving the ship took a backseat to the planning and tactics, as well as the radar work.

Becoming highly proficient in the mathematics and physics of radar was a fun challenge. Kimberly's best time was in the combat information center (CIC). Aegis is a highly integrated system. Off watch when she was not sleeping, she was doing physical training or reading everything she could find on the combat weapon systems. Except for Billie Jo, who frequently joined her, the junior officers teased her about her obsession with exercise. The reading of manuals and anything else Navy was also seen as strange by her fellow junior officers. Duty onshore at Norfolk was not as much fun as at sea, but Kimberly understood its importance. She was learning and determined to be an excellent seagoing officer. A good recommendation here would be a path to the SEALs.

Chapter Three: It Gets Real

After her initial sea duty, Kimberly received an assignment to ADOC, the Advanced Division Officer Courses in Newport, Rhode Island. That was a good next step as it would upgrade her qualifications. She judged that it was too soon to reapply for the SEALs.

The trip north on her bike was fun. She settled in at Newport, beginning her ADOC classes. Much of it was like the basic course but more advanced, utilizing what they had learned aboard. Her knowledge of the ship and the combat systems was far better than most of her classmates. At the academy, she discovered her ability to calculate complex mathematics rapidly. Much of it she could do in her head. Her skill with mathematics astounded the instructors.

One week into the course, she was bored. A notice on a post board told her of a martial arts program that a Marine Gunnery Sergeant named Lambert ran. As civilians were involved, it was off base. They were starting a new class. Kimberly did not have her taekwondo robes, so a T-shirt, sweats, and sneakers would have to do. Likely they would work in bare feet. Having told the woman at registration that she had a taekwondo black belt, she was put into one of the advanced groups, but not the top group that the Gunny Lambert was instructing. Her group's instructor was one of his buddies, another Marine Gunnery Sergeant, Gunny Klecka.

Klecka paired up two of the guys so they could demonstrate their abilities. In Kimberly's estimation, it was tame even though anything went. It was martial arts, not taekwondo. She wanted in the more advanced group. The only way to do that was to impress Gunny Lambert. She was paired with a civilian male who talked a lot but appeared out of shape.

His initial posture was ridiculous, and he had a smirk. Likely he thought that beating a woman was going to be easy. She had to be sure she was not getting sucked into something. For the next several moments, she moved and watched him. He did not know what he was doing. With a shriek and using her left foot, she kicked at his midriff. As her left foot landed on the floor, she was up on her toes, spinning and lashing out with her right foot, a back-kick. He had toppled forward more than she anticipated. Her right foot was going to smash his jaw. At last moment she tried to change course and struck him on his right shoulder resulting in a loud crack. He was down.

Lambert was right there. He told her group to sit on some benches at the side of the room while they called EMS. Kimberly was not surprised that the others in her cohort gave her some space. Lambert approached the group. He was looking at her.

"Okay, I'm not sure how you could've avoided that, he wasn't ready for your kick at his middle. I saw you try to change the direction of your second kick when you realized what'd happened. That's almost impossible to do. You did change it enough that you didn't kick his head. Had that happened, I suspect his injuries would be worse. The rest of you back to class with Gunny Klecka. You wait here." The last sentence he directed at Kimberly.

The others moved off. Shit, it was not a smart way to start. She had been in Newport for a week and was already in trouble. He looked at the stick-on badge with her first name.

"Okay, Kimberly, how many black belts, obviously not just one."

"No, Gunny, fourth degree."

"Shit, I should've asked when I heard you say black belt at registration. Okay, don't worry, that guy is an ass anyway. Thinks he knows more than he does. Likely a good lesson for him. Who are you?"

She knew he meant more than her name; likely he'd busted her. "Ensign Kimberly Callahan, Gunny."

"Damn, that also occurred to me too late. Sorry, ma'am. You're Academy?"

"Yes, Gunny."

"Do martial arts there?"

"Some, mostly taekwondo at home, junior high and high school."

"How are your nerves, ma'am?"

"I'm fine."

"Would you mind if we found out how good you are? No holds barred."

"No problem Gunny."

As she approached his advanced group, there were four guys, she suspected Marines, eying her like fresh meat. That was not the plan; the Gunny was going to test her personally. Her mind began to race.

He was much more experienced than her and possibly in better shape. She was younger, probably faster, and a bit smaller. The latter might be an advantage. She kept telling herself that. They moved around, taking each other's measure, and watching for an opening. Finally, Lambert attacked. Kimberly was either able to escape, defend the attack, or turn it to her advantage over the next several minutes. Lambert was making a mistake, but she had too much respect for him, likely it was a trap. He kept on doing it, confirming in her mind that it was a trap. Suddenly he lunged, she twisted and flipped out of the way. Kimberly saw the mistake again. She let her body momentum carry her into him, locked his poorly placed leg, then she came up under him, and flipped him. That this was fun crossed her mind; it was hapkido, definitely not taekwondo. Flying after him, she landed on his torso. Kimberly hit her hip, simulating grabbing a knife from her waist and play-acting that she held it against his throat.

"You're fuckin' dead, Gunny."

Hand to hand is much more personal than staring at a radar screen. Her immediate thought was that her instincts to kill were too good. That was her civilian brain talking. She was being trained to kill and needed to be good at it or would be dead herself. The Gunny nodded and smiled at her as they got up. The Marines were grinning, the civilians not sure what to do. She later learned that her civilian victim had nothing more than a broken collarbone and would do well. He never came back, which was okay with Gunny Lambert.

The ADOC course went well, and her remaining time in Newport very well. After encountering them on an early morning run, Kimberly started hanging with the Marines from the martial arts club. They increased her three miles of running each morning before breakfast to five. They also took no mercy on her at the martial arts sessions, nor did she on them. Being bruised up became a way of life. Gunny Lambert was promoted to Master Sergeant and transferred. Gunny Klecka took over the martial arts group.

Chapter Four: Back to Sea

Just after the New Year, with the courses done and having completed the promotion process, Kimberly started sea duty on a different Arleigh-Burke class destroyer, this time as a Lieutenant JG. During periods of introspection, she realized that while respected, she had acquaintances, but no real close buddies. That was the pattern of much of her life. Bobbie Jo was somewhere else. Once again, some of the other officers found her fetish for physical fitness amusing, but Kimberly believed it was what kept her mentally agile. Aside from her brain, she needed her body to be ready. During operations, she was entirely focused on her job, amazed her superiors with solutions, sometimes found quicker than the computers did.

"What the shit?"

Kimberly was on the watch by the Aegis in the combat information center. She was the senior officer there. "Is there a problem, Petty Officer?"

"Think so ma'am; the ADS shows what looks like a contact coming in low and fast."

Kimberly looked at the screen for just a moment. "CIC to Bridge, General Quarters. We have a contact coming in low and fast, one hundred and twenty degrees, about one hundred knots out."

"Who is this?"

"Lieutenant, JG Callahan."

"Are you sure you're not looking at wave tops, Lieutenant?"

"Yes sir, eighty knots out, info flow coming from radar and satellite."

"Why don't you have a senior officer look at that Lieutenant?"

"Because there isn't one here, Sir. I'm on the watch." Kimberly tried to discern who was on the bridge. Lieutenant Commander Carruthers should have the con, and this was not his voice. "Where is Commander Carruthers?" While asking, Kimberly kept looking at the incoming data.

"He just came back. Sir, a JG in CIC, want us to call general quarters."

"What are you looking at, Lieutenant?" asked Carruthers.

"Sir, the Aegis is showing a contact coming in low and fast. The feed is both from the AN/SPY and the satellite. One hundred and twenty degrees, sixty knots out and closing, straight line."

"Shit, you'd better be right, Lieutenant." General quarters sounded.

"The Ruskies have a carrier about two hundred and fifty knots out in that direction, likely where it came from," a different Petty Officer in the CIC said. Kimberly knew that; she just had not expected them to do anything.

"Forty knots out, speed, and course unchanged, but he hasn't lit us up," Kimberly reported

"Got it, Lieutenant, we see it now. We're going to launch SAMs."

"That might be a bad idea, Sir. The contact hasn't lit us up," Kimberly blurted out.

"What the hell?" asked Carruthers.

"Likely, it's just Ruskies playing. It's probably from a carrier they've got out in that direction." Having gone this far, she might as well dig her hole deeper. "They're not even trying to be subtle, just straight-line in."

"She's correct, Commander," came Captain McElrath's voice, "light it up but don't fire, yet. Let's be sure the cameras are operating."

Kimberly was holding her breath, more alert than she had ever been. Her career and possibly the lives of many onboard rested on her being correct. The incoming blip was not moving fast enough. She needed to take a breath.

"Jesus Christ." The exclamation on her headset was Lieutenant Commander Carruthers' voice. The screen showed that the blip had passed them. "Flew right over our chopper LZ." Kimberly watched as the blip made a full U-turn and started back at them.

"He's coming back," someone on the bridge said.

"Holy shit he came right across our bow showing off his belly, that's fuckin' gutsy," Carruthers again.

Kimberly watched as the blip moved away, back toward their aircraft carrier.

"Whoa," one of the female Seamen let her breath out.

The Petty Officer at the Aegis screen laughed," You can breathe now, Seaman."

"And this JG," Kimberly laughed. "Contact is returning toward their carrier," she reported to the bridge.

"Nice call ma'am, you were correct," the Petty Officer told her. "It wasn't being subtle and didn't have us lit up."

"Shit, if I'd been wrong, I could've gotten us all blown up."

"You weren't wrong, ma'am."

Kim's buzz of adrenaline faded over the next half hour as the crew returned to their routine duties.

"Ten' shun, Captain on deck."

Captain McElrath walked up to her. Her adrenaline started again. She saluted, and he returned it.

"Callahan, you the Lieutenant who just prevented a major incident?"

"Sorry, Sir."

"Sorry for what?"

"I was insubordinate."

"My kind of insubordinate, and that took nerves of steel in anyone, let alone a Lieutenant JG. Well done," the Captain told her.

It pleased Kimberly when, in the wardroom, senior officers remarked on her quick assessment of the situation. The Lieutenant, who had had the con for Lieutenant Commander Carruthers, was surly and did not speak to her. Making enemies was never a good idea, but this time she had been correct. Commander Carruthers had no problem with her.

A few months later, Kimberly had a different assignment. She and her bike headed cross-country to her new ship in San Diego, a brand-new state of the art destroyer, the DDG-1000 USS Zumwalt. Despite the debate over the series, it was a plum assignment, a guided missile stealth weapon. The controversy was above Kimberly's pay grade, a fight between the Navy and Congress over building more DDG-1000's or building Arleigh-Burke Flight III destroyers. There had been some engineering problems in the lubrication system for the drive shafts of the Zumwalt. There are so few Zumwalt's built that the few commissioned ones are almost research vessels.

Kimberly was delighted to find a friend, Lieutenant JG Billie Jo Dufrene, aboard, still doing propulsion. The two engineers would be roommates again.

Kimberly hated that she immediately had a problem. The Zumwalt is technology sensitive, which she loved. Her assignment was to the hyper technology-sensitive plotting room. Her superior there, a Lieutenant Anderson, had been a couple of years ahead of her at the Academy. Aware that academically he had barely made it, Kimberly wondered how he got the Zumwalt assignment. She kept her feelings to herself and tried to be helpful.

The bad blood between them started immediately and increased with each exercise. Anderson did not understand the system. Not realizing that she threatened him, Kimberly made the mistake of trying to help him by suggesting what a solution could be when he took too long. The Non-Coms knew how to operate the system and soon started grabbing her suggestions as commands, infuriating Anderson and causing him to revoke the order and issue an incorrect one. Kimberly went quiet. Anderson's errors typically resulted in a visit from an angry Lieutenant-Commander Berg from fire control. Somehow, according to her nemesis, the problem was her.

She learned long ago, likely at the Academy that in the wardroom environment, a junior officer kept their eyes down and spoke only when spoken to. She did not always keep her eyes down, but Lieutenant Anderson not only did not keep his eyes down but mouthed off about his problems with her. One evening during a meal, she missed the look between Lieutenant-Commander Berg and the XO when Anderson was mouthing off. The XO changed the topic of the conversation saying that they would not be going into Okinawa. They had a new assignment that they would learn about the next morning. Dismissing the officers, the XO indicated that he wanted to talk to her in private. Kimberly's heart started to race again. She took a deep breath.

"What's going on between you and Anderson?"

"Not sure, sir, but I've been trying to help, and he takes offense."

"He makes a lot of mistakes." It was a comment, not a question, Kimberly felt no need to reply. "Look, a ship is a small environment.

I know what's been going on. Master Chief is pissed, to say the least," the XO told her. "I never said this, but Anderson's an idiot. He's being reassigned and won't be here in the morning. You now have command in the plotting room." There was not even a for now.

In their quarters later, Billie Jo Dufrene filled her in. "What's the deal? They pissed at you?" Billie Jo asked.

"Don't think so, likely it's at Anderson as he's no longer the command in plotting," Kimberly told her.

"Who's in charge there if not Anderson?"

"Me, I guess." A big smile broke out on Billie Jo's face. "What?"

"Damn, girl, you don't listen to anything, do you?" Billie Jo laughed.

"What do you mean?" Kimberly asked her.

"Ship scuttlebutt has it that you've been trying to help the idiot. He wouldn't listen to you, so the non-coms just started doing what you said. A helicopter took him off the ship as the XO was talking to you. If he'd just shut up, he would've been okay 'cause I hear that you had it right every time."

"Where the hell did you hear that?"

"Overheard a heated conversation between one of your non-coms and the Master Chief, you got friends, girl."

The next morning at breakfast, the Captain gave them more explanation of their mission northward. They were going to be testing the ship's stealth capabilities.

"We're going to see if we can irritate the Russians' off the Kamchatka Peninsula," the Captain explained. "We're going to cruise in international waters to see when the Russians figure out we're there. Let's be damn sure we remain in international waters. Callahan follow protocol with your radars at first but be ready when we ask you to turn up the power. We want to get caught. If they don't find us using normal protocols, we want to know where they do find us. I'll give you the study protocols after dinner."

Kimberly's first inclination was to suggest they have a more experienced officer play tag with the Russians. Her second inclination was screw it; this was going to be fun.

They were steaming north with no combat anticipated. Smiles greeted her as Kimberly entered the plotting room and relieved an Ensign.

Petty Officer First Class Marcus Brian spoke. "Glad you're here, ma'am."

"Thanks, Petty Officer, we've work to do."

Brian knew his stuff. Before this assignment, he had done tours on Arleigh-Burke class destroyers, all in plotting. Kimberly shared the new mission. She and PO Brian decided how to complete the tests the Pentagon wanted, and a plan of how to train to do the tests. By mid-afternoon, their work complete, they began speculating.

At supper, her superior, Lieutenant Commander Kalvin Berg, sat beside her.

"I understand that we have to do the tests that the Navy wants, but can we do more?" Kimberly asked him.

"Like what?" he asked.

She briefly outlined her and Marcus Brian's ideas. "It involves going off protocol and using non-standard settings."

"Why would we do that?" the Lieutenant Commander asked her.

"If they figure out our protocols, we may need a different approach. As a minimum, it'll confuse them." He just looked at her. They explained her ideas to the XO at the end of the meal.

Shortly after joining the ship, Kimberly realized how good the plotting team was. Marcus Brian had the non-coms and seamen together as the new watch started the next morning.

"Pleased you're in command now, ma'am," one of the Petty Officers ventured.

"Thanks, but let's nail the Russians."

"Yes, ma'am."

Kimberly and Brian outlined what they were going to do and a schedule of training that they would do before arriving off Kamchatka. As they worked that morning, she began to appreciate how fast the Petty Officers processed when they were allowed. Kimberly missed it, but a noncom later told her that during the morning, Berg came in, spoke with a seaman by the hatch, and left. Berg returned just as they broke for lunch.

"Captain wants to see you." It was us; Berg was also going. The XO was there.

"XO tells me you want to expand the work," the Captain addressed to Kimberly.

"Yes, sir."

"Explain."

She explained what they had in mind and how they were going to go about it, even adding a few thoughts and arguing why.

"This making sense, Berg?"

"Yes, sir, a lot of sense."

The Captain was concerned about the mission. "It is imperative that we get the testing done that the Pentagon wants."

"Understood sir, but my crew can do both," Kimberly told him.

The Captain smiled. "Berg?"

"No doubt, Sir, she had them drilling this morning."

That brought another smile. "Yeah, I'm not accustomed to being told that a Lieutenant JG is too busy to meet with me."

Oh God, that was why Berg had come to the plotting room in mid-morning. Fortunately, the Captain was amused.

For the next few days, they drilled, modified their plans, and drilled some more. They could quickly complete the information that the Pentagon wanted, even if the Russians were alert. The rest of it was going to be a treasure trove of data. Berg was a bit skeptical when Kimberly showed him how she wanted to modify the equipment to maximize the data acquisition.

"Didn't someone tell you that you aren't allowed to tamper with government equipment?" he asked her.

"Yeah, I guess," she sighed.

"Damn Callahan don't give up so easily. Undoing the modifications would be straight forward?"

"Absolutely, no one would see anything on the equipment."

"But if they knew what they were looking at with the data, they could tell?"

"Yes."

"If I recall history classes correctly, it is the unconventional warrior who wins battles. Let's do it." Kimberly looked at Berg trying to decide if he would cover his ass or back her. "It's okay; you'll be a cute brigmate." She was inclined to slug his shoulder for that remark but decided she had pushed far enough.

Even having to turn their plotting radars on a few times to drill, they arrived off Kamchatka undetected. Her crew had trained and trained and had their plan down cold. Brian had not even had to push, they liked him, they liked what they were doing, and they were excited about the tests. Hell, they liked her. Her crew was focused.

The tests started, and the Russians had no idea they were there until they ramped up their radar signal to look well into the Sea of Okhotsk. Then they played cat and mouse for a few days, continually acquiring data. On a few occasions, the Russians thought they knew where the ship was, but by the time their planes were on that location, the destroyer was gone, and they did not know where. The Russians started using more fighters to do more comprehensive looks. On the Zumwalt, the crew could drop the signal and move, causing the Russians to lose them. The Zumwalt was faster than the Russians thought, and oceans are enormous. A ship and some planes weren't going to find them. Kimberly wasn't sure why Russian satellites hadn't spotted them. She and Berg decided that the answer was the Zumwalt's stealth configuration, but that question was above their pay grade. It was fun, even though deadly serious. Kimberly and her crew accumulated a lot of data before the Zumwalt sailed away.

During the days returning to San Diego, the Captain worked with Kimberly and Berg as they completed entering the data on the forms the Pentagon wanted.

"Some puke at the Pentagon probably took a year to construct this form." The Captain was not a fan of the Pentagon.

Once what the Pentagon wanted was completed, they started collating the additional data, planning to present it as a supplemental. When the Captain was happy, the reports were encrypted and sent. They were heading back to homeport; the mood on board was jovial. The senior officers regarded Kimberly well, and now she was much more relaxed. Privately, but also in the confines of the wardroom, the Captain even referred to her as Kim.

"Girl, who does he think you are, his daughter?" was her roommate's observation.

Once secured dockside at San Diego, all officers except the watch were to report to the wardroom. The Captain walked in with a two-star Rear Admiral and a civilian. The Admiral's name tag said, Snell. The Admiral wanted to congratulate them, allowing as they had done significant work off Kamchatka. They were dismissed, except Kimberly and Berg.

"You two did the additional tests?" The Admiral asked.

"No, Sir, that was all Lieutenant Callahan," Berg said. The Admiral turned his gaze on her. He was smiling. Kimberly did not think they were in trouble.

"Sir, my team, in particular, Petty Officer First Class Brian, really the whole team did it."

"Understood Lieutenant, but the brain behind this was you." Indicating the civilian with him, he continued, "This is Allister Lesher, who's one of the contractor's scientists. He has a few questions."

Shit, the brass had figured out that she had changed some components around. Kimberly decided she had better stop overthinking things; maybe the Admiral also believed Berg's mantra about unconventional warriors.

It was more than a few questions. The guy was an egg head, and Admiral Snell was no slouch. They wanted to know what she had done and why. Far from upset, they seemed excited. Ultimately, Brian was brought in with Snell going over all the technology with him.

"Okay, I am sorry to have delayed you, but we needed to know what your thinking was behind these other numbers and how you did it," the Admiral finally told them. "At first, the pukes at the Pentagon were pissed, likely because they hadn't thought this through clearly. Captain MacLean was always supposed to send me a copy of your report, so, despite the Pentagon, we brought in the contractor. I'm not sure that I'd say too much about rearranging government property Lieutenant, but good work. I've looked at each of your personnel files. Brian let's deal with you first. Exemplary record and you're due a promotion to Chief Petty Officer; it's done. Get this on your uniform, and you'll need to go back to school, dismissed. Berg was also allowed to go.

"Now, Lieutenant Callahan, what are we going to do with you? Do you know a Marine First Sargent Lambert?"

"I knew a Gunnery Sargent named Lambert in Newport."

"Yes, well, he says you're dangerous." Kimberly was not sure how to respond. "That you excel is confirmed by your physical and weapons instructors when you were a midshipman. Your performance onboard has been remarkable. On your last assignment, you risked an insubordination charge to prevent a disaster. For those reasons, we've got a couple of options in mind for you. We've some problems out on the horizon that we're planning for, and where we could use you. The first step would be for you to go through SEAL training." He stopped awaiting a response.

Kimberly's heart was beating quickly. Her dream, obsession, was about to be possible. She needed to stay non-responsive until she heard the other options, she nodded.

"Option two is that we keep you in Surface Warfare and give you a bit more to do. There is an option three that I'm not excited about but involves you going to a defense contractor as a liaison." Admiral Snell stopped and was looking at her. He wanted an immediate response.

Kimberly agreed with him about option three. That was not on the table unless she received a direct order. The second option would likely lead to a good but predictable career. The SEAL option was full of hazards, not the least of which was washing out. Eighty percent of candidates did. It was also the most exciting with, from what the Admiral had suggested, potential for something more. The SEALs were also where Kimberly believed she had her best chance to avenge the deaths of Layla and the others. That fact alone determined the decision.

"I'd like the SEAL option, Sir."

"Good, I was hoping that you'd say that."

"Yes, sir."

"Oh, by the way, here, I have these for you." The Admiral reached into his pocket and pulled out two silver bars. Once she completed her rank training, she would be a full Lieutenant.

Captain MacLean chuckled. "May I Lieutenant?"

The Captain replaced her single silver bar with the double bars; both senior officers saluted her; she returned the salute.

"You've got a couple of weeks leave and then report to my office in San Diego until your rank training starts," the Admiral told her.

Chapter Five: Leave

Having only two weeks, Maine was too far away for her bike. Kimberly did not want to remain on base in San Diego. She wanted to go somewhere that was nice and within a reasonable distance. There needed to be an adequate gym as she needed intense workouts before reporting to the SEALS. Kimberly finally settled on the Pacific Coast north of Los Angeles.

Driving through Los Angeles traffic was a trick, but she had learned her lessons from Rocky well. Soon enough, she was in Santa Monica where she picked up The One, the Pacific Coast Highway heading north. She stopped for the night at Orcutt where a couple of Airmen from the Vandenberg base tried to pick her up. Chuckling the next morning, she wondered what their reaction would have been if she had told them she was a Lieutenant in the Navy.

She had in mind to go to Big Sur but stopped at Lucia as there she would have access east to San Ardo or San Miguel. They were more populous thus more likely to have a good gym. As it was, Kimberly found a perfectly good gym in Lucia, not a brand name, and somewhat rustic but perfectly adequate, as was the motel. She registered at both.

The next morning, she ran five miles at a punishing pace and then went to the gym where she worked out on the ropes, in the weight room, and did pull-ups on the bar. She and a fellow customer spotted each other doing the bench presses. Not particularly hungry, she decided she had better have a high protein lunch anyway. After lunch, she headed for Big Sur.

She had never been there before but had heard a lot about the place. It was beautiful, especially the rocks along the coastal cliffs. It also was beautiful inland where she found a park. There were trails to hike.

The trees, birds, and the rest of flora and fauna relaxed her. There were several hikers, but it was quiet and not crowded. Kimberly was calm. The whole time aboard the Zumwalt had been stressful. She laughed at herself. It had been nothing compared to what she would encounter over the next couple of years with the SEALs. She had damn well better relax. She tripped over something, someone who was crouching down photographing. They both recovered their balance.

"Oh my God, I'm sorry." Kimberly blurted out.

A male unfolded his length to well over her five feet ten inches. Four things popped into her head: he was good-looking, slim, well-built, and likely about thirty.

"No problem, actually, I'm sorry. I should've crouched down off the path instead of obstructing it." His eyes were looking her over.

"That's a serious camera," Kimberly told him.

"Yeah," he laughed, "a Nikon D-700. Are you a photographer?"

"No." Shit Kimberly, say something quickly. Hell, no girl, shut up and keep walking. He laughed.

"Harrison Jusack," he put his hand out. She shook it.

"Kimberly Callahan."

"Hi, you're a biker?" As it was a bit cold, she had her jacket with her, along with the leather pants, and her boots. His was a natural conclusion.

"Ride a bike, hardly a biker in the traditional sense. What do you do?" Oh, damn girl, that was dumb as it invites him to ask the same question.

"Ride a nice safe car, but that isn't what you were asking. I'm a physicist at Stanford."

"Wow, okay, student or faculty."

"Research faculty, they decided to keep me on after my post-doc. I do teach a bit, seminars. What do you do?"

Okay, girl, you cannot pause, and you cannot mention the SEALs, likely not the Navy. "Mechanical Engineer."

"Cool, biker chick who's a mechanical engineer. Whoops, that was decidedly uncool."

"Why?"

"The chick part, I apologize."

"Not a problem if I can call you hunk," she replied.

That got a smile and a blush. "You're funny. Care to walk along with me?" Harrison asked.

Each believed themselves to be a workaholic, so neither wanted to talk about work.

"They threw me out of the lab telling me to go relax," Harrison told her.

Kimberly laughed, "We'll need to find other things to talk about, mechanical engineers don't know a lot about quantum physics. You go by Harry?"

"Never have and not sure why, but always Harrison. You go by Kim?"

"Yes, and Kimberly, and any number of epithets."

"You ride a bike? What kind?"

"A 2015 Harley-Davidson® Softail Classic."

"Cool, nice bike, something just under 1700 cc displacement."

"You a biker?"

"No, just curious. I find motorcycle engines fascinating."

"Okay, and photography, and flora and fauna?"

"Mostly flora."

"After Queen Anne's lace, I'm lost," Kimberly admitted.

He did know about the flora and loved to talk about it. Either he knew his stuff, or he was bullshitting her. Kim didn't care. She enjoyed listening to his baritone voice.

Kimberly did admit to being from the east coast. Harrison was from Chicago, the eldest son of a man of German heritage and a woman of British background. Kimberly talked a bit about her pharmacist father and para-legal mother as well as her business type older brother and her younger sister. His Dad was a machinist, and his mother, an artist who did a variety of jobs. His younger brother was a welder, and his sister, the youngest, was still in school.

Hesitatingly he asked her to dinner. He owned one of the last of the little Geos. She followed it to the restaurant.

He knew quite a bit about food. Kimberly had one glass of Pinot Noir with her entrée.

"You going to be okay on the bike with the wine?"

"One glass won't be a problem," Kimberly told him.

"Could we exchange contact information?" Harrison asked.

"Sure, but I'm frequently, regularly, not available," Kimberly allowed. They exchanged cell phone numbers.

Returning to Lucia, Kimberly drove slowly and carefully, partially because she was not sure about the wine but mostly as it was dark. There was a big moon providing some light and not a lot of traffic. She managed the twenty-nine miles to Lucia without difficulty.

"Hey, I'm back in Lucia." Harrison had asked her to call him when she got back to the motel.

"Good, I had a wonderful evening."

"So did I," Kimberly admitted.

"Could I see you again tomorrow?" Harrison asked. He could, starting in the early afternoon. They spent the afternoons and evenings of the rest of the week together.

The week was terrific. Kimberly discovered that she liked Harrison, a lot; he professed the return sentiment. The Navy has strict rules, and she was engaged in the job to the degree that she never regarded any of the other people as anything but colleagues. She had no sense that Harrison was on the make, just that he enjoyed being with her. They did get him a motorcycle helmet so he could ride with her. Harrison admitted that it was more fun than driving about in his little Geo. Toward the end of the week, after she had started to wonder if he was going to get around to it, he kissed her. It happened at the end of an evening as she was about to drive home.

The drive home was likely the least safe she had done. She had not had anything to drink, but her mind was almost entirely on Harrison. She liked him. Thinking about him made her warm and fuzzy. He did more than that. Her long-neglected libido was rising. The problem was that he was a nice guy and she liked him a lot.

How the hell does one tell a likable theoretical physicist that the girl he is dating is a United States Naval Officer trained in surface warfare and about to embark on SEAL training. You do not. Or do you just tell him you're a Naval Officer, maybe not? Some of his work was for the Defense Department, so neither could talk about their work. She did not correct his belief that she was a civilian mechanical engineer.

It took her the drive back south to San Diego to clear her brain of Harrison. On their last night, things became a bit more torrid, but they never had sex. Kimberly hoped that they would never have sex, that if it happened, it would be making love. He was hunky and fun to wrestle with, but the attraction was his sharp mind discussing the flora, fauna, cameras, motorcycles, and a variety of other topics. On the other hand, he was a civilian, and she needed to have a discussion with him about Naval personnel, and that they can be at sea for weeks and months at a time.

Her assignment with the Admiral was temporary until her rank training started, after which she was due on Coronado. There were a few days when she did useful work going with the Admiral to the defense contractor's offices to go over the experience with the radar targeting systems.

Chapter Six: Sea, Air, and Land

Rank training could be a glitch. It did not involve physical fitness, and Kimberly believed she needed that. Her evenings were in the gym or the pool, and her early morning included a five-mile run, now wearing her combat boots. Soon she was off to Coronado. She had to succeed. Since junior high, her whole deal was to be a Navy SEAL and destroy terrorists. That was an oversimplification, the SEALs did so much more, and Kimberly wanted, needed, to be a part of that.

She was back to square one. The SEAL instructors did not give a damn who she was or what she had accomplished. Someone in an office in one of the buildings knew her record. She suspected many of the SEAL candidates had similar excellent records. To the instructors, she was, like the other officers, just an officer who was a candidate. She had no clue who was who and liked it that way. One of the males was making a deal about being Academy and a Lieutenant JG. She did not recall him from the Academy and secretly hoped he washed out fast.

SEAL training is about a bunch of things: mental and physical toughness and stamina, but also skill sets that allow them to function at an exceptionally high level on the sea, in the air, and on land. The most important was the teamwork. Despite her propensity for being a loner, collaboration was the easiest for Kimberly. Her fellow trainees reciprocated her helping.

A lot of it was mental; most of the eighty percent of candidates who washed out beat themselves mentally. Despite the preparation at Great Lakes, some of the enlisted were not ready physically. Some candidates, who by their brown belt were officers, also were insufficiently physically fit. Women were new to the program, but the instructors gave no indication they cared one way or the other. Most of the women were determined to prove the old ideas wrong. Despite that, there were washouts. The number of female candidates was low to start with, so the percentage of drops compared to the men was unfair.

Her insistence, before coming to the program, on working in gyms with ropes and doing weightlifting helped. Her upper body strength was better than some of the guys. That had been true since she started lifting in high school. Kimberly knew that if she beat herself mentally, it would be during the grueling first phase of the Basic Underwater Demolition/SEAL (BUD/S).   It was eight weeks of conditioning. She had been preparing for years and talked herself out of panic as Hell Week approached.   Teamwork was crucial. Kimberly was able to block her mind to the pain and alternating wet-cold.

"Hell Week is secured," the instructor yelled the four words that Kimberly badly wanted to hear. She was still in the program. The following sleep-deprived four weeks of training was not significantly more manageable than Hell Week. She never felt like dropping her helmet liner by the bell pole, the signal for a drop on request.

Still in the program after the completion of phase one of the BUD/S training, she had short leave, and she had no idea what to do. She called Harrison.

"Hey, Harrison, I've got a bit of free time. Want to meet somewhere?"

"Sure."

Good, he was still talking to her. She had checked a map. "Santa Maria or Santa Barbara are vaguely halfway."

"Okay," Harrison told her, "how about Santa Barbara?"

The problem was her feet. Due to all the punishment for the last several weeks, they had swollen. She borrowed a pair of flats, one size too big for her, from another female officer.

Kimberly had no idea how to approach the time in Santa Barbara. Harrison reserved a room for each of them at The Fess Parker on Cabrillo Boulevard. His deal was that it had a pool. Kimberly was not sure she wanted to be in more water. That was the least of her problems. During their last time together, things had become torrid. She could not deal with that now; she needed to focus on the four-wheel drivers and keeping her bike on the road.

She arrived exhausted, texting Harrison after parking. Meeting her in the lobby, he wrapped her in an embrace; his lips felt nice. She registered.

"Rodney's Grill's a full restaurant, and The Set's an outdoor bistro-style," he told her.

The evening was warm, and a full restaurant did not appeal to Kimberly. "Let's try outdoors."

There was a beautiful view of the ocean, several tables, and a small fire pit at the center. Kimberly collapsed in a chair. She was trying to decide between the lobster roll and the grilled chicken club when the server brought them each a draft Bud Light. Harrison was going to have their burger. Kimberly settled on the lobster roll.

"How've you been?" Kimberly asked him.

She was barely listening as he talked about the lab and a generic version of his project. "How about you?" he asked her, jolting her awake. She looked up at him. "You're exhausted, aren't you?"

"Yes, sorry, we've been busy," she replied.

"Fun busy and productive, I hope."

Kimberly laughed, "definitely, God, I'm sorry."

"No problem that a good night's sleep won't fix."

Kimberly was not sure of Harrison's assertion. During the prior four weeks, they had had very little sleep and almost continuously been on their feet, running, swimming, and small boat handling. She was even less sure when Harrison had to wake her halfway through her lobster roll. She finished the roll and some of the beer before he escorted her to her room.

They kissed. Kimberly wanted to invite him in but had no desire beyond the invitation and decided that falling asleep in the middle of sex would be a bad idea.

It was light outside when she awoke. She was wearing her travel clothes. At some point, she had pulled a blanket around her. The clock said nine-fifteen. Initially, she thought in the evening then realized it was morning. Oh, God, Harrison.

"OMG, I'm so sorry," she texted him.

"NP, there's a breakfast buffet in the lobby," came Harrison's return text.

"Meet you there in twenty minutes," she told him. Sailor girl SEAL candidate or not, it was more like twenty-five minutes before she had showered, put on make-up, something not allowed at Coronado, and pulled on jeans, a blouse, and tried to put her feet into a pair of three-inch heels. They were the lowest she had, not trusting herself in anything higher, both because she was fuzzy and because she had worn only combat boots the past several weeks. Due to all the punishment, her feet had swollen, she managed the size too large low flats. Harrison was at a table seated in a funky highback chair. He stood as she approached.

"Good morning."

"Oh God, I'm so sorry about last evening, good morning."

"You were tired. Likely you still are, so let's take it easy today."

The Santa Barbara Zoo was the perfect activity. It is not huge, like the San Diego Zoo, but has a beautiful collection. Harrison liked the antics of the otters; Kimberly preferred the big cats.

They toured some more that afternoon and ate supper at a restaurant away from the hotel. Harrison kept worriedly looking at Kimberly.

"What?"

"You're still tired," he told her.

"I'm fine," Kimberly asserted.

Back at the hotel, they crossed the road and walked along the beach. Both carried their shoes. Kimberly was able to snuggle into Harrison.

"I'm glad you called. We should try to do this more frequently," Harrison told her.

Kimberly thought she would like that; the logistics might be a problem. "I'm going to be very busy for the next several months, but yes, I'd like to." That was satisfactorily vague.

"In academia, we're spoiled; the pace is slow compared to an engineering office."

Kimberly agreed and wondered what he would think if she told him what she really did. Kimberly did not care. Stopping, Kimberly turned into him and put her lips up for a kiss; he kissed well; she recalled that. They walked along the beach a bit and then kissed and then walked again, each kiss becoming more torrid.

They tried Rodney's for dinner. Kimberly managed steak and a couple of glasses of Pinot Noir. After eating, Harrison thought he was only accompanying Kimberly to her room. She unlocked the door and moved to kiss him, then pulled him into the room behind her as their kiss again became torrid.

They divested each other of their clothing, and she pulled him to the bed where they kissed and touched. He was so gentle, kissing and caressing her gently, slowly. He was driving her crazy. She tried for slow but soon pushed him onto his back and mounted him.

He felt terrific in her. Kimberly knew she was aggressive. During high school, Brad did not like her being aggressive and would have already climaxed. Harrison moved with her and remained hard when she climaxed. She collapsed onto him. He flipped them and placed her ankles on his shoulders.

"Oh fuck, oh God, yes, fuck yes, Harrison, oh God."

Showing no sign of coming, he moved vigorously. Kimberly came and instantly came again, screaming as she went into a string of climaxes. He was moaning louder and then roared and climaxed as her world blew up.

She recalled them tumbling apart, both covered in sweat. Harrison moved to her, and she crawled onto his chest.

It was morning. Harrison was still there and awake.

"Hey, good morning," Kimberly heard. Harrison was smiling at her.

"And to you, physicist guy." She moved. He was hard. Reaching for him made her instantly wet. "Oh, God, oh God, make love to me."

He entered her, and balancing over her, moved slowly in her. Kimberly had never experienced sensations like these. Her brain managed nothing else until it exploded, and her whole body convulsed. Harrison came. She collapsed. The only sound in the room was of their heavy breathing.

Harrison was running fingers over her arms. She opened her eyes to look at him. He was carefully looking at her bruised skin.

"I'm a fitness nut, and sometimes I get banged up," Kimberly told him. He bought it or, so it seemed.

Too soon, Kimberly and her bike were back on the 101 heading south. The time had been fantastic. The time had been all wrong. She had a plan, and neither Harrison nor her hormones could get in the way.

The eight weeks of diving in phase two and the eight weeks of land warfare, including weapons training, went well. Hell Week had convinced her that she could do anything. She enjoyed all the swimming and SCUBA training in phase two. She loved being a water rat. At seventy minutes, she comfortably qualified during the timed two-mile swim with fins. There was training on land as well. She accomplished the four-mile run with combat boots in just over twenty-four minutes.

Kimberly did well with weapons as a midshipman, but in phase three, the rifle training was at a much higher standard. Having not handled rifles before plebe summer, she found it curious that she did so well during weapons training. Recalling lessons about breathing offered by one of her instructors at the Academy allowed her to improve her accuracy. She could not deal with the curiosities. She needed to accept and push ahead. She became an expert marksman, the top qualification.

Soon they were off to San Clemente Island and the last part of Phase Three. Of all the skills she was learning an essential feature for Kimberly, and most of the other candidates was teamwork. Most who had not learned that by now were gone, including the Academy braggart.

She loved the three weeks after BUDS, the fundamentals of parachuting, both on a static line and free fall. Kimberly loved jumping and resolved to join a skydiving team once she was out of training. SCUBA was something else she wanted to pursue.

At the end of phases two and three, she and Harrison had a few days together. He was cute, fun, and great to talk to; the sex was terrific. She liked him. That was a problem as Harrison professed more. Kimberly could not decide if her plan was in the way or if he would become what some girlfriends had referred to as a fuck buddy. That would not work for Harrison.

SEAL Qualification Training (SQT), the last phase is twenty-six weeks, where the candidates are to pull it all together.

"Callahan, Ewing, Carlos, Martinek, and Rodriquez, you're the final team," the instructor called. They had no time to think but were to secure a mock-up village immediately.

"Carlos point, Martinek close the door, no Ewing close the door. Let's go," Rodriquez called. He was out of line, both Kimberly and Ewing had brown belts on. Kimberly decided to let it be, and Ewing did not attempt to correct him. Damn Navy had teamed up two female officers with a couple of male Hispanic hard asses.

Kimberly did not like the set up as they moved forward. She called for a halt expecting trouble from Rodriquez or Carlos. She waved for everyone to move into an area of bushes.

"What did you see?" Rodriquez asked her.

"Nothing, but they expect us to go straight up the hill," Kimberly told him. Rodriquez nodded.

"Suddenly, you're in charge," Carlos challenged Kimberly.

"Carlos, first, Ewing and I are officers, so yes, we're in charge. But I like non-comms to think."

Rodriquez added, "Think about this Carlos, they've put two Hispanics with two women. They expect us to fight. We'll all wash out if that happens. We work together. Callahan, as an officer, was correct to stop us; my gut also started feeling not right. I'm sorry, my initial charge up the hill was just wrong."

"What now?" Carlos asked.

Kimberly had been surveying the hill and the village's location. "We stay out of sight, spread out, and move up the hill on the north. Up in that grove, two of us can cross to the south without being seen. We get above them on both sides and work in from a rear high point." They worked out what would happen once they got there.

What happened was they encountered a nervous enemy unit who had not seen them for twenty minutes. Suddenly the candidate team was there virtually killing the enemy. Two women were being used as shields by the alleged hostiles.   Using hand signs, Kimberly and Martinek coordinated and got headshots on both hostiles. It was over.

"That never happens the first go," the instructor debriefing them said. "Rodriquez and Carlos, how come you guys are taking orders from women?"

"What women Sir? I see only SEAL officers," Carlos barked. Kimberly saw Rodriquez smirk.

The instructor gave them a long stare. "I guess there is a reason we are supposed to keep you guys together." The team had a break.

"Hey."

"Hey yourself, Callahan," Janie Ewing replied.

"Having fun yet?" Kimberly asked her.

"This is boring after Hell Week," Ewing replied.

"Oh my God, don't let the instructors hear you say that," Kimberly laughed. "What's with this togetherness?"

"Not sure," Ewing replied. "You mustang?"

"Academy."

"Okay, I'm a new JG. I was a Petty Officer First Class when recommended for Officer Candidate School, so a mustang."

Kimberly learned that Janie was thirty. It crossed her mind that Janie was a bit old for SEAL training, and, earlier in the program, Kimberly had thought that at five foot six Ewing was too short. The woman was in great physical shape and had proved Kimberly wrong on all counts. The males were Luis Rodriquez, Warren Martinek, and Anthony Carlos, all Petty Officers. After twenty-six weeks of SQT, they all received their Trident insignia. They might not be operational for another eighteen months or more. They had leave.

The guys headed to their families. Janie Ewing went to San Clemente to see her kids, Montana eighteen and Amanda nine. Amanda lived with her father in San Clemente, and conveniently Montana lived in the same city, estranged from her father. She left home the day she turned eighteen.

For Kimberly, Harrison was a problem. Neither was sure of the relationship, though Harrison was more confident. For that reason, and despite her libido, Kimberly did not want to get too involved. Kimberly was amazed that they were still talking. The guy was patient; there had been huge gaps between when she had been able to see him. Kimberly headed north to Palo Alto. She found the physics building.

Taking long, confident strides, looking as though she belonged, even when wearing biker leathers, she strode in. She got to Harrison's office. The young administrative assistant did not question her, just directed her to Professor Jusack's lab. He was there with two guys his age and an older man.

"Hey."

They all looked up. "Oh, my goodness, Kimberly. I wasn't expecting you. How in the world did you get in here?" Harrison exclaimed.

"Walked."

The two younger guys thought that was funny, the older guy frowned. Likely, she was not supposed to be there. Kimberly decided that staying back and not showing too much interest in their computer screens was prudent.

Harrison moved to her. "Okay, so guys, this is my girlfriend, Kimberly Callahan." The girlfriend was good, even if they rarely saw each other. He had not added mechanical engineer; maybe he liked that she projected a biker girl image, she could do that. He introduced his two colleagues; the older guy was the Head of the Department.

"So, how come you're here?" Harrison asked.

"I finally had a break, so I decided to see if I could get your nose out of your electrons and have you buy me supper."

All three of his colleagues laughed. Neither she nor Harrison let on that the time apart had been many months. He agreed to supper, as he and his colleagues finished work. It was a surprise to his colleagues that he had a helmet in a file cabinet in his office. With Harrison on the back, she departed the parking lot with a roar and a flourish.

They settled on a restaurant not far from the campus that was not so upscale that she would need to change. She was starving. The menu said entrecote, and it was ten ounces. A big steak, even with a fancy name, sounded good to Kimberly. Harrison settled on the veal al la Oscar.

"How long do you have?"

"Rest of the week. I need to be back next Monday."

"Okay, good. You'll drive back on Sunday?"

"Yep."

The food was excellent, and Harrison his usual charming self. He did not push when Kimberly did not talk about her work. He generically spoke about his work. Though their meetings were sporadic, there unquestionably was an attraction on both their parts, regardless of Kimberly's misgivings.

"There is a classical quartet playing this evening, and I planned on going. Would you like to come?" Harrison asked.

"Am I okay in biker stuff?"

"Sure, people wear anything. Tomorrow, I must work in the morning but have the afternoon off. Would you like to spend it on the beach?"

"Sure." She surprised herself; the water rat did want to be at the beach.

The wear anything was not entirely correct. Some of the students were wearing what Kimberly called student grunge, but all of Harrison's colleagues were well dressed. She did not feel awkward; instead, she found it amusing.

The quartet played classical music, mostly Beethoven and Brahms. From Kimberly's perspective, they excelled. The juxtaposition was strange. She had just come from a course where she learned to be very proficient at killing enemies. For some unknown reason, the History Channel's images of Jewish musical groups playing in Nazi death camps played across her brain.

During intermission, she met several of Harrison's colleagues and their spouses. Some had seen them arrive at the concert, so they knew that she drove a motorcycle. One of the men asked about the model.

"Harley Davidson Softail Classic," Kimberly told him. He nodded appreciatively.

"What do you do, dear?" one of the older wives asked. Okay, the dear was unnecessary.

"I'm a mechanical engineer." That surprised a few and, stereotypically, of the way people think of motorcyclists, likely some did not believe her.

"Where do you work?" Kimberly decided it was natural but was concerned that there was altogether too much curiosity about her. Kimberly paused. Harrison rescued her.

"She works for a defense contractor," offered Harrison. Okay, that was what she had told him, and technically it had been, sometimes, vaguely correct. Admiral Snell had said that she was going to have to spend some more time at the defense contractor's when she got back to San Diego. Kimberly invoked the hard stare. It worked, the woman backed down and asked no more questions.

"Where did you folks meet?" Another female spouse asked. Kimberly thought she would have some fun.

"I assaulted him out in the woods, you know, flora and fauna, birds and bees and all that stuff." Harrison just grinned; some were a bit shocked; most were not sure how to take her. That was fine with Kimberly. Intermission was over.

At the end of the concert, Harrison and Kimberly left the parking lot with a flourish waving goodbye to anyone who might be looking.

"I hope I didn't cause you trouble with your colleagues," she asked over the intercom.

Harrison laughed. "No, not at all."

"I get that you like the biker chick image."

"Well, you very much played on that tonight."

Kimberly surprised herself at Harrison's apartment. She did not immediately want to jump in bed. They each had a beer while talking about the music. Harrison changed the subject.

"How have your last six months been?"

It was that long, and Kimberly did not want to go there. Explaining that she had been practicing blowing up things and doing sniper training, was not a good idea. Fortunately, they were seated beside each other, and Kimberly could divert him. That was when her libido showed up.

For months all her swimming was in Navy issue and much of it in battle dress. In the morning, Harrison was teaching, so Kimberly spent the time bikini shopping and purchased a pair of oversized sneakers. The time was an opportunity to try and work through her feelings about him and, in her mind, try out scenarios about work questions. Kimberly arrived back at the Physics Building at noon. Security was much tighter, Kimberly had to wait at the desk in the main lobby for him to come down. She wondered if that would have happened if she had been wearing a business suit the day before. A couple of men greeted her during her wait. Finally, they headed out to lunch.

"What were you teaching this morning?" she asked Harrison.

"A seminar that's part of a senior physics course dealing with particles, this morning antielectrons."

"Dirac equation." His head snapped up. "What, you think old Paul's equation is too complex for a mechanical engineer? Were you teaching how in Colorado, Carl Anderson proved the existence of the antielectron that the equation predicted and discovered the muon in the process?"

He stared at Kimberly. "I'm not sure that most of our grad students could have pulled that out of thin air. Damn, the seniors hardly know what an electron is." She laughed.

One would have thought that she had enough water with her training, but she enjoyed the bay beach and swimming. Harrison was a good swimmer but without her power. He bought her semi-accurate story about the high school swim team and state records. The tricky part of the afternoon came when, in the bright sunlight, he could discern more healing cuts and bruises.

"They're nothing, just got a bit banged up," she explained.

"Had to put your bike down?" he asked very concernedly. Kimberly's brain, too into her training, she had not thought of that obvious explanation. She did not lie; she shrugged and did not respond, letting Harrison think what he wanted to. She hoped that he would not notice the lack of marks on her bike.

They joined a group in a beach volleyball game. Volleyball was another place where Harrison was okay. When she started accurately playing balls that she either had to dive or leap for, she got another look from him.

"You're a heck of an athlete," Harrison noted. They had won, and the group was breaking up.

"Thanks, what are we doing for supper?" A high school friend had argued that diverting a male was easy with food. Kimberly had discovered the axiom to be correct, food, or sex.

They settled on a bar and a beer and burger supper. When they left the bar, a skinny male was sitting on her bike, showing off to a couple of girls. Without thinking, she grabbed his shirtfront, lifted him off the bike, spun, and set him down, pushing his back against the wall.

"What the fuck were you doing on my bike?" The guy was about thirty, five feet six or so.

His jovial face was now white and scared. "Oh shit, I'm sorry, I'm sorry."

She let go and watched as he slipped down the wall. Though tempted, kicking him might cause legal problems, plus if any of this got back to base, she would be in trouble.

"Don't ever fuckin' do that again, or some meaner biker might beat the shit out of you."

The guy scrambled to his feet and slunk off alone; the girls had disappeared into the bar. Harrison was trying to look severe; it was sort of funny. She dug their helmets out of the saddlebag. They left.

"Remind me never to piss you off," came over her headset. Harrison sounded amused, maybe.

"Sorry about that, but I can't stand pricks like that."

"He had no business touching your bike, and you're correct that if it had been a meaner biker, he would've been in bad trouble."

"Meaner ... so I'm mean now?"

"Probably the wrong word, and it was your word, but as I said, remind me never to piss you off."

"I wonder what your colleague's wives would've said if they'd seen that?"

"It would've just added to your legend."

"What the geeky theoretical physicist and the biker chick?"

"Pretty much," he laughed. Fortunately, he was not upset.

Chapter Seven: The Admiral's Office

An email recalled her to San Diego early, not the Naval Special Warfare Center on Coronado, but to Admiral Snell's office. The Navy and the defense contractor wanted more from her on the radar systems, and she had a few days before having to report to Coronado. During the drive back, her mind kept going to the Harrison problem. Her evenings were free. That gave her more time to fret over Harrison. She refused to call him. She had to work this out. To her, he was a great guy and a fuck buddy. She had perceived, he had said, that to him she was becoming much more.

A few days later, she and Admiral Snell, along with Allister Lesher, drove to Moffett Field. Kimberly could do nothing about her orders. It occurred to her that she rarely wore her service blues. The meeting was going to get awkward.   They were flying to Pala Alto on the Admiral's C-20D. It was a lot more luxurious and faster than her bike. Allister Lesher tried to engage her in a conversation about sub-atomic particles and radar interference; she was only half-listening. She needed to close things with Harrison before it all got out of hand. It was already out of hand. None of it was fair to Harrison.

Admiral Snell wanted Allister's spot and indicated that Allister should go aft. "Tell me about Harrison Jusack."

Damn, was there anything that the Navy did not know? "A guy I met on leave a couple of years ago."

"Serious relationship?"

'Somewhat, more on his part more than mine. I've been trying to discern what I should do about him. That's even more of a problem now that I know they're part of the radar work."

"At a very theoretical level but, yes, he doesn't do work that the average guy does. Your SEAL missions might endanger him and, ultimately, the physics department."

"One of my angsts," Kimberly admitted. The Admiral left it there.

The receptionist was too nervous and excited about the Admiral to give Kimberly a good look, so she was not recognized until the introductions. That was not true; Harrison spotted her. From under her cap's visor, she wiggled her eyebrows at him and wondered how that might be received.

"...and Professor, I believe you know Lieutenant Callahan," Admiral Snell continued. "She can most easily be explained as an end-user of the plotting radar and has done field tests of the equipment."

It was slowly dawning on the other physicists that the Naval Lieutenant was the biker chick engineer. The Head of the Department's eyebrows furled, jeez, okay, now he thought that her waltzing in had been a Navy security check. How did that explain Harrison?

What the theoretical physicists were doing was very interesting. Allister and Kimberly kept exchanging looks. Allister was shaking his head no as he listened and looked. Okay, that was because he was an applied physicist, it was up to engineers to problem solve.

"Lieutenant, Allister, what do you think?" Allister's frown deepened with Admiral Snell's question.

Kimberly stepped in. "Subatomic particle physics is, for the most part, theoretical. It's also fascinating, and likely understanding the particles in gaseous states will ultimately be important to our work, Admiral," Kimberly started. "However, currently, there's no discernable application. Just so you guys understand our problems," she addressed the physicists, "we work in the X band eight to twelve gigahertz, and as you know, it's all about electromagnetic waves. I understand the whole wave/particle argument. If you are not aware, plotting radars are a part of our fire control in that they seek out a target and guide the missiles. Air targets and land targets are different entities, and particularly with land targets interference in the usual one-meter squared RCS beam is a problem."

One of the guys did not understand the RCS reference. "Sorry," Kimberly said. "We tend to talk in acronyms, Radar Cross Section. Within that narrow beam over twenty to thirty miles, we get interference from a variety of things. Dealing sea to sea, the most obvious is a bounce of the signal off the water surface at the horizon. I suspect that some, likely a lot, of it is a variety of disturbed energies in your sub-atomic particles occurring for a variety of reasons. However, until you understand them better and in some, several cases, even confirm their existence, we won't be able to apply the information to interference solutions."

Allister was smiling. They listened as the physicists got into a highly theoretical discussion of waveforms and sub-atomic particles. They were all heading for lunch. Admiral Snell slid up beside her.

"Well done, I was afraid Allister was going to tell them there was no application. You gave them something to chew on. Sit separately from the rest of us with your young man."

Kimberly slid up beside Harrison. "If you're still talking to me, the Admiral suggested we eat at a separate table." Harrison grinned at her, okay so far.

"Look, I'm sorry," Kimberly started, "but I had no clue what I could tell you and what I couldn't. Before you say anything, let me bring you up to date. How much I can say is limited by security, but I can tell you a bit more than usual because you too have a security clearance. You can't say most of this to anyone. My engineering degree is from the Naval Academy, and I was a surface warfare officer; that can be public. As you now know, I did plotting. My ship and the plotting team were involved with a bunch of tests on the plotting radar system. Thus, my involvement with the Admiral and the defense contractor. Now comes the difficult part. This Trident insignia means I am a SEAL. A very new one in need of a lot more training. What you and I have had is great, but my best advice is that you drop me like a hot potato as sailors tend to deploy at sea for extended time frames, and the SEAL shit is dangerous stuff."

She had known that if she was to get into any serious relationship, but particularly with a civilian, these conversations would be difficult. Harrison had not processed the latter part and was all but laughing at her. "It was a surprise, but now I understand all the security checks after you waltzed into the lab."

"That had nothing to do with me. Your Head of Department turned you guys in. I just happened to waltz in. The Navy wasn't testing your security."

"Damn, I've lucked into one amazing woman. I guess that explains all the cuts and bruises."

"Or a real crazy. Drop me, find a nice science major, or even an art major who's not crazy, and have bright kids who become scientists."

"No way, but I understand keeping my mouth shut about what you do."

"Harrison, it's a hell of a lot more complicated than that. My work as a SEAL covers a lot of stuff, and most of it is highly classified and dangerous. It was pointed out to me that should we allow this to go on, it could bring unwanted attention to this facility. I never told you about a friend that was killed in a terrorist attack back in junior high. I'm about fighting terrorists. Our being together will bring a security risk to this facility but, more importantly, to me, and you. As I said, find a nice science major that's not crazy, and have bright kids who become scientists." She hated that she had allowed things to go this far when she saw Harrison's face drop. She was not going to back down; her advice to him was correct.

"How was Harrison?" They were back on the C-20D heading for San Diego when the Admiral brought it up.

"Okay, I guess. Hell, there are times I hate being a sailor girl."

Soon she was back at Coronado.   For the next six months, Kimberly was very busy with the individual specialty training. Though there were opportunities, Kimberly resisted the urge to contact and get together again with Harrison. The Navy had decided that she was an excellent marksman, so she was assigned to high-level sniper training. Those guys were even crazier.

The following six months, Kimberly, along with Ewing, Carlos, Martinek, and Rodriquez, were together again doing the unit-level training. Then they went through the six months of task group level training.   Finally, as a group, they were assigned to a Special Operations Task Force, based in Hawaii. It had been fifteen years since the cafeteria bombing.

The drilling began on a mock-up. A couple of weeks later, there was a briefing, including satellite pictures of a compound. They were in the air when Kimberly learned that they were on a real mission. An American family, a couple with their three children ranging in age from seven to fifteen, had been sailing in the Pacific when they were captured. A known terrorist organization was trying to bargain for their release, which the United States would not do. Intelligence was that they did not know who they had; the father was a scientist at Los Alamos. The team's task was recovering them, more specifically, Dr. Baker, the Los Alamos scientist.

At Subic Bay in the Philippines, they transferred to a submarine. There was no moon when they surfaced and started paddling small boats toward the island. They could see some lights up at the compound as they pulled onto a rocky beach below the cliff. There was an inlet and a route to the top that intelligence had mapped correctly. Thus far, not a word had been spoken. They split into their component teams. Kimberly had Ewing, Carlos, Martinek, and Rodriquez with her.

Every intelligence indication that the compound was lightly guarded was correct. The team had to move fast as there was a larger camp just minutes away. Everyone was in position.

"Go," came the command over Kimberly's headset. Her team moved up either side of the small hut where the hostages were believed to be held. A click in her headset told her Martinek had silently taken out a sentry, as planned. The sentry at the front door of the hut was bored and lax; his back turned to Kimberly.

Kimberly grasped his head with her left arm covering his mouth with her hand then cut his throat with her combat knife. The dying man could not shout and was spurting blood as Kimberly shoved him aside.   As she opened the door, she had the thought that that was for Tommy James.

Janie Ewing, coming from the opposite side of the hut, was right behind her when she entered the cabin. It was pitch black, and Kimberly could hear crying. Janie turned a flashlight with a hooded beam on that she pointed at the floor. There were no guards; only the family was in the hut.

"You're okay, quiet; we're American's coming to rescue you."

They identified each of the kids and both parents, including Dr. Baker, the Los Alamos scientist. There was an extra pair.

"Who are you?" Ewing asked the frightened pair.

"They don't speak English very well," Dr. Baker told them. "They were brought here after we were captured. Apparently, from the mainland." Kimberly had a problem. They could not be left there, even if they were there to spy on the Baker's.

"Do you want to come with us?" she asked slowly.

"You are American?" the man asked.

"Yes, sent to rescue this family," Kimberly replied, indicating the Bakers.

"Get away from here?" the man asked.

"Yes."

The man spoke to the woman in a language Kimberly did not recognize. She nodded affirmatively.

"Yes, go with you," the man said.

"Okay," she told her team, "but if one of them makes a sound, kill them."

"How'd you get past the guards?" Chuck Baker, the thirteen-year-old son, asked?" Kimberly ignored him.

"Okay,' Kimberly said, addressing them all, "when we leave here, there'll be one or two bodies to pass. Ignore them. We'll be climbing down a narrow path to the shore. Anyone have a physical problem to prevent them from doing that?"

The answers from the Anderson's were all negative. "The lady is elderly, at least she's infirmed," Dr. Anderson told them.

"We'll see," was Kimberly's reply, "let's go."

With Rodriquez leading the way, they got back to the path where they came up the cliff. Twenty meters later, it was clear that the older woman could not make it. One of the component teams was already by the water, and they were risking the back-door guys by taking too long to get down the cliff. The lady was frail and light. Using some harnesses, they strapped her to Kimberly's back, Carlos took Kimberly's pack.

"Damn, who are you guys, SEALs?" Carolyn Baker, the eldest daughter, asked in awe.

"Haven't you figured that out yet? But you never talk about this," Janie Ewing said.

The next problem was at the bottom of the cliff, where the older woman was afraid of getting into the small boat. Fortunately, her husband promptly and emphatically talked her into the boat.

Kimberly wondered if he had understood her order that they could not be left behind alive.

"May I paddle, I'm good in a canoe," Carolyn asked.

Kimberly nodded, and Martinek handed her one of the spare paddles. If the girl kept up, it might help resolve the problem of losing time due to the extra couple. Carolyn kept up, but Kimberly could see that it was only with great effort. Captivity had weakened her.

There was no noise from the compound as they paddled out of range. Finally, all the small boats stopped and waited. They were now a few minutes ahead of schedule. With almost no noise, only a slight splash, the submarine resurfaced in the dark. Soon everyone was safe inside, and they were on their way back to the Philippines.

The mission commander sat beside Kimberly. "The kids okay? I'm going to give them the talk."

"Good, considering what they've been through. Could I do the talk, Sir? I've got a bit of rapport with them." Kimberly added. The commander agreed. Kimberly moved to where the family was and squatted down so that she was in the kids' faces.

"Carolyn correctly guessed that we're a SEAL team," she told the family. "You're to forget that now. Talking about this part of your life is a bad idea unless it's to counselors. At no time can you mention us, or how many of us, and should you ever see any of us again, you do not, under any circumstances, know us. The secrecy is for your safety as well as ours. Understood?" Everyone nodded that they did. Kimberly had them each talk about their time in captivity.

Back on Coronado, de-briefers told the team that they had scored a coup. The male of the extra couple was a senior Malaysian police officer whose life the terrorists had been trying to ransom.

The Bachelor Officers Quarters was relatively lonely. Kimberly and Lieutenant JG Janie Ewing were apartment-mates. Janie talked about her family life. Montana's father was bullshit about Janie pushing the idea of Montana going to the Naval Academy. Janie denied pushing the idea; it was what Montana wanted. Montana's father had never taken his eldest daughter seriously despite her excellent math and science marks. As the Academy required, she did have two languages, English and Spanish.

"She's trying to one-up Mommy?" Kimberly asked Janie.

"No, I don't think so."

"He has custody because ...?"

"The court decided her father would have custody because, as a sailor, my life is too unstable. Montana has always talked Navy and is very interested in what I do. That was particularly true when I got to Officer Candidate School. Her father's a prick. They fight all the time. She walked out as soon as she legally could. If she's trying to do anything about her parents, it's directed at her father."

Janie decided to learn to ride a motorcycle. Kimberly accompanied her to a school to check it out. The guy running it was no Rocky Lachance but would do a good job.

One evening while Janie was at motorcycle school, Kimberly became bored and headed downtown to a bar for a drink. There were only a few patrons in the bar. That was probably usual on a Sunday night. As uniforms are not permitted off base, she had on a blouse and slacks. Sitting up on the barstool, Kimberly tried to decide what to drink, finally settling on a Pina Colada. The big bar mirror gave her a chance to survey things. The bar was dead, which was okay by her as she was not looking for trouble.

Almost finished with her drink, she decided that coming was a mistake, and she would go back to the base. Inertia won.

"May I sit here?"

"Free country," Kimberly replied.

The guy was about fifty, bulky, with a ridiculous wig, yacking on about something. Kimberly was not listening. He expected a reply to something as he started getting belligerent toward her. She stood up and moved to the end of the bar. He followed her.

"Hey, bitch, I was talking to you."

"Get lost."

"You can't talk to me like that."

"Wanna bet ... just get lost." Kimberly put both hands on her drink and gripped it tightly. The base was too damn close, and whoever this guy was, if she belted him, she would be in trouble.

"Sir, why don't you go sit down at the other end of the bar and have another drink on the house," the bartender chimed in trying to settle the guy.

"Fuck you. I was talking to the whore."

Kimberly did not see the man come up behind her, but suddenly there was a tall, slightly balding guy in a very nice tan suit standing somewhat off the two stools where she and the troublemaker were sitting.

"Sir, I'd suggest that you leave the lady alone. She clearly asked you not to bother her."

"Stay the fuck out'a this."

"The bartender has kindly offered you a free drink if you just go to the other end of the bar and behave yourself."

"I told you to stay the fuck out of this."

The guy in the suit put his hand on the man's right shoulder and did something with his fingers.

"Ow, you're fuckin' hurting me."

"Clean up the language, and apologize to the lady, then I'll let you go." He glanced at the bartender and nodded his head toward the door. The bartender nodded affirmatively.

"Your fuckin' hurting me, let go." The massive guy started to swing with his left hand, but the guy in the suit blocked it with his other hand then pressed down harder.

"Ow, fuck, stop that." The suit guy let the pressure off a bit; Kimberly was fascinated as she watched, the bartender was intrigued as well.

"Now, get up, turn away slowly, and walk out of here. If you want to argue, I'm going to hurt you again. Don't come back in here, or the bartender will call the cops. I'll deal with you before they arrive in a way that you will be pleased to see them. Understood?"

"Fuck you. Ow, shit, yes, okay." The guy slid off the stool and turned his back on them as he walked out.

"Thank you, sir," the bartender said, "but we prefer if customers didn't get involved like that."

"I know, but he was no match, so it was safe." He turned to Kimberly. "I'm Malcolm Greene. It would be an honor if you would come to the booth with me. However, should you prefer to sit here, please do."

The evening was looking up. "Kimberly Callahan," she offered her hand to shake, "and I'd be pleased to join you. Thank you for getting rid of the pest." He shook her hand and stepped back, pointing to his booth. Once there, she slid into the side opposite to where his drink was.

"That was awkward. Thanks for the rescue," she told him.

"It's my pleasure to rescue a beautiful damsel in distress."

"Oh, oh, Sir Malcolm, the Knight on his trusty white steed, came to the rescue."

"You have a vivid imagination." They laughed. Somehow this guy made her feel comfortable.

"So, what's a Malcolm Greene?" He sighed and looked at her for a moment.

"A bored, probably boring aging male who, until he was able to rescue you, was having a perfectly awful evening."

"Where did you learn that trick with the fingers in his shoulder?"

She got a different look. "With your imagination, I probably should have some quick-witted answer about going to the local martial arts academy."

"That'll do for now."

"So, what's a Kimberly Callahan?"

Now it was Kimberly's turn to pause. She looked down. Very unsure of how to answer, she decided to be entirely forthright. No, she could not talk about successes or even the Navy. Aside from the Navy and her agenda, there was, in her estimation, little. "I don't have a clue," she replied. Greene said nothing, just looked at her eyes. "I really don't. It's a long, sad tale that you don't want to hear."

"We've all night." She pursed her lips for a moment and looked down again. Greene continued, "at the risk of being told to get lost, which would be a perfectly good response, I'll tell you what little I know." Kimberly looked up at him, surprised that a stranger might know anything about her.

"Let's start with you're an amazing Navy officer who earned her Lieutenant bars well ahead of her Academy classmates and blew the brass out of the water during SEAL training."

There had been a massive security breach; no one was within earshot. Kimberly paused too long. "Talk about a vivid imagination. A story like that would sure pep up a girl's life." Crap, that was not good. "So how many rescue or sniper thingies have I done in this story? Isn't that what SEALs do?"

"One rescue and, for the record, you did well, and you're a hell of a marksman." Wishing she had a firearm, Kimberly reached into her purse and pulled out a cell phone. The man watched her mildly amused.

"What are you doing?"

"Calling the Masters at Arms."

He nodded. "You realize that I could seriously injure you before you even start to dial."

"Yeah, with that finger trick, maybe, but I'm no drunk."

"Give me a second." He brought out his cell and dialed. "Charles, Mack, Lieutenant Callahan is calling the Masters at Arms on me."

"No, really, I should have shown her my ID? Hang on." He passed his phone to her. It was Rear Admiral Smallwood, commanding officer of the Naval Special Warfare Center. He even had the password for the day. Malcolm Green was someone to whom she was supposed to listen.

"So, do people call you Mack or Malcolm?"

"My friends call me Mack. You're trying to change the subject."

"Yeah. What are you?"

"We can get to me later; this is about you."

"No big deal. A sailor who enjoys a lot that the Navy has to offer."

"Then rationalize the math genius with the surface warfare officer and the physical warrior."

"Not much physical."

"We're already established that you did SEAL training and did it very well. You likely don't know that I'm aware that you whipped Gunnery Sergeant Lambert the first night you walked in his gym in Newport."

"Jesus, what are you a PI?"

He laughed. "No, and I said that we'd get to me later."

Kimberly thought a moment. Whoever this guy was, he knew an awful lot about her. Bullshit was likely not going to work. "Okay, but you're supposed to show me some I.D."

He pulled out an identification that looked very authentic. He was Malcolm Greene and a Deputy Director of Homeland Security. What the hell did they have to do with the Navy?

"Okay. I'm not sure what you're looking for, but likely you know that I grew up in Augusta, Maine. Never particularly happy in school up through high school as the work was too easy, and the other kids thought I was a brainiac and bullied. My parents let me take taekwondo in junior high school through high school. A small group of us did some additional disciplines. In grade seven, I had a confrontation with a big kid who was a bully. He threw one too many punches, so I kickboxed him and sat him down. He was okay, likely too afraid to tell his father, another bully, that he had been beaten up by a girl. Nothing happened to me, but physical bullying stopped. I enjoyed martial arts, running, weights, ropes, and swimming; I was on the high school swim team and the track team, we won state in both. Both are loner sports, so I played basketball for the Rams because I thought I needed to learn how to be a part of a team. Unfortunately, my athleticism was such that the coach's solution to winning was that everyone was to pass me the ball as I would score. She would yell at me when I passed it off to someone else, particularly if they didn't score. Plebe summer taught me some teamwork, then the Academy did, and the SEAL training certainly did."

"You left out the thirteen-year-old Girl Scout hero and that in SEAL training, your team had solutions whenever you were in charge."

Kimberly winced; this guy knew how many breaths she took each minute. "Both true, what about you? What's a forty-something guy, who, despite being Homeland Security, knows too much about me, doing by himself in a bar Sunday night?"

He snorted. "Sometimes, I think I'm just watching the parade go by. Let's see, not much to tell, but given where our conversation is going, I should answer. I went to the Academy; engineering degree, and later an MBA; Marine Corps. Attracted the attention of some people and went FBI, was there when the CIA became interested. From there, I wound up at Homeland Security. Now I'm in this bar because we need to talk to you."

"Okay, a hell of a pedigree, but why do you know how many breaths of air I take?"

"You're a fascinating mix of a lot of talent. That mix will be wasted mainline Navy even with the SEALs, so we have an offer. By the way, the number of breaths is different if you're in San Diego as opposed to Palo Alto and curiously goes down, not up when you're dropping through the sky."

Shit, he knew about Harrison, that was not even subtle. Of course, he knew about Harrison; he knew everything else. "You said offer."

"The Coast Guard and Border Patrol do a hell of a job, but their resources are extended, and there is a lot of coastlines. We've caught a couple of terrorist teams landing or inland, but the catches were as much fluke as a thought-out mission. Do you know what the Freedom-class ships are?"

"The LCS's, yeah, small warships, a bit like the old frigates or more the World War Two corvettes, but with a hell of a lot more punch including chopper capability."

"More than capability, there're two choppers on board. What good are they?"

"Bunch of stuff, but mostly they're intended to support land-based operations in shallow coastal areas, anti-submarine, and minesweeping. They've got a couple of missiles on board as well; both, I believe, are Hellfire's."

"We're setting up teams to do coastal patrol to augment the Coast Guard. The whole mission is classified, so only Coast Guard senior command knows."

"Why classified?"

"Operating in U.S. waters and with teams that will take the fight to the land if needed."

"Illegal as shit."

"Arguably, but yes, the military's not allowed to do combat operations on U.S. soil, which makes no sense if someone's invading us. That is why, to be legal, you'll be Coast Guard, or FBI, depending on the situation. However, the same team may suddenly be CIA or even Navy. Some of the seamen and probably Petty Officers will be Coast Guard."

"Congressional oversight?"

"Very limited and secure, so far other than their Chairman, no one trusts any of them."

"We are expendable?"

"I thought the other question would be first."

"Which is – oh - how much does the President know?"

"You got it. POTUS knows all of it, and there is no plausible deniability on his part or on the part of the Congressional Chair. That leads to your other question; you are not expendable. If something goes bad, every effort will be made to extract you."

Some of what was happening with assignments was starting to make sense to Kimberly. "So, I'm with Lt. Ewing, plus PO's Rodriquez, Martinek, and Carlos."

"That's your team leadership. Depending on the mission you may, likely will need, others or in a few scenarios we have imagined different personnel."

To Kimberly, this was an Oh, My God moment; it was beyond exciting and closer to what she had wanted to do since junior high. It would not just be drilling and waiting for a war. "What happens to my Navy career?"

"That remains intact with regular promotions and the standard benefits. Despite the questionable legality and even though we're going to fix that, you will remain Navy. We suspect few will care about legal technicalities as you'll be keeping terrorists away from the country, particularly as Posse Comitatus was passed to allow Jim Crow and designates the Army but not the Navy. It's a new kind of warfare, and we need exceptionally trained people who are highly flexible. Even the SEAL paradigm won't work for this."

"But, it's why we all did SEAL training?"

"Yes."

"Standards were not lowered?"

"Hell no, if you hadn't made it, you'd be going back to the plotting room, and we wouldn't be having this conversation. The same goes for the others. That was not the end of your training. You're going to Quantico."

"Really? Okay, FBI training?"

"And the CIA."

"Shit, so we really will be all of the above operating under the heading of Homeland Security."

"Usually." Kimberly decided to leave that alone for now. "What about your boyfriend?" Greene continued.

"What about him?"

"He has security clearance nowhere near as high as yours, but we don't want the lab to start guessing why his biker engineer girlfriend disappears for extended periods."

"I pretty much disappeared for a year, so I doubt your premise. That said, this is where your info is out of date. Harrison is history and will remain so."

Chapter Eight: Quantico

Janie Ewing had an equally strange discussion with Malcolm Greene. Kimberly and Janie, but not the Petty Officers, were detached from their SEAL team and spent the next few weeks attached to Admiral Sutherland's office at Coronado either underwater with SCUBA gear or free-falling through the sky. Sometimes the guys were with them, sometimes not. Kimberly developed a love of jumping, mainly when she had to free-fall to just above the surface before deploying her chute and moments later be on the ground or in the water.

Finally, Kimberly and Janie had their new orders. They were assigned to Quantico for an undefined training period. Leaving her bike at Janie's on a Friday morning, they went to the airport by cab. Being at Janie's allowed her to meet Janie's two daughters.

Janie had pictures of them at the apartment but rarely talked about them. Kimberly watched and listened to them over breakfast. Montana, the eighteen-year-old, was a beautiful reproduction of her mother. Amanda, who was nine, had exotic features and would be a mankiller when she grew up. Montana was in charge for the weekend as their father also had to be away. They loaded Janie's luggage into the cab, and the two women were off.

"Your daughters are beautiful."

"Thank you. I'm biased, but I think so too. That Amanda's going to do some serious heartbreaking in a few years, not that Montana isn't already."

"You're surprised?"

"No, but Montana's too damn grown-up for eighteen, and Amanda's not far behind. Sometimes I think they are bringing me up rather than the other way around." Kimberly decided to let that drop; they were almost at Departures.

At Quantico, the two women were pleased they had each other for support. Initially, assigned to the FBI Academy, they found that a lot of it was new, criminology, and about the law. For much of it, notably the weapons and physical stuff, they were advance placed through, having qualified at a higher level as SEALs. That shortened their training time, though there was a concern that they know how to handle weapons in civilian environments.

"Jeez, you'd kill these FBI recruits doing martial arts," Janie laughed.

"Yeah, likely you would as well," Kimberly told her.

As they were in a defined program, they covered what they needed by Christmas. The women did well, and, in his office, the Director swore them in as agents. They each got home for Christmas, Janie to San Clemente and Kimberly to Maine.

"You look fitter than I've ever seen you. I guess the Navy keeps you busy," her Dad laughed the day after she arrived.

"Yeah, they do," Kimberly laughed.

"Which ship are you on now?"

Kimberly had not told anyone in her family that she was a SEAL. "Come on, Dad, you know I can't talk about it."

Her brother was his usual quiet self. Meredith, now in junior high, seemed not to know that Kimberly was there. To Kimberly, her baby sister was very narcissistic, self-absorbed with her friends. Her mother's comments about marriage and babies were awkward. Dumping, because that was what she had done, Harrison was a regret. The regret was not so much about Harrison, though that would have been nice. The relationship would now be even more impossible with him on the west coast and her on the east coast. Being a sailor had forced her into a paradigm usually reserved for males. She wondered if she would ever be a mother.

Camp Perry, a former naval facility that allegedly no longer existed, was something else. During CIA training, the teaching was the clandestine crafts. She found the business about information drops funny, even while realizing that they could be deadly serious. She excelled at the drops and all the training. Unlike the FBI, the instruction was not about what one could do legally; it was about functioning in an inhospitable world where there were few rules. Both women found it strange that they liked the CIA training much more than the FBI training. Possibly that was not so strange, working on U.S. soil, the FBI was bound up in rules. At the end of their training, Janie headed to San Clemente on leave. This time Kimberly went with her, initially to get her bike, but she ended up staying with her.

One morning Janie was with her kids, and nothing was happening for Kimberly, so she went riding. She considered going to Palo Alto but immediately rejected it as a lousy idea, only going to Orange County. The big vibrating engine between her legs would have to do. Heading for the coastal hills, she passed a bar with several bikes out front, Grumpy's. She had seen it while riding one day after she was first posted to San Diego and wondered about the place. She argued with herself then turned her bike around. She knew bikers had a bad reputation and that some were into criminal activity, including drugs. She knew she could not and did not want to get involved with that. How would checking out the bar hurt? Parking on the side of the property, she sat on her bike for a minute and looked at the bikes lined up. She wondered if she was getting into more trouble than she needed. Well, a girl had to eat. She walked into the bar.

It was dark inside. Kimberly's eyes took a few moments to adapt. There was a counter straight in front of her. She sat down.

"Whadda ya want honey," the bartender, a heavyset woman in her fifties, asked. Her badge identified her as "Ruby."

"Bud Light draft and a cheeseburger?"

"Coming right up." She hollered back into the kitchen and poured the beer.

Sitting at the counter was a mistake. Kimberly knew better than to turn her back on possible danger. There was no mirror for her to survey the scene behind her. She considered moving but decided to focus on listening as she sipped on the beer.

A couple of minutes later, a guy was standing to her left, his back to the counter. "Seems a shame that a pretty girl like you is eating all alone. Would you like to join us?"

She turned her head to look him over. About five-ten, she guessed and not the typically substantial image of a biker. She figured his weight at about one-eighty. He did have black leather pants, a red Harley Davidson t-shirt, with a red bandanna on his head.

"Who's us?"

"The Easy Riders, over there in the corner."

She looked toward the corner. There were about ten people there, mostly guys; three were women. The age range looked like the early twenties to late forties. "Okay, what're you guys about?"

"Eatin', and then we're doing some ridin'."

"Where're you riding to?"

"Just a circuit into the hills, up to Lake Elsinore and back."

"Why?"

"For fun and to run our bikes. Come on over."

"Okay."

"Mike Steele, they call me Ironman," he put his hand out to shake. "Hey, Ruby, bring the lady's food over to our table."

"Kimberly and I've been called all sorts of things."

"Everybody, this is Kimberly, and these folks are..." He listed off a bunch of names. Halfway through, Kimberly could not recall the first name. They seemed open enough.

"I'd be careful of this bunch of ne're-do-wells lady," was Ruby's comment when she served the cheeseburger.

"Aw Ruby, it's terrible business to diss on your customers," came from a guy who Kimberly thought might be the leader. They called him Doggie. He seemed to be with the older lady they called Pasta.

It was a friendly group, intent on relaxing and having fun. They explained that they were a bunch of motorcycle enthusiasts who liked to ride together on weekends.

"Do you wanna come on the ride tonight?" asked Michael, a.k.a. Ironman.

"Sure," Kimberly replied.

The twenty-five miles to Lake Elsinore was a good ride. Contrary to the usual relatively flat land near the coast, they were in hills. Talking back and forth with them on the radios was a blast. As they passed cars, she enjoyed the various reactions of the people in the vehicles, civilians as Ironman called them. Riding solo, she had not paid much attention. She wondered how Ironman would react if he knew she was a SEAL. There was another bar at Lake Elsinore. Inside, Kimberly decided on another Bud and another cheeseburger. This bunch was fun.

"You guys don't know me, why invite me along?" Kimberly asked.

"We're a group of bikers, sort of a family, all with regular jobs," Doggie explained. "When you drove in, you seemed to be an okay option to go with us. We enjoy biking and pride ourselves on being good bikers, the ability to ride, and to all be clean legally."

Kimberly was in a strange mood, possibly just being free had done it. She wondered what she was going to say if they asked her what she did.

"Oh jeez, will you look at that now." One of the women, Dixie, was looking across the café where one of the guys, Weasel, had been cornered by a couple of women.

"Louise is not going to like that," was Pasta's response.

"Jeez, no, and she's not here to look after it," Dixie said.

"You don't like that local women are cutting in on Weasel?" Kimberly asked.

"Shit no, he's Louise's boyfriend."

"What're we going to do about it?" Kimberly asked.

The woman called Brownie looked at Kimberly for a moment. Kimberly had to think for a bit; her name was Natalie Pigoris. "You mean we should look after Louise's business?" Brownie asked. Things were getting interesting.

"Sounds like what friends are for," Kimberly replied.

"What happens if other locals object?"

"I think we could handle that, and then we all run like hell," was Doggie's comment. "We'd have to leave soon after anyway, in case someone decides to screw with the bikes."

"What are we going to do?" Dixie asked.

"Follow my lead, but let's not attract the cops. Pasta and the guys stay here," Kimberly told them.

She stood, thinking this could be fun or a whole lot of trouble. Kimberly had no clue why she was getting into their shit, just seemed like fun. Likely she was bored given the intensity of the prior months, years. Damn, aside from the Navy, she was FBI, this could be stupid and bad. Likely the bartender was going to call the cops the moment the first punch was thrown. With Kimberly in the lead, the three women headed across the room to Weasel.

"Hey, blonde cunt, what d'ya think you're doing?" demanded Kimberly. By then, the blonde had her hands all over Weasel.

"Weasel, back to the group," Brownie ordered him. "Louise's going to tear your balls fuckin' off."

"Hey, what's your problem, bitch?" The blonde was just a little shorter than Kimberly. She moved into the blonde's face, her leather jacket brushing the blonde's ample chest.

"That's right cunt, I'm da bitch, and you don't get to mess with any of our men. You were messing."

The blonde's two girlfriends backed away. One spoke up. "Hey, you don't need to talk like that."

"Shut up, cunt two," barked Brownie.

"Jeez, I'm sorry."

"Say it fuckin' louder cunt," Dixie ordered.

"I'm sorry," the girl almost hollered. She was close to crying.

"Just don't fuckin' mess with our guys again, capisce?" Kimberly said.

She wheeled and returned to the table. Everyone got up. Doggie handed the waitress enough money for the food and beers plus a good tip as they walked out to their bikes. Kimberly was still doing attitude as she strutted to her bike.

"You're fuckin' awesome," Mike told her over the headset as they headed back.

"Shit, being a pretend badass is fun," Kimberly replied.

Brownie was still laughing when they got back to the Grumpy' s.

"Hey Bitch, that's what we're calling you from now on, 'The Bitch.' You were awesome. Shit, that was fun."

Kimberly just laughed, "I da Bitch." Damn, she was sounding Chicago.

"Yeah, so Weasel, do we tell Louise about this?" Doggie asked him.

"Fuck, no, I was just having a little funning."

"Yeah, well, you know how jealous she gets, besides you just about got us into a fight."

"Shit it was The Bitch that came charging across."

"Yeah, with me, and Dixie," pointed out Brownie, "someone has to look out for Louise."

"Bull shit, you guys were just looking for a fight."

"Yeah, but we had so much fun doing it," agreed Dixie.

"You did okay, Kimberly," said Pasta. "You're fun to have around. We never asked what you do?"

"Is that important?"

"No…" There was a definite but there.

Kimberly admitted to be an engineer. The group went over their real names again for Kimberly. Antonio Isabelli, Doggie, was a machinist, and Pasta worked at a dry-cleaning establishment. Ironman was an insurance guy and his girlfriend, Brownie, Natalie Pigoris, a bartender. Pasta did not explain Cheryl Phillips, a.k.a. Dixie, the nickname likely due to her southern drawl. Dixie spoke up.

"I'm kinda a sometimes rider; I'm Navy,"

"Cool, what do you do for the Navy?" Kimberly asked.

Dixie paused slightly before answering. "Ordnance."

"Oh, okay, hey, I've got to get going."

"Come on back." Pasta offered. Michael accompanied her to her bike.

"This is a good night?"

"'fraid so Ironman, just wanted to ride with some good people. Besides, I think Brownie would take exception."

"Yeah, probably, come on back anytime. Can't blame a guy for trying."

"Sure, thanks."

That Phillips said ordnance, got Kimberly thinking about her mission personnel. The question the next morning was who to ask. Kimberly decided that the Admiral was only going along with the secret stuff, better that she should ask Greene. Getting ahold of him was amazingly simple. She told him a bit about the encounter with the Easy Riders and Cheryl Phillips.

"Trying to be a badass?"

"I can do badass."

"Yes, you can. Let me find out about Phillips. You're correct that with the ordnance training and a bad-ass attitude, she might just fit our plans. I gather you like her."

Kimberly decided she had better tell Greene the whole story. Fortunately, he was laughing.

"Damn it, one of these days, I'm going to have to dream up some plausible story to bust you out of the brig after a Master at Arms picks you up."

He called back two hours later. Phillips was an excellent Chief Petty Officer whose specialty was ordnance, and she was good at it. She just might fit in with the team. That was the first time Green had called them a team. Kimberly was to call Phillips and invite her to dinner on a yacht called the Destiny II that would be birthed at Newport Beach, no uniforms. She called the number Greene gave her. CPO Phillips was not available, but they would give her the message. Kimberly's phone rang fifty minutes later.

"This is CPO Phillips."

"Hey, Dixie, this is Da Bitch, a.k.a Lieutenant Kimberly Callahan."

"Shit."

"Oh, babe, it's not even started."

"No ma'am, I don't imagine, not with you calling from an Admiral's office."

"Whatever you're doing Thursday night, forget it. You have a dinner date on a yacht named Destiny II that's docked at the marina in Newport Beach. No uniforms, in fact, biker dress. My bike and I'll join you at a bar called The Place on the East Coast Highway in Corona Del Mar."

Kimberly arrived early. The parking lot in front of the bar was a reasonable size. She parked her bike well away from the building and checked the area. As Cheryl drove up, Kimberly started her engine. Making it visible, she pulled her headset plug.

Cheryl pulled up close to her. "What's going on?" They could converse with the engines throttled down.

"How's your physical shape?" It was a question Greene had asked to which Kimberly had not been able to give specifics.

"Good, I like to be in good condition. It helps me think clearly around the ordnance. I run five miles each morning and work out in a gym."

She was a girl after Kimberly's own heart. "Relationship?"

"Never married and just threw the last bum out."

"K, we have plans for you to consider, come with me." They headed up The Five to Newport Beach.

When they arrived at the pier, security had descriptions of the bikes and license numbers. Janie was waiting for them. The guy at the gate gave them parking passes to display. It was a beautiful warm day, so they parked their bikes and walked to slip thirty-nine and Destiny II. Kimberly introduced Dixie to Janie, both as CPO Cheryl Phillips and as Dixie.

Dixie stopped walking. "Okay, Lieutenants, when the shit do I find out what this is all about, ma'am?"

"Once we get on board Destiny II," Kimberly told her.

"I feel like some fuckin' party girl going on a rich guy's yacht."

"That's what it's supposed to look like," replied Janie.

Greene was there with a couple of associates. He introduced Willian A. Sanburg as a senior partner at something called Watsoo Financial Group on the east coast. Kimberly suspected a front; the stupid name could be better. Maybe not, a ridiculous name like that wouldn't be a front. Kimberly guessed him to be six feet in height, probably around fifty, grey hair, and with only a hint of a middle-age spread. A woman, Miranda Davidson, who was in her mid-forties, about five feet nine, trim, and stunning, with short jet-black hair cut pageboy style, and very pale skin, was there. No one had even a fake explanation as to why she was there. Admiral Sutherland was there but in civilian clothing. He and Greene were the only ones to show identification to CPO Phillips. The Admiral first asked Cheryl how much she had been told and if she was at all interested in terrorist interdiction.

"Virtually nothing, and this is the first time I have heard terrorist interdiction. Am I interested? Thus far, I'm intrigued. I'd have no problem with a reassignment as long as I remain Navy," CPO Phillips told the Admiral. He assured her that she would remain Navy. The Davidson woman was a bit sharp, wanting Phillips to understand that all this was confidential.

"I've figured that out ma'am, and Lieutenant Callahan explained that."

"It's not only confidential Chief, but some of it may be clandestine. It's all legal, but you cannot talk to anyone about any of this, including this meeting," Greene explained.

"Understood, sir."

"Where is Walter Giddings in all this?"

"Very past tense, sir, he's not ever coming back." Kimberly guessed he was the ex-boyfriend.

"You understand that your security clearance has been ratcheted up," Davidson asked her.

"For this stuff, I would imagine ma'am."

"You cleared the surveillance easily except for questions about this Giddings person," Davidson told her.

"He's an asshole ma'am, and as I said very past tense." Davidson smiled at the CPO.

"Would it surprise you that Lieutenants Callahan and Ewing are SEALs?" Greene asked her.

"Not at all, sir."

"We want you in the next SEAL class."

"That would be great, sir," she glanced at the Admiral who nodded.

"You have to qualify to continue here," Davidson told her. That told Kimberly that she would need another ordnance person for a couple of years.

"Yes, ma'am," Phillips told Davidson.

"Okay, Admiral, CPO Phillips goes to the next SEAL training class."

"Fine, you're dismissed, CPO Phillips." Cheryl wheeled around to leave, glancing at Kimberly. She was smiling. The Admiral continued after Cheryl left. "Now, Lieutenant Ewing, something has come up. I understand that your daughter is anxious to attend the Naval Academy."

"Yes, Sir."

"Her application was fouled up. We got that sorted out; she's to report for plebe summer next week." Montana would be getting a letter the following day.

The remainder of the evening was discussing how operational they were. Considering that the unit had never functioned as a team,

Kimberly's assessment was not very functional. Before they started to put the mission package together, Kimberly and Janie had Navy training to do. They were both receiving promotions. The Admiral understood that he had to assign an ordnance specialist to them temporarily.

The next morning Kimberly received a call from Montana. The girl wanted to have lunch. Her mother was not to know.

They had barely sat down in the restaurant. "I got a letter today."

"Okay"

"It's from the Naval Academy. I've been accepted this fall; in fact, I have to report this weekend."

"Congratulations, didn't I say it would all work out?"

Montana ignored Kimberly, "One problem, though."

"What's that?"

"They had told me that I'd have to wait out at least a year as my application got screwed up."

"Well, probably it was a Congressional appointment through your high school."

"You're gonna bull shit me?"

"What are you really asking?"

"Mom knew about this last night. She was happy for me but wouldn't say any more, like she wasn't supposed to know for some reason. The acceptance comes out of the blue after my application got screwed up' likely because my fuckin' father had our Congressman intercede, so the effing opposite of your lousy reason. You guys are doing strange stuff, and I don't mean your bike rides. What the hell is going on?"

"We'll have lunch, and then I'll answer your question."

"Somehow, I suspected that would happen. I'm not hungry." The waiter arrived to take their order. They had changed their minds; Kimberly left a tip. Once out on the street, Kimberly waited until they could walk down an alley where there were no windows on the buildings.

"Okay, you're correct, but stop guessing and forget any guessing you've done to date. Things aren't all they appear to be for excellent reasons. I assure you, it's all legal."

"Yeah, well, I didn't think the drug cartels could get me an appointment to Annapolis. You wouldn't talk in the restaurant because you were concerned with being overheard?"

"Yes, and FYI it's tough to bug an alley with no windows when the target keeps walking."

"You guys mixed up with the CIA?"

"I told you to stop guessing and forget all this."

"Why is Mom going to be away after I go to plebe summer?"

"Training, we both will. We're being promoted and have to go back to class to learn how to function at the new ranks."

"Okay, makes sense. If Amanda wants to know where Mom is, what do I say?"

"You say the truth, that she's in training for her new rank. But Amanda won't be able to ask you because you'll be out of touch as a midshipman plebe. You're probably not seeing anyone until Thanksgiving or later."

"And I tell my classmates that my mother is a spook?" she laughed.

"What do you tell your classmates, or your best girlfriend, or Amanda, for that matter?"

"That my mother is a Lieutenant in the U.S. Navy and is often away."

"You're learning. Realize that there's a lot in their job that any Lieutenant can't divulge. Even as a Mid, you'll have a security clearance, and screwing that up is a career stopper."

"Shit, I can't say anything to anybody, and this conversation never happened, right?"

"What conversation? We're going to the Foot Locker to get you some new running shoes, and we're cutting through the alley as a shortcut."

"Weird."

They did buy running shoes. Montana was a bit upset that she was going to be so far away from her friends and particularly Amanda, but she had had Annapolis as a goal for a long time. She could call.

"Really, who told you that?" Kimberly asked.

"Just assumed."

"That's the first mistake, assume nothing. The Firsties will take your phone at the start of plebe summer. After that, you get three calls to your family for no more than thirty minutes. You get your phone back at the end of the summer but can't use it for media. If you're in Bancroft Hall, the cell phone reception is poor to non-existent," Kimberly told her.

Montana stopped and looked at Kimberly. "Makes sense. If I'm going to do this, the focus is on what the Navy wants me doing."

"You got it."

Montana even had a story as to why she had not told her friends that she had applied there. As she thought about it, some of them knew, just not about the foul-up. She was going to be okay.

Chapter Nine: Back East

In the Navy, the rank of Lieutenant Commander covers all sorts of work from combat missions to heading the payroll office. Ultimately the rank specific training was about leadership and team building. As she had been a loner, Kimberly's take was that she needed the classes, despite all the teamwork training she had done. As usual, she did very well and soon could legally wear the gold oak leaf. Janie Ewing did well in her classes and now had two silver bars, a full Lieutenant.

The next step for both women was the Advanced Medical Training Course 18D required before going operational. It was more comprehensive than the medical training they had as SEALs.

In July, Alex Howle made another attempt to get his daughter removed from the Academy. His lawyer explained that as she was nineteen, there was nothing he could do. He even warned Howle that his attempt to use the Congressman's office could land him in legal hot water, should Montana choose. A guy from the FBI had called his lawyer and explained that in no uncertain terms. That stopped her father. She did well at plebe summer, and come fall was at Annapolis.

Well into fall, Kimberly and Janie were assigned to Norfolk. For Kimberly, it was like being back at surface warfare school as they were substituting for assigned core personnel on littorals, the Freedom Class Warships. They were the mission package but undergoing cross-training to drive the LCS. Janie had done boat handling as a Petty Officer but nothing as small as a littoral. Of the three modules available, these littorals had the configuration for surface warfare.

The Commissioned Officer's Mess at Norfolk is impressive, as massive as the one in San Diego's, but likely with more brass given their proximity to Washington. Kimberly and Janie went to the bar the second night they were on the base. While sitting at the bar, one observing from the rear could not see their collars.

"Hey gorgeous, the evening's looking up." A male Lieutenant with a broad gold band and narrow band on his sleeve moved in on Kimberly's left side. As he did so, she turned to Janie on her right, her back to him, to signal the guy to back off. "Come on, babe, let me buy you a fresh beer."

Kimberly turned her stool to face the Lieutenant, checking his name badge. His eyes went immediately to the Gold Leaf on her collar and then to the Trident insignia. "Fuck." His fellow Lieutenant, who had been grinning, went pale.

"Really, Lieutenant JG Ward, that's your best? Try an apology," Kimberly said. "If I ever see you here, or anywhere else in the world, talking like a jerk like that to a fellow officer, an enlisted or a civilian you're going on report."

"Yes, ma'am. Sorry, ma'am." Both men left quickly.

The boat handling training on the littorals continued up to Christmas. During leave over Christmas, Kimberly chose to fly home, not trusting the weather and her motorcycle.

"You're more relaxed than I've seen you in a few years," her dad commented.

"Yeah, things are going well. Since fall, I've been at sea for multiple short periods, and I like that."

"Do you have your Lieutenant bars, or am I not allowed to ask?"

"Gold Oak Leaf."

"You lost me, what's that?"

"Lieutenant Commander."

Her Dad broke into a big smile, clearly proud, "You're moving fast."

"Working hard."

"So, you're on a destroyer ... cruiser...?"

"Jeez, Dad, you know you can't ask that." Her father nodded.

The petty officers had their new rank training. After Christmas CPO Luis Rodriquez, PO-1 Warren Martinek, and PO-2 Anthony Carlos joined Janie Ewing and Kimberly in Norfolk. They were assigned a combination of office and warehouse space in a land building.

"As I understand the orders," Luis said at their first meeting, "we're tasked with putting together a mission team of fifteen to twenty that will work from a littoral reinforcing the Coast Guard and Border Patrol with terrorist interdiction?"

"Yes, the others are coming in next week," Kimberly told them.

"SEALs?" Warren asked.

"No," Kimberly told them, "as far as they've told me, excepting an ordnance specialist, we'll be the only SEALs. But the mission package needs to be trained to work on water or land. They'll be selected Navy and Coast Guard non-coms and seamen."

"No air?" Anthony Carlos asked.

"Thus far, not that I'm aware of, or we're going to do it if needed. We're not training novices to jump."

"We need to train the Seamen in land ops then?" Rodriquez asked.

"Both Navy and Coast Guard, we're to train the Seamen and NCO's in land ops, and advanced sea maneuvers," Kimberly told them.

"Is there a curriculum?" Rodriquez asked.

"Up to us, that's what we do over the next week," Kimberly told them.

"And beyond," Ewing added, "we'll get a start this week, but the curriculum will be under constant modification. Lieutenant Commander Callahan has told me that we need to be working out plausible and implausible scenarios, figure out how to react, and then train for it."

"An intelligence officer is going to be working with us this week on scenario development," Kimberly told them.

"Aren't intelligence and Navy oxymorons?" one of the Petty officers joked.

"Who said the officer was Navy?" Kimberly asked, getting stares from the Petty Officers.

Kimberly was the only one who knew that the male in civilians who joined them was CIA. He had several possible scenarios and helped them develop many more. Lieutenant Ewing working with the Petty Officers, began to create basic training for the mission package and scenario-specific training. Twice a day, Kimberly met with them, but she needed to review all the candidates who volunteered. They were assigned a SEAL PO-1 ordnance specialist on an interim basis.

Several Petty Officers and Seamen, both Coast Guard and Navy, applied. There were no recruits or even apprentice seamen. She expected some would drop or wash out so selected thirty to the first class. The next several weeks confirmed to her how solid the choice of SEALs heading the team had been. They started designing all the classroom tabletop scenarios and land/sea training exercises. Thus far, the Navy was allowing them to develop and modify the curriculum. Kimberly was able to share ideas with other units. The new team members quickly got over their awe of the SEALs and trained well; there were only a few drops. Kimberly coordinated with several other mission package commanders on Norfolk for the venues for ordnance and live-fire drills. A couple of the commanders she recognized from SEAL training and a few from the Academy. Similar teams were being developed in Louisiana for the Gulf Coast and in San Diego for the West Coast.

One afternoon they came ashore at Norfolk at 2100 hrs. Zulu, 1700 hrs. Eastern. Kimberly and Janie decided to head to the Commissioned Officer's Mess. Their route cut across the back of the building. A guy was there with a beer truck.

"Whoa, Kim?"

Kimberly looked; it was Brad Watson. Kimberly had not heard that he moved to Virginia. With a distributor's uniform on, he was, as he had at home, loading beer. "Oh, hi," Kimberly replied.

"Jeez, you look great. I tried to see you back home, but your folks said you were in California. You Navy now?"

Duh, they were wearing their service khaki uniforms. Kimberly doubted Brad would have a clue about the insignia on her collar. "Yes."

"What're you doing here?"

"I've been posted to this base."

"Wow, shit, you look great."

Two enlisted men passed. As they did, they snapped salutes at the two officers that the women returned.

"Shit, like, are you someone important?" Brad asked.

"We're officers; they're enlisted."

"Oh. Shit, you have a lot of stuff."

He was referring to her ribbon rack. She hoped that he had no idea about the Budweiser pin. He asked for her new address; the answer was no, and that they needed to get on with their business. There was no need to explain that they were going to the mess.

"An ex-friend?" Janie asked as they walked to the front and the mess entrance.

"Yeah, an ex-boyfriend from my high school stupid days. I knew he was delivering beer back home, but I've no idea what he's doing here. Probably chasing women, though he's supposedly married."

Kimberly did receive one set of orders that the others in her team did not get. One morning she was to report to Patuxent River Naval Air Station, a Naval Air test pilot station. She had no clue. Service Dress Whites were the order of the day.

Ten mission team commanders, all Lieutenant Commanders and all of whom Kimberly knew from Norfolk, assembled in one of the hangers. All had the Budweiser pin. There is almost always airplane noise around an air station, so Kimberly paid no attention to the helicopter noise. A Vice Admiral suddenly entered the hanger with a familiar person, the President of the United States. There were no news people. POTUS wanted to meet them, speaking for a few minutes about their costal rapid response units to protect the homeland. He did assure them that he had approved the program and that though highly secret, he had a legal opinion that it was legal. He would back them. Greene had told her that, but this was a higher authority. Kimberly thought she heard the noise of Marine One leave. A Captain advised them that they could admit to meeting POTUS, but not where, when, or why.

After six months of training, Kimberly's team was assigned to a very new Freedom-class ship, a littoral, the USS Detroit. It is one and a third football fields long but has a draft of only thirteen feet so that it can operate in shallow water. Now fully constituted, they were the mission package of twenty over and above the core crew of fifty who managed the ship.

The next morning, they reported aboard their ship. Kimberly found Lieutenant-Commander Hans Shorheim, the ship's Captain on the bridge, preparing to get underway.

"I heard that you were my mission package," Shorheim said, smiling at her. She knew and liked Shorheim. He had been a year ahead of her at the Academy.

"Congrats, I heard that you just got this baby," Kimberly told him.

"Yeah, it's brand new right out of Wisconsin where they build them. She handles nicely. It has the surface warfare module. Come." They stepped into a small space that was his sea cabin. He was smiling. "Damn, I couldn't believe it when they told me who was going to be in command of the mission package. This is going to be fun. I knew bits of what you've achieved but had no clue about most of what they told us at the briefing. I want to be very clear; my responsibility is the ship, yours the mission. We're just the driver for you and your team. I'll be delighted to accommodate whatever you guys need."

"That's good because I'm good at SEAL stuff, but despite driving school, I don't know much about driving this thing or any other ship."

He laughed. "Okay, I don't know much about special ops. I'm told that you have command over the weapons."

"Or one of my people unless all of us with that authority, meaning myself and Lieutenant Ewing, are off the ship, in which case it'll fall to you and your fire officer. The reality is that we'll all work together."

"K, which is what I understand as well. It's kinda tricky working in our waters."

His question went to the legal issue. Kimberly wondered how much he had been told. "We're legal. We need fast, flexible units to respond to these creeps. Neither the Coast Guard nor the Border Patrol has the assets to cover it fully."

"Yeah, I was told that as well." He still appeared concerned.

"Look, I have assurance from POTUS that we're legal, but be careful of that info as the meeting never happened. Don't worry about your career; we have to keep these assholes off our shore or minimally on it and always being watched."

"If they land, we call the FBI?"

That told Kimberly that he did not know that she was FBI. "Only if they get past us and then we'll all be in deep shit. My team will be using your longboats and inflatables."

The immediate task was for everyone to get bunked in and to start familiarizing themselves with the ship. The electronics were terrific, and most of the information was available on the bridge, unlike the destroyers, where the bridge sees the results with most of the detail held in the combat information center. CPO Luis Rodriquez made friends with the plotting guys. One of the new people, Navy PO-1 Susan Rife, was another plotting room expert. If they encountered hostiles, she and Rodriquez would be doing a lot of the radar operations. The littoral's crew were accustomed to low gain surveillance radar. They theoretically knew how to increase the gain and focus on a single target, but Kimberly's team would be doing that.

They were at sea checking ships, most of the time, for the next eighteen months. No one tried to land a terrorist team, but they encountered several suspicious situations about which they notified the Coast Guard or the Border Patrol. Kimberly liked the time at sea. Their time at sea was typically only a few days at a time rather than the long deployments of the task force ships. The time ashore, they spent drilling and honing skills.

The coastal patrolling continued to be fun but quiet. Almost two years after their mission on the USS Detroit started, CPO Cheryl Phillips, a.k.a. Dixie, complete with her Trident insignia, joined them. She had seniority, so was the top CPO. Kimberly and Lieutenant Ewing had to get imaginative with the drills to keep the team sharp. Rodriquez and Rife focused their time with the littoral's plotting crew developing radar, infrared, and other electronic image capabilities using unsuspecting maritime traffic.

With a strong onshore wind, the USS Detroit was sailing north back to Norfolk. The wind blew up just after noon; it was not expected to get any worse. Despite the forecast, it did get worse, to Sea State Force Six conditions. None of that bothered the littoral. The rough seas would be an excellent opportunity to train. Kimberly knew that the Littoral Class was rated to at least Sea Force Nine, a strong gale with ten-foot waves. Hans was not concerned. The watch had on battle dress uniform, including helmets and life preservers. Though not on watch, Kimberly, wearing BDU's and life jacket, while carrying her helmet, was on the bridge.

"What's that?" Janie suddenly asked. She looked with her binoculars. "Shit, someone's in trouble." With her binoculars,

Kimberly saw only waves until she saw the small cabin cruiser bobbing on the six-foot waves.

"The Coast Guard issued an advisory this morning. Small crafts aren't supposed to be out here," Shorheim said. He ordered a minor course shift to head toward the craft and had a seaman inform the Coast Guard of the sighting. There were no reports of a missing craft or distress calls. Moments later, they were closing on the craft. Somebody, the idiot did not have a life jacket on, was frantically waving their arms from the stern.

"CPO Phillips to the wheelhouse," Kimberly announced.

They showed the CPO the problem. "Do you think you can get an RHIB launched in this?" Kimberly asked.

What she was asking was beyond training in rough seas, but the CPO thought they could safely launch a rigid hull inflatable boat and get a line to the craft. Shorheim and Castillo, his CPO, agreed. Aside from likely saving lives, it would be a good, albeit dangerous exercise. Shorheim decided that due to their SEAL training, Kimberly's crew would attempt the rescue with Phillips in command of the inflatable. Shorheim's team would handle deck duties.

"Those people are idiots," Kimberly told both CPOs. "I don't want any of our people hurt, so don't take unnecessary chances. Dixie, get life jackets on the idiots as soon as possible. Shit, I know you know that I'm sorry. Let's get everyone back aboard alive."

"Aye, aye, ma'am."

Hans maneuvered the ship so the bow remained into the wind, but the stern would block some of the wind and waves. He kept the LCS lined up with the pleasure craft, which appeared to be an about twenty-foot cruiser. Phillips, Rodriquez, Martinek, and Carlos got an inflatable boat into the water and maneuvered it to the other craft, securing alongside it. With her binoculars, Kimberly watched as they passed life jackets to the two guys on board and then brought them into the inflatable. She was unhappy as they moved the inflatable forward on the pleasure craft and secured a tow line. Saving the boat had been Phillip's call based on what was happening in the water but seemed an unnecessary danger. The little cruiser was close; one of the guys was Brad Watson.

"Shit."

"S'cuse me, ma'am?" the seaman at the helm asked.

"Nothing helm, sorry, nice job handling her."

Hans' crew recovered the inflatable at the stern, getting the two guys and the SEALs safely onto the littoral's deck and then below. The towline to the cabin cruiser was secured, and Hans ordered a course change to the Coast Guard base. Kimberly felt like hiding and leaving Janie to deal with it. Even with him dripping wet and disheveled, Janie might recognize Watson. Kimberly could not hide anyway; this was her responsibility. She went below.

"Who was in command of the boat?" she asked, ignoring Brad's wide-eyed stare. She could smell the beer. The other guy replied.

"Wally."

"That you? Who's Wally?"

"No Wallace Davis, he owns the boat."

"They told us that he went overboard about two hours ago ma'am, no life jacket. We checked ma'am, there are no more people on board," Phillips told her.

"What happened to your engine?" Kimberly asked.

"Quit about an hour ago," the other guy replied.

"Before or after Davis went over?"

"Before."

Kimberly called to the wheelhouse. "Captain, there was a man overboard from the cruiser, the survivors said about an hour ago. See if the Coast Guard can get a chopper to do a broad sweep of the area." The wind might be a problem. His navigator was going to calculate the drift for the hour.

"What's your name?" Kimberly asked the man.

"Danny Alfonso."

"Okay, from the start, what happened?"

"Do we have to answer these questions? I want to speak to the man in charge," Brad wined.

"You are speaking to her, and yes, you have to answer the questions," Kimberly growled.

Slowly she got the picture of the three guys taking off in the calm of the morning in their small craft with an outboard motor. They had no radio, no life jackets, and no idea how far they were from shore. Their story was that they had kept the coastline in view. Kimberly thought they had been watching the hills inland because one sure as hell could not see the coast from here. Later the navigator established that they had been blown further out to sea than they thought. The Coast Guard base confirmed his drift calculations and launched a helicopter to search even though it was almost dark.

"Did Davis have a flashlight?"

"I don't think so; he just had shorts on."

"Jesus, you idiots. I don't suppose anyone has taken the Coast Guard seamanship course?"

"Come on, Kim lay off. Our buddy's probably dead."

"Kim, you fuckin' know her?" Alfonso asked Brad in amazement.

"She's my fuckin' high school girlfriend."

"You'll address her as Commander," Phillips barked, "and yes, your buddy has likely drowned, which is why we have to find out what happened."

"I need to go to the bridge and brief the Captain. Lieutenant Ewing, try to unravel more of this." Later she heard that Brad had said something derogatory about her as she left. That got him barked at by Phillips and, nose to nose, dressed down sharply by Chief Castillo, Shorheim's male Chief Petty Officer, causing Brad to sulk even more.

In the wheelhouse, Kimberly advised Hans of their findings and suggested they have someone at the CG base do breathalyzer tests on the two survivors. Shorheim told her that he learned that there were media all over the shore next to the Coast Guard station.

"Who the hell notified the media?" Kimberly demanded of the Coast Guard base. The apologetic station commander came back, indicating that the media had picked it up on a police radio scanner when the Coast Guard called for EMS. He was no happier about the situation than she was.

"Do you have a cutter that we can get these guys on as soon as possible then we'll sail away. None of my guys nor this ship are to be seen by media." Kimberly wondered about her assertion. The mission was secret; that a naval ship was in the Atlantic hardly would be. She decided that the less seen, the better.

"Roger that." They diverted a cutter that had been out successfully searching for another yacht and was coming into the port.

"They're gonna fuckin' love the transfer on a boson's chair," Kimberly muttered. Hans laughed.

"What are you going to do about your ex? After you and Ewing encountered him, you told me he had a mouth," Shorheim asked.

"Tie him under the hull. Damn, I have no clue." She got back on the radio and appraised the station commander that one of the survivors was known and that they were concerned with his overactive mouth. They agreed that the best course was to scare the hell out of him.

Hans stepped in. "Chief Castillo, would you bring Mr. Watson to the wheelhouse please," he called on the intercom, addressing his own CPO. When they arrived, Hans had the Chief walk Watson to the back of the wheelhouse.

"Commander Callahan, would you take the con please." Damn, now Hans was playing games.

"Aye, aye', Commander Callahan relieving Commander Shorheim at 0835 Zulu." Shorheim moved to the rear of the wheelhouse.

"Sober enough to understand?" Shorheim asked Watson.

"I guess."

"We have a huge problem called your mouth, which Commander Callahan tells me flaps. Our mission is about nothing public, but we stopped to save your life. There are media all around the Coast Guard station. We are going to try to get you and your buddy ashore without anyone seeing you. However, eventually, someone will discover who we rescued. The problem is that you cannot know anyone on this ship, our names, our sex, what we look like, or that this ship even exists. Nothing and no one, particularly not Commander Callahan. Do you understand?"

"Why the fuck not?"

Chief Castillo looked as though he was going to slug Watson. Hans shook his head no, but Brad had seen the move and became scared.

"Because, if you open your mouth, the federal government will be very unhappy with you. It could have serious long-term consequences," Shorheim explained. Kimberly wondering what she had ever seen in the piece of trash. "Do you clearly understand?"

"Yeah."

"You say 'aye, aye Sir' and you'd better damn well mean it," Chief Castillo barked at Watson. He looked for an instant at the glaring Chief and then back to Commander Shorheim.

"Aye, aye, Sir."

Hans took the con back. An hour later, they met the Coast Guard cutter. The Coast Guard took control of the pleasure craft following which the transfer of the two men occurred. Kimberly chuckled as she saw the Coast Guard cutter, to put the men ashore, set a course for somewhere other than their home Coast Guard base.

The morning news had speculation of all kinds as to what had happened the evening before. Most of the scenarios were that the Coast Guard had done a rescue of some sort, but there was a lot of curiosity as to why they had not publicized the rescue as they usually did. One news channel offered a theory that a Senator and his girlfriend were rescued. So far, neither Brad nor his buddy had surfaced in the media. Later Kimberly learned from Malcolm Greene that the two were moved to a federal interrogation center and, at the time of the television reports, were still being held. Kimberly did not think the scare tactic would work. She started to believe that too much was being made of the incident, that in itself would become suspicious. Wednesday morning, they were on shore at the base. The day was going along as usual until noon.

"Hey, the media found one of those guys that we rescued on the weekend," one of the noncoms called from the office. They gathered around the television.

A reporter was interviewing Watson. Someone had done an excellent job with him, he was clean-shaven, dressed in a shirt and tie, which was most unusual for him. Yes, he had involvement in the rescue; no, he could not say anything about it. No, he was not aware of the involvement of any Senator. Yes, as far as anyone could determine, the boat owner had drowned at sea. No, that person was not a government official. No, he could not say what part he had played in the rescue. Kimberly almost choked. The report was good, someone had given Brad stories that he could build on and make himself seem important, but all were fabricated. Janie had an amused grin on her face.

"Looks like we'll get away with this one," she whispered to Kimberly as they returned to their desks.

Over the next few months, the USS Detroit ran patrols on irregular courses and at irregular times but mostly waited for actionable intelligence. There was little chatter. There were a couple of homegrown incidents well away from the coast that the FBI handled. Kimberly was restless. They had done so much training, and other than the training exercises, this was almost like being on a destroyer waiting for a war. Kimberly told her thirteen-year-old self that it was a good thing that the shield against terrorists was so good that they had no incidents. Adult Kimberly did not quite believe that. The rest of the month was quiet excepting a few evenings of rough seas.

Montana's letters to her mother were excited. Now a Midshipman Second Class, she loved Annapolis and was doing very well with her course material. Janie did get to chat with her by phone briefly at the end of October. Montana was going to have two weeks' leave at Christmas.

It poured rain the entire last week of October. Patrolling was next to useless. They needed radar to move on the water and often could not see more than five meters away from the ship. Kimberly and Janie did develop confidence in handling the vessel in bad weather.

The evenings cooled a bit after Halloween, but the days remained hot. One afternoon early in November, they learned of intelligence that a terrorist organization was going to land a party from an oil tanker on the eastern coast. Initially, there were few other details other than that the threat level was believed high, and the information believed good. The littoral was to patrol from Hilton Head to Cape Fear, where further intelligence indicated that this party was planning to go ashore. Although that was over three hundred nautical miles of coast to patrol, confidence was high that the landing would occur the evening of November twenty-third. They had aerial recon support.

The plan was that they would check every tanker in the area for the next month with radar, infrared, and sonography. Once Kimberly's team and the littoral crew located the attempt, if possible, a ground-based homeland security unit would be brought to the scene to interdict the terrorists. The LCS crew was to monitor the situation and advise the homeland security team of any terrorists approaching. It was going to be finding a needle in a haystack, thought Kimberly. The crew was ready, but they had a lot of water to cover.

During the next week, they established their specific operations plans and coordinated with other units. Some days there were many tankers and other times only a few. No matter the time of day, they could get near enough to all of them to check them. Kimberly thought it was ineffective because if there were several tankers, they were only able to monitor them for part of the distance. The Coast Guard tried to keep tabs on most of them, which appeared more routine. The intelligence became firmer, allowing the littoral to station just south of Cape Fear and monitor the northern sector to Norfolk.

"Intelligence has no clue which tanker?" Kimberly asked Greene.

"We aren't even sure if this is real or misinformation, including if it's even a tanker," Green told her.

"We've been told the intelligence is good," Kimberly replied, astonished.

"It was, and then it wasn't," was the best Greene could do.

They would have to check everything that moved in the two hundred and eighty nautical miles of the northern sector. A Coast Guard cutter was covering the southern region. Kimberly hoped the intelligence was at least correct about the attempt being in the northern sector as the CG did not have the resources to take on a landing party. They had two weeks before November twenty-third when, as far as Kimberly could discern, nothing was going to happen around them, or all hell was going to break loose.

Chapter Ten: Cape Romain

The area was quiet; it was ten days until the twenty-third. Two oil tankers would be in their area on the night of the fourteenth. One would not be near the coastal region until morning. The other approached from the sea and then turned south. That was strange. Information as to where it originated was sketchy, but intelligence had it coming from Venezuela. There were several freighters in the area, none of which were believed a threat. Arial surveillance reported no other tankers. There was no moon. Kimberly's gut told her something was wrong with the boat going south.

They were just north of Cape Romain. Based on the course of the tanker, Kimberly asked Commander Shorheim to position the littoral close to the coast just north of the Santee River estuary and slowly move south with, but slightly north of, the tanker. Hiding a three hundred and seventy-eight-foot ship, and still be close enough to watch the tanker was tricky. The angled semi-stealth superstructure of the Detroit and its funky camo paint helped to hide it from observation in the dark. There were hills west of them, so a silhouette would not be a problem even if there had been a moon, and certainly not in the minimal light of the night.

"Shit."

"What?" Kimberly asked the petty officer who had been operating the infra-red surveillance equipment.

"Sorry, ma'am, for a second I thought I saw something. No dammit, I did." Kimberly went to the seaman's console to see. There was a light thermal image of the tanker, likely the hull cooling from the day's sun but superimposed on that were thermal dots moving from the deck to the water. In some instances, the thermal dots were going in the opposite direction.

"They are loading or offloading something, likely offloading."

"Looks that way, ma'am."

"Damn."

Kimberly radioed Homeland, who had Malcolm back to her within a minute. The crew sent the infrared images to Greene. His interpretation of what they were watching was the same as Kimberly's.

"I have to go after them, Sir."

"No dice. We'll get a Marine unit from Cherry Point."

"Shit, that's over one hundred and sixty miles away. The Marines won't make it on time, and you'll lose whoever this is inland. Plus, the Marines will have legal problems without the FBI being with them. I'll take a team ashore and hit them just after they land. They'll never know what hit them," Kimberly told Greene.

"Damn, you're a hard head, but you're likely correct. Coordinate with the USCG base at Charleston."

"Copy that. I'll keep you informed."

She contacted USCG Charleston. A petty officer would find the duty officer. It took a long time for the officer, a male officer, one Lieutenant Dixon, to responded.

"This is Naval Lieutenant Commander Callahan on the USS Detroit. We're supporting the Coast Guard and have a party suspected to be terrorists trying to come ashore from an oil tanker just north of Cape Romain. I need you on standby for assistance with both sea and land operations should we need it."

"Who the hell is this?"

"The USS Detroit requesting standby should we need assistance."

"I don't know about any damn patrol off Cape Romain. If there were Coast Guard in the Seventh District waters, I would fuckin' know about it. We have nothing up at Cape Romain."

"Lieutenant, we're Navy supporting the Coast Guard mission."

"This is a fuckin' hoax. Get off the fuckin' air."

"Lieutenant listen carefully, do you have a computer in front of you?" He did. She told him the URL he needed then continued.

"Put in the following, Whiskey Whiskey Four Two Six Eight Bravo Seven Zulu." She could hear him keying in and then the faint curse. "Now you are going to do exactly as I instruct. We have a potential terrorist situation with what looks like a team coming ashore in the Santee River estuary area. We do not know their exact landing site yet, but we'll keep you posted. We need a backup team on land but back of the shore, quiet, and hidden until we say so. Got it?"

"Yes, ma'am."

"We may also need a cutter to intercept the tanker, so get a crew on standby for that." She got the same response.

By then, Janie and Dixie were both in the wheelhouse wearing battle dress uniforms, camos, helmets, and life preservers. Everyone wore their camos most of the time aboard. The three reviewed the situation deciding that it would be best to be near the shore in a small boat as soon as possible. The plotting crew aboard the littoral would monitor the thermal images and advise them of the landing site. Kimberly's squad, wearing combat gear and armed to the hilt, set out for shore in rigid-hulled inflatables. Looking at the coast, Kimberly decided to go in on the north side of the estuary.

The littoral advised that the group from the tanker was moving and heading straight for a cove between the Santee and PeeDee rivers. With her team paddling quietly, Kimberly moved the inflatable into the mouth of the PeeDee, where they disembarked. As they started overland for the cove, a truck came down a road to the cove.

"There are light signals from the cove beach out toward the landing party," came the report from the observers on the Detroit. "The landing party responded."

"Truck just came down to the cove," Kimberly replied.

The light signals gave Kimberly's team a fix on the exact landing site. Spreading out, they moved west and then to the dirt road and walked down it toward the cove a little over a mile away.

"Vehicle coming," came over Kimberly's headset. The speaker was a seaman in the rear. They moved off the road.

"Police vehicle," the seaman reported.

Kimberly had no idea what a police car was doing there but did not want a police officer stumbling into something. Stepping out onto the road with a hooded flashlight, she signaled the vehicle to stop. It did, and the flashers came on as he rolled his window down.

"Shit turn those damn things off now," Kimberly ordered as she flipped her night-vision goggles up.

He was staring at Kimberly's M4A1 assault rifle but complied, making no effort to get out of the car. "Ma'am Coast Guard said there was some sort of problem here."

"Shit! Are you the backup? Goddamn. I'm Lieutenant Commander Kimberly Callahan." She showed him her identification. "We likely have a terrorist party coming ashore here. Dammit."

She changed her radio to track three, Greene. "This is Callahan. We've got a huge problem here. USCG Charleston's watch commander's idea of back up is to send us a police officer from Georgetown."

"Damn," Malcolm cursed at the other end, "I'm calling Cherry Point. But keep the officer there."

"Cherry Point will probably get here to mop up. I don't want their unit coming in and screwing up the operation. Have the unit commander hold ten miles out and have them contact me on track four."

The police officer was out of the squad. His name badge said, "Hennet." Kimberly did not need this problem now, concerned that he was very pale and sweaty; he was overweight and out of shape.

"Shit, I'd better call this in," Hennet said.

"No, stay off your damn radio. It's likely not secure." Counties were not known for spending money on sophisticated secure radio equipment.

"Status on the landing party," she asked the watch on the littoral who reported that the paddlers were still at least a mile out, continuing to head for the cove. Kimberly guessed that the trees had hidden the squad's flashing lights. She switched her radio to track one.

"Rodriquez take two seamen and get down near the beach. Don't do a damn thing except keep me apprised of what's happening. Everyone keep covered. If that truck is involved and they start back, let us know and close the door behind them. Keep your damn heads down. We have a Marine unit coming, but they'll probably get here late."

"Lieutenant Ewing take a squad and cover the north side of the road, my group will be north about one hundred meters up, Carlos south side across from Lieutenant Ewing's squad and Martinek across from me. Once the shooting starts, shoot for the wheels of the vehicle or if they're on foot, go for their legs. We need to stop them

here, but I want these bastards alive. Watch the crossfire. Capeesh?"
Kimberly heard the 10-4's.

"Shit, there's going to be shooting?" the police officer asked.

"Probably yes," Kimberly told him. "You stay with me. Keep your ass down and out of sight."

She keyed her mic again, "Martinek, get the squad car off the road and hidden somewhere."

"You don't want that truck past here?" the policeman asked.

"Of course not."

"The road narrows just up the way; we could put the squad there as a blockade."

"Your Chief will have your hide if you get a dint in it," Kimberly said sarcastically.

"Yeah, probably, but I'm getting to the point of not giving a shit."

Kimberly was still worried about the guy and added to the worries was that he might try to drive out of there and cause all sorts of problems.

"How far is just up the way?" she asked the police officer.

"'Bout a quarter of a mile, maybe less."

"You have a portable bullhorn in the squad?

"Yes."

"Okay, go form the blockade and bring back the bullhorn. Keep damn quiet. Rife go with Officer Hennet. If he tries to leave the area, shoot him. Once you create the blockade, both of you get back here immediately. I want Hennet where I can see him, and for some reason, headquarters also wants him here." She keyed her mic, "Martinek, hold on, the police officer and Rife are going to move the squad."

Petty Officer Susan Rife nudged the cop with her M4A1. He all but ran to the car. With Rife seated on the passenger side, he began to move slowly without turning on any lights. Ewing and Rodriquez moved their squads out.

Kimberly began to position her squad away from the road along a line parallel to it. There was a bit of a rise in the ground. She changed her mind and decided the best tactic was to hit them hard and fast where the road rose to go over the little ridge. She moved her people closer to the roadside.

"Dixie, come with me. Can you put ordnance across the road here where we want them stopped but alive and then thirty meters downhill to close their rear?"

"No problem." Chief Petty Officer Phillips laid the two lines of plastic explosive.

As the group out on the water kept coming and as the party on land was not doing anything, the guess was that the paddlers had seen nothing. Rodriquez had them all in sight. He reported two sports utility vehicles and the truck at the landing site. That brought up the possibility of a secondary route, but the police officer had said that this was the only route to the cove. Likely the SUVs had been pre-parked there. Kimberly hoped like hell that the police officer was correct. Her map suggested he was.

Once the boat from the tanker got there, Rodriquez counted eight paddlers plus the three drivers from the vehicles. He reported that the driver of the Explorer was giving orders suggesting that he was the leader. As they guessed, the terrorists had freight, multiple crates of varying sizes. They offloaded the boxes into the truck. Some of the uncovered cargo was assault weapons, which they loaded into the back of the vehicle. No personnel were in the back of the truck. Rodriquez reported that they seemed at ease joking amongst themselves. Four lit up cigarettes.

The Explorer left with five people in it, followed by the truck, and then a Navigator with five people.

"Explorer shotgun likely the leader from the tanker. He greeted the guy on land and didn't do any of the lifting," Rodriquez reported. They had loaded all the assault weapons that Rodriquez saw into the back of the truck. Unless they had weapons in the vehicles before arriving, he did not believe any of them carried more than handguns.

Rife and the cop were back. The Marine team was at least twenty minutes out. Kimberly pressed her mic key.

"Okay, here we go. Don't anybody get caught in the crossfire. Rodriquez don't come past that second bend east of us until the road explodes. Disable the vehicles; we want these guys alive. After a five-count of firing to disable the vehicles stop and our police officer friend is going to order them out of the vehicles. We'll give them a ten count to comply and then, or if they return fire at any time, resume firing. Initially fire on the vehicles but after a ten-count fire a bit over the vehicles, and we'll move in low and fast to secure each vehicle. We need to be precise and move fast; I don't want them on radios or cell phones. Keep your damn heads down. Remember that we have teams on both sides."

"I could try for a grenade in the back of that truck if we need," came Petty Officer Second Class Anthony Carlos' transmission.

"Is the back closed, Rodriquez?"

"Yeah, but not locked."

"Too risky Tony, I want you around to make Chief, so don't play hero. If things go south, we'll need to disable their stuff. If you have a clean shot, then okay. Ideally, I'd like the evidence."

"Who do I say we are?" the cop asked.

"Government of the United States."

"Do I arrest them?"

"They'll be taken into federal custody."

Now it was a short waiting game. Kimberly ran over her plan again and again. It was the best she could do. For a moment, Kimberly realized that she was scared out of her mind. She did not have time for that she told herself and ran the plan over in her mind again.

The three vehicles were moving together as they came around the corner to their east. The vehicles were perfectly positioned when Dixie blew the road away in front and behind them. The ordnance job was precise. Unless they had some very sophisticated equipment, there was no big flash nor a lot of noise that might be detected back at the tanker. Tires were blown away when all the M4A1s opened up. The Explorer's engine started smoking. There was silence.

"This is the Government of the United States. Come out of the vehicles with your hands in the air."

A door on the passenger side of the Navigator opened. Even with night vision goggles, Kimberly did not see anybody move. Someone at the Navigator fired a shot. The flash was just over the engine hood. The person had to have crouched down beside the south side of the vehicle. A single shot came from the southeast, from Rodriquez's group. Someone at the Navigator screamed. The ten-count passed. Fire now came from Rodriquez's group across the east and Ewing's group to the central north as well as Kimberly's group on the northwest. Then the fire lines rose to just over the vehicles.

Moving under the fire, Kimberly and a seaman got to the front passenger door of the Explorer. Petty Officer Third Class Lois Flanagan and a seaman from Martinek's group were at the driver's door. The seamen opened the doors simultaneously. Kimberly could grab the arm of the guy in the passenger seat and pull him out. He had been trying to make a call on his cell phone, not yet talking. Flanagan did the same thing with the driver. A passenger in the back seat tried to fire a handgun, but another seaman, who had moved up behind Flanagan, neutralized him. The other passengers surrendered.

A burst of fire came from the truck cab. Kimberly heard a female voice over her radio swear as Ewing's team, and Carlos's team trained fire on the cab.

"Explorer north secure," Kimberly radioed.

"Truck cab secure with one very dead driver," was Petty Officer Carlos's report.

"Navigator south secure." Chief Petty Officer Rodriquez.

"Everyone okay?" Kimberly asked.

"Lieutenant Ewing's hit," reported Petty Officer Carlos.

"Shut up, Carlos, it's just a flesh wound to my right arm. Arm's functioning," came Janie's disgusted voice. Kimberly grinned; the tone of voice told her that Janie was okay.

"Secure all the prisoners. Carlos check the back of the truck. Be careful there may be someone in there, or it may be booby-trapped. Have people cover you."

The Marine team radioed that they were at the ten-mile mark. Kimberly had forgotten all about them.

"Action's done. Come on in but stay quiet and dark. If we can avoid it, I don't want anyone on the tanker alerted that we have their people. There're no power lines, but there're trees just beside the road. Can you land on the road?"

"Affirmative."

Kimberly checked on Janie. Her arm was grazed, but as she said, everything worked. Petty Officer Third Class Alonzo Taylor, their Pharmacy Mate, was dressing her wound. Kimberly switched to track three, Greene.

"Action's over. One minor causality for us. Two dead enemies and two injured. Enemy prisoners are all secured. We have eleven, including the dead guys, eight believed to be from the boat. We've preserved most of their stuff. Sorry, we kinda shot up their vehicles. Marines are on the way, coming in dark, to secure the zone. We made a mess of the road."

"Great work," Malcolm replied enthusiastically. "Miranda and I are at Edwards and will be there shortly. Keep the area secure. How much of a mess is the road?"

"Big holes from plastic."

"K, I'll get a Seabee unit in there right now to repair it before morning. Any tourists?"

"Not yet, I'll have the officer go back to his car and send any away."

"Tell him to stay dark until I get there and talk to him. He is NOT, repeat NOT, to report anything on his radio." Kimberly relayed the information, and the officer started for his squad car. He was much more co-operative than when he arrived. Who in hell was Miranda? Shit, Miranda Davidson, the spooky CIA type.

Moments later, two Blackhawk helicopters landed on the road, one east and the other west of the site. The Marines secured the perimeter. A Marine Captain strode over to Kimberly, a Gunny Sergeant in tow. "You in charge?

"Yeah. Lt Commander Callahan."

"Captain Allard," the marine replied and saluted. "I need to see your ID, ma'am."

Kim returned the salute and held out her identifications for inspection.

He looked both of hers, the Navy one and the FBI one, over carefully, and raised an eyebrow. He pointed to something on one to show the Gunny. Kimberly's thought was, careful Captain baby, I outrank you, don't say an effing word.

"I gather the area is secure."

"We believe so. Our Pharmacy Mate is working on a couple of prisoners. If you have a medic, perhaps they could help. There are two dead terrorists."

"We'll get your injured prisoners evacuated."

"I don't think so, Captain. We have another chopper coming. We may need your equipment, but this gang is ours," Kimberly told him.

"Navy's supposed to stick to the sea and let us do the land stuff, Commander."

"Yeah, well, we're FBI/Homeland Security, and our unit is helping the Coast Guard, and this is the coast, Captain. Besides, none of you Marine types are supposed to be in action on US soil."

"Yeah, they're, ah, FBI, Gunny. Instruct the troops that tonight never happened. Not ever. They tell no one or I'll personally kill them before the United States Government puts them in prison for the rest of their lives."

"Yes, sir."

"How're you going to explain the road, Commander?" the Marine officer asked.

"We're not. A Seabee unit is coming, and they'll have it fixed by dawn. The county will be pleased that their potholed road is repaired."

The Captain just nodded with the wry grin on his face. Kimberly and the Captain checked out the scene. "Hell, of a unit you're running Commander. Nice work." It was Kimberly's turn to nod.

A smaller helicopter came in dark, landing between the Explorer and the Marine Helicopter. Kimberly, with the Captain in tow, explained the scene to Malcolm and Miranda Davidson.

Miranda chuckled as she took in the scene. "Well, Da Bitch did it again. When are the assholes of the world going to learn not to mess with you, Callahan?"

Malcolm nodded. "Impressive."

Taylor jogged up to them. "The Marines want to take the injured prisoners ma'am," he reported to Kimberly.

"No, load the two of them on our chopper, the dead ones also," ordered Miranda.

That was interesting, Kimberly thought. She would have expected the order to come from Malcolm.

The group walked west on the road. "Captain, can you load the non-injured prisoners on your chopper and bring them to Edwards for us? And keep all this quiet," said Malcolm.

"Yes, sir," Allard said. "I've already instructed my people that tonight never happened."

As they approached, Hennet climbed out of his squad car.

"Any curiosity seekers? "Kimberly asked.

"One guy who lives nearby. I told him to go back to bed that it was just some dumb military exercise. Sorry sir," he said with a glance at Allard. "Dispatch checked up on me. I told them nothing was happening but that I was checking out the beach area to be sure. I think they bought it."

"Good. This is the guy in charge," Kimberly nodded at Malcolm. Or maybe not, but Kimberly figured Miranda Davis would speak up if she wanted to enlighten anyone.

"Thank you for your excellent service," Malcolm said. "I'll see that it's noted in your record somehow, but you understand that this never happened."

"Very clearly, sir," said Hennet. "The Commander made that abundantly clear to me. No one ever hears this story, sir, 'cause I know the Commander would track me down and kill me without a second thought, sir."

"That's why we call her 'Da Bitch' Officer," Davis said laughing

Hennet glanced at the Marine Captain. "I don't think I should reply to that."

Allard chuckled, "Wise man."

"I want your team to board that tanker," Malcolm told Kimberly.

"With all due respect, sir, why?"

Malcolm looked at Kimberly, puzzled. "Why not?"

"It'll be just another useless search. There isn't anything to see by now, and it'll tip the terrorists off that we know, assuming they haven't seen or heard any of this by now."

"Alright, what would you do?"

"Blow the thing up in about three months when it's empty and somewhere else."

"Shit," said Allard in an awed voice.

"We'll think about it," Greene told her. He turned to Hennet, "there's a Seabee unit coming to repair your road, can you secure it long enough for them to get here or should we leave a couple of Marines behind?"

"Dispatch will get antsy if I'm here much longer, sir."

"Okay." Malcolm looked at Captain Allard, who nodded affirmative and left for his team. Malcolm turned back to Hennet. "You can leave with our thanks. There will be a heroic effort made by you in a few weeks that will win you a commendation. Go with it. Can you do that?"

"The Commander has taught me well, so, yes, sir."

"What's your full name, Officer?"

"Robert Hennet, Sir." Malcolm dictated a note into his phone and headed back to the helicopters.

The team assisted the two forensic specialists who came with Greene and Davis. The Marines continued to secure the area. One of the forensic guys assured Malcolm that the assault team, as he put it, had the evidence well managed. They were not going to do anymore with the vehicles except haul them, intact, to a garage where they could go over them in detail. The Marine helicopters took off back to Edwards, with Malcolm, and the uninjured prisoners. Miranda Davis was in command of the site.

Kimberly got Petty Officer Second Class Anthony Carlos aside. "You okay, Tony?"

"Yes, ma'am."

"Don't do the tough guy shit on me, you okay? You just killed a person."

"I understand the question, ma'am, and I'm fine. The bastard was going to hurt or kill Lieutenant Ewing, plus he was no friend of the United States. I hope he wasn't major evidence."

"Okay, Petty Officer, nice shoot. I think Flanagan got a piece of him also."

"Yes, ma'am, I think she did, his gun arm. Probably kept me from getting shot, ma'am."

"Yes, noted Petty Officer, thank you. You're to see the psychologist when we return to base."

"Yes ma'am, thank you, ma'am." She went to find Miranda.

"Hey, boss spook lady or whatever the hell you are, can I get my crew back to our ship?"

"In a few minutes, Warrior Bitch, once we get the vehicles loaded. These fuckers never knew what hit them. Remind me not to piss you off."

Four large covered trucks arrived a half-hour later. The Seabees winched the terrorist's vehicles into three and the other evidence into the fourth. Vehicles with construction equipment and aggregate arrived. The Seabees dug out the surface of the explosion pits on the road. The material was placed into fifty-five-gallon drum containers and loaded into one of the trucks. Fortunately, it was November; they still had a few hours of dark.

Commander Shorheim kept in contact and had been apprised of the situation as things developed, but he did not like how long the operation was taking. Kimberly told him to cool his jets; they were all okay. Once they were back on board, he was very concerned about Lieutenant Ewing quizzing Alonzo Taylor extensively until Kimberly told him to back off.

For Kimberly, the ship's motion was soothing. She went to the bridge, asking Commander Shorheim's permission to remain there for a while.

"Certainly, Commander."

She was pleased that she did. Five minutes later, Coast Guard Station Charleston called. It was the Commanding Officer, a Lieutenant Commander wishing to speak with one Lieutenant Commander Callahan.

"Commander, I want to apologize for the actions of my Watch Commander tonight. I understand he was very uncooperative. Could you tell me what happened?"

"How are you aware of that, Commander?"

"A William A. Sanburg called from Washington. He is mightily pissed and has good cause. I understand my officer left you in the cold in a dangerous situation."

"Any action report you should probably get through Mr. Sanburg. However, yes, your officer was not happy being bothered. I suspect he was asleep. His response was totally inadequate."

"I gather he called the local police in Georgetown."

"According to the police officer that showed up, yes. Your man could well have gotten that officer killed and blown the whole operation. We truly don't know all the ramifications at this time."

"I've replayed the voice tapes, and I agree. You plainly told my Lieutenant who you were, referenced your authority, and the severity of the situation as you read it at the time. I gather that turned out to be right on. He will be brought up on a variety of charges. You are correct in your assessment that he was asleep on duty. Let me again apologize for my officer. Can we assist you in any way?"

"We're okay, Commander. We will not need a cutter to intercept the tanker, and tonight never happened. Good night." She shut her mic. "Take us home, Commander."

Kimberly's question was, who in the hell is William A. Sanburg? Someone in Washington. For a secret operation, there was a hell of a lot of people who knew at least parts. Kimberly did not like that; there were a lot of ego-driven loose lips around Washington cocktail parties. Shit no, she recalled that he had been on the Destiny II, the guy with the strangely named financial company. Likely he was CIA.

Chapter Eleven – Redemption

Months later, Kimberly received orders to appear at Langley wearing civilian clothing. Sanburg was one of the senior CIA people and the person to whom Miranda Davidson reported. Both were meeting with her. She recalled Sanburg from Destiny II; he looked shifty enough to be a lawyer.

"Your team's action at the Santee River estuary was clean," Sanburg told her. "Intercepts indicated that the terrorists knew their team disappeared but have no clue when or where. They're sure it was in South Carolina somewhere as the team missed a check-in. The tanker continued to Venezuela where it loaded fuel then went to Africa."

"You had an idea in the field about blowing up the tanker?" Davidson asked her.

"It was a thought," Kimberly said. Sanburg was watching her, his face blank. Kimberly decided he was creepy.

"Have you expanded on the thought?" Davidson asked.

Kimberly wondered where Davidson was going with this, but she had expanded her thoughts. "It might be meaningless depending on who owns the tanker or who's funding this group of terrorists. That said, they know which tanker was off our shore and when, plus they know that their team disappeared. If that tanker suddenly blew up and sank for no good reason, it would send a message. They would figure it out. Probably not stop them, but it might slow them up. On the other hand, it might show them what we know and be detrimental to our intelligence gathering."

"How would you do this?" Sanburg asked her.

"Ideally, we'd need to see some design information on the tanker referencing if there were bulkheads that could be immediately closed to limit flooding, but likely explosives on the hull," Kimberly said, thinking out loud. "The bit we saw of it off Cape Romain suggests that it's old, so likely they don't have electronics that could automatically close bulkheads. Probably not relevant as typically, the hold of a tanker is several large tanks. The explosive would need to be under a couple of sections with enough potential to crack the hull, not just make a hole. Not being detected would be tricky."

"You're comfortable working with CPO Cheryl Phillips, a.k.a. Dixie? I doubt we'll ever be able to get her to speak with an Arabic accent." Davidson laughed at her little joke about Cheryl's southern accent.

"Absolutely," Kimberly told Davidson.

"You're correct about the detection issue," Sanburg suddenly spoke up, "but they rarely worry too much about tankers. I would be more concerned with port security. A highly undetectable manner would be putting them on the hull while the ship is in motion."

"That would be dangerous, those propellers are huge," Davidson stated.

"The timing would have to be perfect," Sanburg amended.

Janie took over the mission team on the littoral for an undetermined time. Their temporarily assigned ordnance guy returned. Kimberly and Dixie went to Newport, where Navy divers trained them in underwater methods beyond what they had learned during SEAL training. Their days consisted of underwater exercises with sleds and learning how to escape the screws. Sanburg had been correct; it was all about timing. Straight up from the bottom, apply the explosive, and then straight down. It was feasible. They ran tests with a couple of tankers coming into Boston. It was possible, but the timing was critical. An advantage was that oil tankers move slowly compared to container ships with perishable cargo. They tried on oil tankers leaving Boston empty, traveling faster, and it still worked. A CIA operative learned where the terrorist's tanker was built and obtained adequate details to determine where to locate the explosives on the hull. It had taken a few months, but a plan was coming together.

The tanker was in Iran. It appeared that it was going to load more oil. Mossad intel shared with the CIA said that it did not. Mossad determined that weapons were loaded on the tanker and that it headed for northern Syria. Interdiction by the U.S. was politically not possible. The Israelis had no such compunctions. The Israelis removed the weapons from the vessel off southern Syria and released the ship, which started west in the Mediterranean heading for the Atlantic.

Kimberly preferred to fly commercial. That would appear a lot less military. Based on time issues and the ordnance with them, looking like a tourist on a commercial flight was not possible. They did change into civilian tourist like garb on the plane. They flew to the French military airport at Salon-de-Provence, near Marseilles. They did not taxi to the hanger area, but far from the hanger, men in civilian clothing with two SUVs met them.

"Bonjour, I am Jean-Marc Pitien from the DGSE. We will be assisting you." The DGSE is the French version of the CIA. Kimberly worried about too many people in the loop but operating from French soil they needed French cooperation.

"Lieutenant Commander Kimberly Callahan and this is Chief Petty Officer Cheryl Phillips." The French DGSE officer frowned. "What?"

"We were told the CIA."

Kimberly chuckled, "Your information is correct." She showed her Navy ID and CIA ID. The expression on Pitien's face changed to one of admiration.

"You are a Navy SEAL?"

"We both are."

"Wow, okay. I was unsure of this operation, particularly when they told me two women. It will be a pleasure to assist you."

They offloaded the equipment and ordnance turning it over to the DGSE. In a Renault Captur, the women were driven to a small hotel near the Marseilles old port area. In the Renault, the driver gave them their room keys. They had checked into the hotel two days earlier, as Darlene Smithers and Billy-Jo Meissen. They walked into the hotel. The guy at the desk nodded as they entered. They kept on walking. Luggage that they had never before seen was in their room, all correctly labeled and containing vacation type clothing of appropriate sizes.

"Where the hell did they get this shit, some thrift shop?" Dixie wanted to know. The answer was, likely.

The next morning, they took the train to Nice dressed as two American female tourists. At least, Dixie said, that was what they looked like; the operational plan was to meet male DGSE operatives at a restaurant by the beach.

The sun and the warmth were lovely as the two women relaxed at their outdoor table. Halfway through their plat principal, the main course, two uninvited males suddenly sat in the other two chairs.

"Bonjour mon cheri, how are you today?"

Initially, Kimberly was irritated; these idiots were going to blow the meeting. Looking up, she recognized a casually dressed Jean-Marc. The other guy also had been among the DGSE men who took their equipment and the ordnance from them at the airport.

"You're French," Dixie said, feigning surprise. The girl could play a dumb blond very well.

"Jeez Billy-Jo, of course, they're French, we're in France. What do you guys want?" Kimberly replied, trying to sound a little irritated.

"Ah, two beautiful American women alone on the French Riviera. I am Pierre Lafleur. If you're looking for some fun, we could go on our yacht."

"Yeah, right, you own a yacht," Kimberly hoped that she was convincingly skeptical to anyone listening.

"Ah domage, you're correct, it is not mine. It is my father's."

"Come on, Darlene, it could be fun," Dixie prodded.

Kimberly hoped that she sounded sufficiently unsure before reluctantly agreeing.

The trip to Monto Carlo on the yacht allowed Kimberly and Cheryl to go below. The DGSE had all their gear stowed. The ordnance was there. Jean-Marc a.k.a. Pierre said the sleds were underwater, attached to the side of the yacht. Each woman had a bikini and a t-shirt in her bag. They changed to the bottom half of the bikini, and the t-shirt then went topside to the flybridge.

"We noticed something interesting this morning." Jean-Marc focused their vision on a large yacht, the size of a destroyer, moored at the Monto Carlo harbor.

"Okay."

"Farrokhz Ad Hamedani."

"You're fuckin' kidding," Kimberly exclaimed. Jean-Marc had just named one of the significant money guys believed to not only fund terrorist cells but who was also a big-time lender to companies and even states. "You're sure of your intelligence?"

"Absolutely," Jean-Marc told them. "Mr. Sanburg knows, and he wants a call. Here is your satellite phone."

Kimberly was churning with emotion. Farrokhz Ad Hamedani not only funding terrorists, but the CIA developed intelligence that he funded the terrorists who attacked Augusta's Madison Junior High twenty-one years earlier.

"You okay?" Dixie asked.

It took a moment before Kimberly got her emotions under control. They called Sanburg. The phone transmission was highly encrypted; they need not talk in code.

"Do we have verification that it's Farrokhz Ad Hamedani?" Kimberly asked.

"Yes, it's him. He sailed in yesterday unannounced. The harbormaster didn't know he was coming, so the DGSE didn't know, but both their operatives, Mossad and ourselves, have independently verified that it is his yacht. DGSE and Mossad have confirmed that Farrokhz Ad Hamedani is on board."

"He's anchored just outside the south breakwater."

"Yes, that's what he does. He doesn't like getting in too close. He tends to stay put and have people come to him," Sandburg told her.

"Can I go after him?"

"Are you okay?"

"Damn, yes. This bastard bombed my junior high or enabled it."

"We know. We're just not sure if you'd have your emotions under control."

"Totally."

"Let me speak to CPO Phillips." Kimberly handed Dixie the phone.

"She's good," was all Cheryl said after listening for a moment. She handed the phone back to Kimberly.

"Don't wait for him to get underway," Sanburg told her. "DGSE divers are checking for divers under their hull. We flew additional ordnance in overnight. It's a combined operation. You two will place the ordnance on the hull and then give the DGSE the triggers. They decide when to fire them. He's now the primary target. If you're successful getting ordnance under his hull, go for the tanker as planned."

The added mission was eating up time if they were going to chase the tanker. "We need to get going," Kimberly told Jean-Marc.

"No, don't worry. The tanker's coming north."

"Why, that doesn't make sense."

Jean-Marc grinned. "It's coming up the coast of Italy rather than at an angle across the Mediterranean. They landed a team on the east side of Corsica that we are keeping under observation. Unless we must, we are not going to move on them until we complete this mission."

Once she knew that, Kimberly understood the tankers route. They returned to Nice. The DGSE had surveillance on and under the yacht almost as soon as it anchored. They reported that early each morning, divers from Hamedani's boat checked the hull, again right after the noon hour and once more at supper time. Those had been the only checks. Without arousing suspicion, DGSE divers had been able, during the afternoon, to get under the hull after a noon check by Hamedani's crew and implied that they could have done the job if they had had the ordnance. Kimberly thought that was likely true. However, it was U.S. ordnance, and those decisions were all wrapped in politics. The French would get to pull the trigger.

The tanker would be off the coast steaming west the next afternoon. There would be a very tight window. In the middle of the morning, the team returned to Monte Carlo on their yacht. Kimberly and Cheryl Phillips remained below out of sight, getting mission ready.

Their yacht did not attempt to go into the harbor but proceeded east. Kimberly and Cheryl exited into the water through a lock in the hull below the waterline. They would not need the sleds. The harbor at Monto Carlo is always full of luxury yachts. Farrokhz Ad Hamedani was enough of a megalomaniac that he had to have the biggest yacht. It was easy to discern from underwater as Kimberly and Cheryl skimmed the seabed. They had two tanks, each with a Nitrox mix, even though they would not be that deep. They waited. There was no sign of anyone around the hull. They moved under it and waited again; there was nothing. They rose straight up, carefully controlling their buoyancy control devices so that they did not hit the hull and cause an alert. Even though the DGSE guys had touched the hull, they had not applied metal to it. Carefully they moved the two mines into position. The color of the mines was almost the exact white that the hull was. They were indiscernible from ten feet away.

There was no noise or scuffling of running around to suggest an alarm. Back on the bottom, the women headed out away from the harbor and east. Their alleged boyfriend's yacht had turned and was returning toward Nice. Kimberly and Cheryl joined them through the hatch in the hull. Slowly the boat moved east and out to sea. Jean-Marc came below.

"The tanker is on a 232.58 course," he told them. "That makes sense because if one projects that course west, it'll take them just north of Mallorca and to Gibraltar with a minimal course correction."

Time was of the essence to complete the tanker mission. The other problem was that for them to be successful, the tanker had to have a constant speed or be slowing.

The yacht was parallel to the coast about two kilometers north of the tanker and west of it when Kimberly and Cheryl launched again. On their sleds, they could move, but not as fast as the tanker. If they missed, there would be no second chance that day; their navigating had to be very accurate. The problem would be if the tanker changed course. Given its current heading, that would be unlikely.

They moved to the point where they planned to leave the sleds and started for the top. When they got to the twenty-meter level, Kimberly could not discern the screws in the jumble of sea noise.

She wondered if they had messed up the navigating. Kimberly went up and carefully broke the surface with her eyes. The tanker was a distance away but heading right at them. Back at twenty meters, she gave Cheryl a thumb up. Soon the noise of the screws became obvious. All the planning and training paid off. Going up as the bow approached, applying the explosive, and then getting back below a depth where the screws could cause them trouble, went very smoothly. It was threading a needle, but some days the thread goes right in.

Letting the sleds do all the work, they returned to their boyfriend's yacht. After securing the sleds, they entered the hatch one at a time.

Topside, the French guys were enjoying the sun as the boat was on a course for Nice.

They turned into the Nice harbor, to their mooring. The DGSE reported from Monte Carlo that all was quiet around Hamedani's yacht. It remained isolated, anchored south of the breakwater. There had been no sign of the dive team that checked the hull. That check was not due for an hour. The DGSE did not anticipate collateral damage. Cheryl handed the radio triggers for the mines on Hamedani's yacht to Jean-Marc. Each of the DGSE agents had one and fired them simultaneously. They heard the muffled noise of the explosion several seconds later. Cheryl took the triggers back.

The Captur was at the pier. They needed to get to the military airport near Marseilles so they would be out of French territory and airspace as soon as possible.

For reasons unknown to the four on the yacht, the DGSE and the CIA had changed the plan; there would not be a long drive. They were flying out of Nice. There would be no race, and the Nice Côte de Azur airport was conveniently by the sea out on a point west of town. Jean-Marc told them that the DGSE agents had reported that Hamedani's yacht blew to pieces. Nothing much was left. There had been no collateral damage.

The Gulfstream was waiting. While on the ground, Dixie walked to the tarmac aft of the plane, with the radio trigger for the tanker's mines. They could see the ship. She pushed the trigger. Nothing happened, then they saw huge bubbles come to the surface alongside the ship. The women stepped onto the Gulfstream and were almost immediately in the air. The flight path required the pilot to go east initially, then out to sea, and then turn west. They were well over ten thousand feet, but they could see the tanker sinking rapidly. Its bow was already underwater; the steel mid-ships was contorted.

Kimberly did not feel elated. She wanted proof that they had killed Hamedani. In her mind, as well as in her orders, the tanker had become a secondary target.

Cheryl looked at her, "We got the bastards."

"Yeah."

It was one in the afternoon in Washington, D.C. The phone in the cabin rang. It was Sanburg.

"Congratulations to both of you, job well done. The DGSE has mixed with the Monto Carlo forensic team and is recovering bodies. They have one that they think is Hamedani. I have a friend of yours here."

Malcolm Greene came on the line. "Congratulations, ladies. Kimberly, we have dress whites hanging in the locker that should fit you. We have a new mission for you; you're going to the Portsmouth Naval Yard. Tell CPO Phillips that she is heading back to Norfolk to rejoin the USS Detroit."

Kimberly had no clue what her orders would be at the Naval Yard. She suspected that Greene had been vague as he did not want an argument.

Chapter Twelve – Just a Hometown Girl

After a long nap during her flight over the Atlantic, Kim checked the locker and found not only Dress Whites but a full kit and a set of service khaki. Sizes, rank insignia, and the racks were correct. She changed into service khakis for her arrival in New Hampshire. Dixie remained on the Gulfstream when they dropped Kimberly off at the Pease Air National Guard base in Portsmouth, New Hampshire. A staff car took her to the Portsmouth Naval Yard. She was to report to the base commander.

"How much have you been told of this assignment?" the base commander asked her.

"Nothing," Kimberly told him.

"Really? Do you at least know where you're going?"

"No," replied Kimberly.

"I thought they would have told you in Norfolk."

Okay, Kimberly thought, this guy has no clue, so its time for a little fabrication. "It was a bit of a rush getting off my ship and getting here." In a sense, that was true; she hoped it would not come back to bite her. Possibly the authorities, like Sanburg and Greene, thought they needed to hide her. Maybe she was being buried in the naval yard as an engineer. That did not make sense; she would not need Dress Whites for that.

"Yes, well, you're going home for Veteran's Day. I gather your community makes a big deal of that. They had a retired Captain as the speaker, but he had a heart attack, so someone decided that a hometown girl would make a good stand-in. They sent his speech over for you if you need some ideas. I'll have a car take you up in the morning."

Shit, they had to be kidding. As Kimberly thought about it, the scenario made perfect sense. Unless someone was able to track her continuously, it would be unlikely for anyone to believe that she was in France earlier in the day and here now, let alone making a speech at her hometown Veteran's Day celebration the next morning. Kimberly wondered if the Captain had a heart attack. If not, she hoped that he had not wanted to make the speech.

"Do I have to use his speech?"

"God, no, I read it, and I hope you can do better. The car will be at your quarters at 0800."

Okay, Kimberly thought, they start late here. Once she found her assigned room in the Single Officers' Quarters, she read the speech and immediately agreed with the base commander. By nine, she had written a new one and fallen into bed.

At 0600, she awoke to a crisp autumn New England morning. Guessing at the five miles, Kimberly enjoyed her run. After a shower, she donned her service khakis and headed for the mess. She sat down with her breakfast within earshot of a television tuned to CNN. Their major story of the morning was of two maritime disasters off France. One was in Monte Carlo, where the yacht of a wealthy Persian financier had blown up. He was alleged to have terrorist ties through Iran, but the main concern was how the global financial markets would react. The other story was that an oil tanker off Nice had exploded and rapidly sunk. No one knew why.

At 0750 hours, Seaman Gleeson arrived, ready to drive her north to her parent's home. He was huge with three red stripes on his sleeve representing the rank of a full Seaman. His orders were to be at her service as needed and to have her back to the Pease Air National Guard base by 2300 hours that evening. She took the drive time to rework her speech.

The Captain's speech was about sacrifices during World War II, Korea, and Vietnam. Kimberly understood that and those of Iraqi and Afghanistan. She decided to acknowledge those sacrifices but talk about why people chose to defend the country. The draft Kimberly wrote the evening prior sounded more like a recruiting speech; it needed reworking. She kept mentally reminding herself of the brevity and yet impact of the Gettysburg Address. By the time the Seaman parked in front of her parent's home, she thought the speech was okay.

Kimberly invited Seaman Gleeson to accompany her into the house. He declined. She took her garment bag and proceeded to the house. Meredith answered the door. At seventeen, her baby sister was becoming a lovely young woman. Kimberly knew that she was a junior in high school.

"Yeah, whoa Kim. You a cop now?"

"Good morning Meredith. No, I'm what I've been for a while, a Naval Officer." The girl continued to stare at her, apparently perplexed. "May I come in?" Meredith stepped back.

"Who is it, dear?" Her mother came from the kitchen. "Oh my goodness, Kimberly. Are you going to a party?"

Really? Kimberly thought. Well, it was getting toward Halloween, and her mother had been in denial about her being a Naval Officer, admitting only to engineer. She was going to have to spend more time at home.

"Yeah, Mom, it's called Veteran's Day. It's why Meredith has the day off."

"Is that Kimberly?" her Dad called from the dining room; the family had just started breakfast. She hugged her Mom and continued into the dining room. She should not be surprised at either Meredith or her Mom's response, except at her graduation from the Naval Academy, no one in the family had seen her in uniform. Her Dad hugged her and then looked her uniform over.

"Good to see you again, Dad."

"You look great! We didn't expect you."

"I didn't expect me. The Captain scheduled to give the talk at the Veteran's Day celebrations had a heart attack, so someone decided to send a hometown girl as a replacement."

The cop thing was still irking her. She should have worn her service blue with the rank stripes on her sleeves as she doubted anyone had any idea what the gold oak leaf on her collar represented. Likely they would not understand the two broad bands with the thin one in the middle on her service blues, and the color might look even more like a cop. At least Meredith was paying attention, watching Kimberly.

"What talk?" Meredith asked.

"At the park after the parade to commemorate Veteran's Day," Kimberly explained.

"Oh."

"Well, we'll all be there. Diane, would you call Dwaine and let him know his sister is here," her father asked her mother.

"We're going to the mall," Meredith announced.

"Who is we?" her father asked Meredith.

"My friends and I."

"You weren't going to the parade and the ceremony?" their father asked, sounding surprised. At least Meredith should now have some sense that she was getting into trouble. Meredith shook her head and frowned, almost pouted.

Their father stared at her. "Well, even if you don't understand it, you're going because your sister is the guest of honor." Now the pouting girl was unhappy, she looked at her father and then her sister.

"Dwaine and Andria are coming right over," their mother announced.

"Okay, who's Andria?" Kimberly started to ask then recalled that weeks prior, Dwaine had said in a letter that he had a new girlfriend. "Oh yes, Dwaine's girlfriend. I've not met her."

"They're going to be married next summer," their mother asserted.

"Well, I've been posted to the East Coast, so that'll make getting home a little easier," Kimberly told them.

"What does that mean 'posted to the East Coast'?" Meredith wanted to know.

"That I was on the west coast and now have an assignment to a ship based at the Norfolk Naval Base in Virginia."

"Oh ... you go on a ship."

Oh God, Kimberly thought, it would be so easy to be flip. "Most of the time, but we do have a building onshore that we use as well."

The girl was frowning. "What do you do on the ship?"

Kimberly did not want to visit the SEAL issue. "I'm a surface warfare officer." The girl just shrugged; she had no clue. "All right, surface as opposed to serving in a submarine; war, we fight the bad guys; officer, I am in charge. The work is in fire control, where we plot the course for the weapons."

"So, you're like a fireman?"

"No, fire control means controlling the firing of our weapons, usually missiles." The girl's eyes got bigger. "My team uses radar to plot the course for the missile from the ship to the target."

Technically not a lie, should they ever have to use the Hellfires on the littoral.

Meredith opened her mouth, but the arrival of Dwaine and his girlfriend cut the conversation short. Dwaine crushed Kimberly in a hug.

"Damn, I'm glad you could get back. Andria, this is my sister Kimberly, sis Andria Pedersen."

Kimberly had heard the gasp behind Dwaine and wondered why the girl's posture was so stiff. There was no hug or extended hand, her dress civilian garb, but these days, that meant nothing.

"Pleased to meet you, Lieutenant Commander."

Kimberly grinned; Andria knew what the Gold Oak Leaf was. "Your experience is Navy, Army, Guard, or Air Force?" Whoops, she had left out the Marines.

"Sorry, ma'am. National Guard ma'am," the woman was still rigid.

"Great, at ease, please relax. What do you do for the Guard?"

"I'm a specialist ma'am. We're an engineer unit, and I do logistics."

"Fabulous, so between the two of us, do you think we can get this family to understand the military?"

"Speaking of your brother, no ma'am." They both laughed. Meredith, Kimberly realized, was carefully watching the whole episode.

"Andria joined so they would pay for her college." As Dwaine spoke, the woman frowned slightly.

"Why I went to the Academy, Dwaine," Kimberly said, "but, Andria, you discovered that you liked it?"

The woman looked at her, unsure of how to respond. "Yes, ma'am."

"Are you from around here?" Kimberly asked.

"Yes, ma'am." She named a nearby small town.

"Is your unit involved in the parade this afternoon?"

"Yes, ma'am, in fact, I have to report in a couple of hours. Our company is the hometown unit."

"Thus, they uncover you and shine you up once a year. Have you been deployed?"

Andria was not offended; she understood Kimberly, grinned, and then became serious again. "Yes ma'am, the Company was a year in Kosovo before I joined, and then we were a year in Iraq."

"If you can say, what were you doing there?" Kimberly asked.

Andria grinned. "Nothing very exciting, ma'am, mostly building barracks and maintaining them, sometimes squads were looking for IED's."

"But, it screwed up your four years of college?"

"Not really ma'am, the university worked around it, and the deployment was a great education. I was different after we got back. That's when I met Dwaine."

"Kimberly's a surface war officer. She fires missiles," Meredith added. Not quite, but at least the girl was listening.

Kimberly had an idea. "Can you get in touch with your CO?"

"Maybe, I could call my Sergeant."

Andria did, telling the Sergeant that one Lieutenant Commander Callahan, United States Navy, wanted to talk to their Captain. The Captain returned the call about ten minutes later. Kimberly explained her idea, and immediately, the Captain assigned SPC Andria Pedersen as her aide for the day.

"What are your dress orders for the day?" Kimberly asked her.

"BDU's."

"K, do you have Dress Blues?"

"With trousers, yes ma'am," Andria replied.

"K, my orders are Dress Whites, so ..."

"I'm in Dress Blues," Andria completed. "I'll be right back, can I borrow your car, Dwaine?"

"Why have Andria with you?" Kimberly's dad wanted to know.

"It was just a thought. A retired captain was supposed to give the speech today, but he had a heart attack. That's when they decided to send me. I was given the Captain's address; it was all about individual sacrifice from World War Two through Vietnam; he forgot about Iraq and Afghanistan. I decided on a different approach, why people join when it can mean that they sacrifice everything. If they want hometown and I'm talking, then having a Guard aide who is also hometown is a great idea."

"Why do you have wings?" Hell, Meredith was getting too observant, maybe Kimberly preferred the totally into herself Meredith. She looked at the girl for a second. Meredith saw the pause, but Kimberly assessed that now she was genuinely interested.

"Typically, only Navy people would recognize that. It isn't secret, or we wouldn't be allowed to wear the insignia publicly. However, the less you talk about it, the better and certainly don't tell Mom or Dad." The girl looked a little surprised as both parents were right there. "Okay, that last part about Mom and Dad was a little joke, but the part about talking very little is not. Shit, I should lie. You can't even tell your BFF. Swear?"

"Yes, God, what?"

"No, this is serious."

"I get that, I swear."

"Okay, look, I am a surface warfare officer, that's this insignia, but I don't do that anymore. This insignia does have wings with the canopy of a parachute, the Neptune harpoon, a rifle, and an anchor. The insignia means I am a SEAL."

Meredith's mouth had been open. She closed it and stared at her sister. Okay, she had seen enough movies.

"What is that dear, aquarium training of some sort?"

Now it was Kimberly's little sister who burst out laughing at her mother's lack of military knowledge. "No, Mom, it means she is a damn dangerous warrior." Their mother appeared confused. "They're like special ops and do scary shit. SEAL stands for something, doesn't it?" Meredith asked.

"Sea, Air, and Land, thus the components of the insignia," Kimberly offered.

"Yeah, that's it – jeez, can you parachute?" Suddenly her little sister was excited.

"Yeah, it's fun. We free fall until just above the target and deploy our chutes at last second."

"Shit … really, why."

"Less time in the air to be seen and targeted." Her sister just looked with awe.

Her father was frowning. "I thought females couldn't do SEAL training?"

"As in too physically tough?" Kimberly asked.

"Well, that too, but I thought you weren't allowed."

"Well, the Navy has proved, several times over now, that females can do the training for all the Navy jobs. Recently Congress, in its infinite wisdom, allowed women to deploy in all combat units, including SEAL teams. The Navy has female sailors on attack subs, and when I was on destroyers, a lucky shot could have blown my ship out of the water, fire control center, and all." Her father appeared concerned. Jeez, Daddy, if you even knew half of what your daughter really does, was Kimberly's thought.

"Don't the men object?" he asked.

"What about having female SEALs?"

"Well, yes."

"Hell no, particularly not when we bail out their sorry asses," Kimberly responded. Meredith started laughing.

"Really, dear, there is no need to talk like that," their mother interjected.

"She's a sailor, Mom, so of course, she'll talk like that," laughed Meredith.

"Not in my house." That seemed to be the end of it. Her mother changed the topic to the current town gossip.

Andria returned, looking very smart in her dress blues. Kimberly's heart sank for a moment. The way Andria and Dwaine were looking at each other showed that they were very much in love. It was a reminder of how lacking her personal life was.

Kimberly was to report at noon, so at eleven, she went upstairs to change. Andria asked to assist and, a bit of a surprise, Meredith also did. It would have been easier just to get dressed. It would not have taken long to put her uniform on if Andria had not insisted on pressing her trousers, and Meredith brushing off her jacket.

"Do you know what that is?" Andria asked Meredith, pointing at the Budweiser insignia.

"No," came the prompt answer.

"I didn't either, but I was curious, so I looked it up," She looked at Kimberly, "you're a SEAL."

Kimberly was about to acknowledge when a frowning Meredith spoke sharply. "Neither of us know anything about that." Andria looked directly at Meredith, who stared back. Suddenly recognition dawned in Andria's eyes, and she nodded. "They shouldn't even let you guys wear that insignia in public," Meredith continued. Andria apologized to Meredith, good move.

It was rare that she wore her dress whites, and when she looked in the full-length mirror, even she had to admit that it looked good. Andria was smiling. Meredith seemed very proud. Okay, good for her, maybe she was tuning in. Downstairs her mother was surprised, and her father very pleased. Possibly her mother was getting it. Kimberly thought that through the years, she should have sent photographs. She made a mental note to rectify that.

Kimberly left with Andria and Meredith in the naval staff car driven by Seaman Gleeson, who had augmented his uniform; he had a Shore Patrol armband on, white web, and a sidearm. Kimberly wondered, a bit much for a driver; possibly, it was even too obvious, but she understood, to the Navy and Homeland Security, she was an asset.

Meredith was on her cell phone as soon as they left. "Yeah, look, I can't go with you guys today."

"Yeah, well, my sister's a Lieutenant Commander in the Navy, and she's the guest of honor at the Veteran's Day celebrations today, so I'm with her. I wasn't expecting her home," Meredith told her friends.

"Yeah, Veteran's Day ... like why we have a holiday, like the people who sacrificed so we can wander around malls."

"Really ... you need to read your fuckin' history books." Meredith disconnected. "Jeez, they're idiots," she fumed.

"Don't be too hard on them, Meredith, only one percent of the families in the US are involved with defending the country, so most people have no clue," was Andria's advice.

"You just happen to be related to two of them." Andria beamed at Kimberly's statement.

It was a beautiful day, clear blue sunny skies, dry, and reasonably warm at sixty-five degrees. The local Chevrolet dealer had a convertible for The Commander to ride in. Kimberly insisted that Charlie Company Engineering Regiment National Guard's SPC Andria Pedersen would ride with her. That was fine with the Chamber of Commerce guys who were parade organizers. Meredith could ride shotgun. The dealer had a friend, a bit of a blowhard, who was going to drive. Seaman Gleeson stepped in and quietly informed everyone that he was driving whatever vehicle the Lieutenant Commander was using. One look at the enormous armed seaman with the Shore Patrol armband, and they stopped arguing.

"Guess we should've brought a Jeep," Kimberly laughed to the seaman.

"In all due respect, no ma'am, then the street crowd might be able to see my sidearm." Okay, so this guy was more than a deckhand and driver.

Another convertible drove up. An older, but still spry male with a VFW blazer got out of the passenger seat. It was the local VFW commander. He came up to Kimberly and saluted.

"Welcome home, Commander Callahan. We're so pleased that you could make it." Kimberly returned the salute. He had copies of the program for them, they cross-checked a few points and then left.

"Why are they calling you Commander," Meredith wanted to know.

"In abbreviated parlance, the Lieutenant is left off, as with Lieutenant JG, where the JG is left off."

"It's like all Generals one star up are usually just addressed as General," added Andria.

Meredith nodded. "What's a JG?"

"Junior Grade, it is the second-lowest Naval commissioned officer rank, after Ensign, a full Lieutenant in the other services," Kimberly explained to her sister.

"Oh."

Soon they were underway, a police cruiser, lights flashing, leading the way followed by the Guard's color unit and then the vehicle with Kimberly, Andria, and Meredith. The VFW Commander's convertible was next, followed by vets carrying service flags, and then a sizable corps of veterans of all ages. It bothered Kimberly that she had been unaware of the number of people in the area who had contributed to the military.

Following them was Charlie Company of the Guard engineer regiment and then the community college marching band. After them, there were some fire and rescue trucks, EMS, and the county police SWAT team with some new armor; then, some civilian floats, then the Boy Scouts, and the high school marching band. Meredith got excited when she spotted some of her friends.

"Are those the ones you dissed on?" Andria asked her.

"No." It turned out that those friends were a few blocks ahead and did see Meredith in the car with her sister.

The Veteran's Monument was in a park, and to one side of it, facing out onto a small plaza, someone had built a platform. The parade broke up there, and the organizers instructed the seaman to park behind the platform's backdrop. Meredith left to find her friends.

The Mayor met them and wanted Kimberly to place a large wreath at the memorial that he was going to hold.

"With apologies, sir, but how good are you at backing up while holding a big wreath?" Seaman Gleeson asked the mayor. The mayor just looked at the big guy. "What say I handle it for her?" the seaman added.

"Sure, of course," the mayor conceded.

"Specialist Pedersen is going to accompany me. Can you find me the Boy Scout leader, not the adult troop leader but the top kid?"

The Mayor certainly could, and ten minutes later, the kid arrived with an adult. Kimberly wheeled to attention and saluted him. He snapped to attention and returned a Scout salute.

"What is your name Scout?"

"Thomas Thorsen, ma'am." She explained to the Scout what was going to happen. The boy knew how to do an about-face. A local pastor joined them; he had been an Army Chaplin during Desert Storm. Ten minutes later, they were ready.

The Mayor went to the microphone and got everyone's attention. He then attempted a command voice while reading off a script, "Color party, present arms, forward march." The community college marching band did a reasonable rendition of the Star-Spangled Banner as the Guards color party marched in, taking the flags to their appointed position.

The pastor went to a microphone on a stone terrace at the front of the top level of the memorial. He got everyone's attention. It took a while as a large crowd had come into the park from the parade. The Pastor spoke for a moment of the sacrifices of both the dead and the living that gave the people of the community of the United States the freedoms they had. He then spoke of the ongoing sacrifices of the people who chose to serve and were now on active duty. He said a prayer for the dead. He nodded at Kimberly.

"Unit, slow march," Kimberly gave the command.

As they slow marched forward, Kimberly saw that Seaman Gleeson could do slow march backward, while correctly carrying the awkwardly large wreath. From Kimberly's peripheral vision, she saw that the Scout was rigidly at attention and in perfect alignment with Andria and her. At the top of the monument steps, they each put a hand on the wreath as the Seaman secured it on an easel. All four stepped back and saluted. A bugler blew taps. The bugler was terrific – the notes just cried. As the last note died away, there was silence.

"Order arms."

All four arms snapped down on Kimberly's command. They about-faced smartly and marched back to the raised platform with the dignitaries. There were three empty chairs in the front row; the Scout was to rejoin his troop, score one for the mayor. Seaman Gleeson stood nearby.

The mayor was so excited in his introduction of her that Kimberly wondered if the Captain's heart attack had been his idea. Unquestionably the guy had spoken with some of her high school teachers. He knew about the police award from junior high. He expressed his pleasure that one of the communities own was a graduate of the Naval Academy and a Surface Warfare Officer.

"Folks, that means that she knows how to use those big steel warships to wreak havoc on our enemies," Well, that was partially true, if she had someone to drive it. She wondered what the Mayor would think if he knew what she really did. "I give you one of our very own, United States Navy Commander Kimberly Callahan." Okay, no need to correct to Lieutenant Commander.

Kimberly acknowledged the sacrifices of those who had served and then started on the reasons why people serve. She did say that, like the National Guard Specialist Pedersen and her, the principal reason to join might be education. Or, like Seaman Gleeson, it was a way to be useful and see the world, something the seaman had told her during their drive from Kittery. For almost all, there was an awareness of 9/11, and for most, there was the satisfaction of defending their country's rights and freedoms. She did talk about the small number, less than one percent of families, that service members come from, a disproportionate sacrifice. The folks in the park listened attentively and cheered her when she ended ten minutes later.

There was nothing more planned, other than the mayor announcing that the program was over, forgetting to retire the color party. People enjoyed milling around the park on one of the last of the beautiful days of the year. Some who wished to talk to her she recalled from high school. For the most part, they just wanted to say hello, some, most, congratulated her on her accomplishments. She saw a group at the periphery staring in. That reminded her of herself years go outside the cool girl's group and staring in.

There was a male on the periphery standing alone. Kimberly recognized Brad Watson. Her immediate question to herself was, why was he back in Augusta, and what the hell did he want? As others moved on, he had an opportunity to come up to her privately.

"Good afternoon, Commander. Nice talk."

"Hello, Brad."

"I want to thank you for Virginia and what you did for Danny and me. I know that it was the Coast Guard and you guys just did them a favor as you happened to be in the area, I still need to thank you. Between Wally dying, they never did find his body, and the pissed-off

Coast Guard, it was a very low point in my life. I am an alcoholic. After that, I joined AA. It should stand for Assholes Anonymous as well because I certainly was one of those most of my life. I came back from Virginia and have tried to face my problems and, as much as I can, make restitution. It's kinda part of the program. I was a complete asshole to you in high school, and that night, and other times, and I want to apologize."

Kimberly nodded. She did not doubt his sincerity but hoped he was not going to try to reconnect.

"Since I returned, I've met a woman," he continued. "I've told her everything. That I'm an alcoholic and that I have a daughter. We are trying to get custody of her because her mother is an alcoholic and unfit. She has left her in dangerous situations. Well, the court will decide all that. For the record, my girlfriend also knows about you, including that you were somehow involved in my rescue in Virginia. I have a new job in a warehouse, and I've returned to the community college to try and get an associate degree in business."

"Brad, I'm pleased that you're getting your life in order." She noticed a woman standing off them who had stepped up shortly after Brad started talking to her.

"Would you like to meet Nancy?" he asked.

Kimberly shifted her feet. "Sure."

Brad looked at the woman and signaled her to approach.

"Kim, Nancy Morris," Brad made the introductions.

"I am pleased to meet you, Commander. You're kinda amazing. Anyway, I want to thank you and your crew for rescuing Brad and his friend and getting them to the Coast Guard."

"You're welcome. Brad, can I tell the crew what you are doing now?"

"Sure, but why?"

"Your story isn't unusual. Usually, the Coast Guard deals with things like that, but now and then, we run into something while we are doing our other work. You were not in good shape; it'd be nice for them to learn that you've turned it around."

Brad bit his lip. "Sure, but I'm not sure I have."

"As I understand it, if you have those genes, you're never sure, but with work, you can stay sober."

"He works hard at it," Nancy offered.

Brad nodded. "Yes, and the minute I start thinking it's easy is when I'll fail, so yes, it's constant. Anyway, others want to talk to you, I just, we, wanted to say hi."

She recognized one of the others, her history, and government affairs teacher, Mr. Howell. Meredith was with him.

"Hello, Kimberly, very effective talk. We always knew that you'd do well. I've followed your career through the Academy but lost track of you after that. It makes a teacher feel good to have a student do so well."

"Thank you, Sir."

"Your sister has an idea that we would like you to consider." He looked at Meredith.

"Kim, my friends, are dorks, really, they are so clueless. Mr. Howell tries to make them understand, but it's difficult. I include myself in that difficult group. To be honest, I never really thought about what you and the other military do for us until today. Mr. Howell tries to make it real and alive and not just something in a book, but I think that if you could come to the class in uniform for one period that it would really, really help."

Mr. Howell smiled at Meredith and then looked at Kimberly and nodded. Recruiting pieces were not a part of her mission. She understood the education potential; this would not be recruiting. It might mean a lot of paperwork.

"I'm an active-duty sea-going officer, not PR. I'll have to check to see if I'd even be allowed to do that."

"Can we help with that?" Howell asked.

"Not sure, I may need a letter requesting me to come, but let's just see."

Her parents arrived with a couple of technologists from her dad's pharmacy and, to her surprise, a couple of women from her mother's office.

If the day had accomplished nothing else, her mother now accepted that she was a naval officer and was proud of her daughter.

Most of the people with her parents just wanted to meet her. A male she did not know came up.

"Oh, honey, this is Mr. Skirlin, one of the lawyers," her mother introduced. Kimberly nodded at the man.

"You're a surface warfare officer?"

"Yes."

"I thought women weren't allowed in combat."

"For a variety of times and now in all the services we are. There are female Sappers, combat engineers; we have female fighter pilots in the Navy, as does the Air Force. Navy women are on both surface combat ships and submarines. The world is changing." She grinned, hoping not to get into an argument.

The man frowned. "What does a Surface Warfare Officer do?"

"Command various aspects of surface ship missions, in my case, the fire control and, more specifically, the plotting."

His frown deepened. "Those two don't seem logical?"

"Why"

"Well, dealing with fires and navigation?"

Kimberly laughed. "No, plotting uses radar and other technologies to discern our target and get a missile onto it. Fire control is controlling the firing from our ship, both missiles, and standard weapons."

"Oh," he seemed confused. "So, how do you decide targets?"

"The easy way is that someone fires at us, but they might be targets designated by intelligence."

"Oh."

The conversation helped Kimberly decide that her younger sister and Andria were correct; most people had no clue of the military protecting them or how it functioned.

Back at their parent's home, Meredith had more on her mind. "Jesus, they're idiots. Holly and Sue were the only ones who came with me to the park. The others thought it was all inconvenient. They wanted to go shopping. Shit, they and their parents would be the first to start screaming if terrorists blew up the mall."

"Meredith, where did you learn language like that?"

"At school, Mom, and really, I have to include myself in my comments because I had no clue what you did sis. Damn, that trumpet was eerie."

"Yeah, the trumpeter was really good," Andria added.

"That's weird, both my sister and my brother's girlfriend are soldiers," Meredith said in awe.

"That'll get you in a whole lot of trouble with your sister," Andria told Meredith.

"What?"

"Calling a sailor, a soldier," Andria laughed.

"Oh, so what do I say?"

"I suppose the safest and most politically correct is a warrior," their father offered.

"Likely, and it's a term used for centuries," acknowledged Andria.

Early in the evening, Kimberly spoke with Meredith alone. "Two things, Meredith. First, it's easy to diss on people. I used to do that, still do sometimes. But you must understand that folks are free to make their individual choices, malls versus homework as an example. The military defends their freedom to make those choices, even if you and I think they're making bad choices. Second, it's easy to become angry with your classmates or friends and lash out with the knowledge you have sworn to keep secret. It takes discipline not to do that." Meredith assured her that she understood both points.

Back in Norfolk, Kimberly rejoined the team. The littorals had set up a screen along the coast with the Coast Guard cutters inside that. Because the ships were perfect for operations near the coast, the Coast Guard was asking for Congress for littorals as fleet additions.

Alone in her sea cabin, Kimberly started reflecting. The body the DGSE found at the Monto Carlo harbor had been confirmed as Hamedani's. For Kimberly, that was not even close to closure. She did not know what would be. Some of her withdrawal from her hometown, even her family, likely had been due to the incident at the junior high. Some issues were that, like many, she wanted to, and had achieved getting away from where she grew up. She did not understand why she had distanced herself from her family. Some of that was that as a SEAL, she could not talk about what she did, and certainly did not want to have that discussion with her parents. As telephoning her at sea was impossible, her family never tried. She hadn't even sent pictures of her at her graduation from the Naval Academy. She should try to connect when ashore. During the last visit home, the distance closed, particularly with Meredith. Kimberly had started to ask, and likely it would not be difficult for her to talk to Meredith's class. She'd follow up ashore. Meredith's other request might be a lot trickier. She had asked to visit Kimberly on base.

Chapter Thirteen – Sisters

Due to Kimberly's multiple roles, Meredith and Mr. Howell's request was a bit complicated. The Navy had no real problem if she remained within her publicly allowed parameters. Malcolm Greene dealt with most of the other flack. The FBI was not sure if they had a problem. Due to her operation in France and as a generality, the CIA did not like it at all. Greene liked the idea. It took until just before Christmas, but everyone gave her permission.

Due to exams, the school could not accommodate the request while Kimberly was home for Christmas. It was late January before she could talk to Meredith's class. By the time the day came, the principal had turned her presentation into an assembly. Meredith, backed by Mr. Howell, insisted to the Principal that Kimberly would also speak to Meredith's history class. For Kimberly, the uniform code was dress whites.

As Kimberly talked, she thought that her assembly speech sounded more like the rah-rah recruiting stuff. That had a role. The smaller history class venue worked better as she described her training and what a surface warfare officer did. There were multiple questions, most of which she answered. No one recognized the trident insignia, and Meredith did not go there.

From anything Kimberly had seen over the prior years, she never considered Meredith more than a flaky teenager. On Veteran's Day and during Kimberly's school visit, Meredith said things suggesting that was no longer true. Unfortunately, Kimberly had to leave for Norfolk as soon as she completed the school presentations. As she was going, Meredith again asked, implored her, to find a way to allow her to visit Kimberly on base. That would be possible only in the public areas. They had never had a serious what do you want to do conversation. While returning to Norfolk, she wondered why Meredith wished to visit the base. Likely it was just curiosity.

"The Navy wants to move the littorals further out to sea as a first cover and have the Coast Guard cover closer," Greene told her one day at a meeting ashore.

"Do the CG have the resources?" Kimberly asked.

"To do that and cover all the ports, not really."

"They have Border Patrol."

"Yes, and you guys at sea, but they're still stretched."

"So, what's the Navy concerned with?"

"I'm not sure, possibly Posse Comitatus; maybe, they don't see guarding the immediate coast as their mission."

"I can see that, but I believe we're doing valuable service," Kimberly told him.

"Just a heads up, likely nothing until you hear something official from the Navy. You had something?"

"Personal deal. My sister's a junior in high school and wants to spend a day at work with her older sister."

Greene frowned and paused. "She as crazy as you are?"

"I respectfully object to the characterization, sir, but truly, I have no idea. For reasons I am not sure of, my family and I are not close. It's okay, good even when I'm at home, but we don't communicate, I don't communicate."

"Thus, you're not sure what your sister's request is about?"

"Correct."

Greene thought for a moment. "Depending on her reasons, we might be able to make it work."

That evening in her apartment in the Single Officers Quarters, she decided to call. Meredith was home, but their Mom and Dad were perplexed that Kimberly wanted to talk to her.

"Your end secure?" she asked Meredith.

"As in are parents listening, no, I'll go to my room."

"Good, still be careful as I'm on an unsecured cell phone." Kimberly waited until Meredith came back on. "I've been thinking about you and your request to spend some time with me. I realized that I have no clue about what you might want to do career-wise."

"Okay, well, really neither do I," Meredith replied. "I sort of know what I don't want to do, and that is office stuff like Mom or a shop like Dad. When you were home Veteran's Day, I realized that I hadn't been paying attention. God, I am so sorry that I thought you were a cop."

"They do good stuff."

"Yeah, I know, and maybe something like that. I like using my hands, and I like being up moving. After that visit and when we talked at Christmas, I started to think about what you do. Dad says you went to the Naval Academy and are a mechanical engineer. I looked up the SEAL stuff, God, that training is brutal. I can see where the Navy might want their surface warfare officers or SEALS to be engineers. As I thought about it, that whole thing has a lot of appeal. I looked up the Academy online, and I have the courses and grades to get in. I was going to call you as I'm not sure about any of it."

"Most of that I could answer when I am home. Why do you want to spend time with me here?"

"I'd like to, but is that even possible? No, your question was why. It's because my ideas of what you do are likely misinformation from the movies. I want to see the real deal. I started working out in the weight room. Maybe I could qualify as a SEAL?"

"That's a long way out. Let's focus on the Navy in general and Annapolis in particular. The application deadline for Annapolis is the end of next January, but you need to be working on it now. But, to the base, I'm not sure if I could get permission for you to visit. If you're truly interested, I can try."

"I would so love that."

Kimberly wondered what next. She called Malcolm Greene to say that Meredith was interested in a Navy career, Annapolis, and talking SEALs.

"As are six thousand kids who just left a movie about the SEALs."

"True, is that a no?"

"It's we'll see. Find out what the base commander thinks."

Except when she first arrived, she had not interacted with the base commander, a Captain. The week she asked was slow as Kimberly got an appointment with her the next morning at 1500 hours Zulu, ten in the morning local time.

"Good morning, Commander, what can I do for you?" Had the Captain wanted to do attitude, she would have added the Lieutenant. Kimberly outlined what she wanted.

"What you guys do with the littorals is highly classified. Even I'm not fully read in."

"True, so to do this, I would have to also go to my direct commanders off base; however, I decided that I needed to start here."

"I would have little problem if you got those permissions. Do you need anything from me?"

"Likely a base pass for her if I get the okay. If it's a go, Malcolm Greene will give you the okay."

That got Kimberly a long stare while the Captain decided what to say. "The Deputy Director of Homeland Security?"

"Yes, ma'am."

"Wow, I had heard a bit of this. You report directly to Greene?"

"Yes, ma'am."

"But I didn't hear that from you."

"Or anybody, ma'am."

The Captain pulled up something on her computer. "My stuff says that you report to Admiral Mike Mann in San Diego."

"For Navy, yes."

"Need we involve him?"

"If it would make you feel more comfortable, certainly."

"But not necessary?"

"No, ma'am."

"Okay, you'll contact Greene?"

"Yes, ma'am. I've already floated the idea at him."

She called Greene back. He was more enthusiastic. During the discussion, Kimberly stated a negative, that her kid sister was a narcissistic idiot. She learned two things. Due to her, Meredith and all her family had already undergone security checks so getting clearance would not be as difficult as she had imagined, and that Greene thought Meredith was just a typical teenager.

"She's more like you than I think you want to admit," Greene told her. That set Kimberly back a bit. Until recently, neither of them had been paying attention to the other.

As an afterthought, she called Admiral Mann, who thought it a good idea. While very specific about where Meredith could go and what she could see, he authorized Meredith to have abridged visits aboard the USS Detroit as well as an Arleigh-Burke destroyer. By

2000 Zulu both Greene and Mann had communicated their approval to the base commander.

Kimberly called Meredith. "So, here's the deal. When you're able to come, I'll get you a flight going from Portsmouth to Norfolk. I'll pick you up at the Norfolk airport."

"Okay, likely March, when we have an early release on a Thursday as the teachers have a thing the next day. I started the application process for the Academy SAT stuff."

"What happens if you hate your visit here?"

"Unlikely, but I'm not required to complete the process."

"Okay."

"Dad is excited. Mom has no clue, does she?"

"It came in stages with me. Mom easily got her mind around that I was going to engineering school. I suspect the whole Navy thing bothers her. Some people cope by shutting out thinking about the danger. Even at my graduation from the Naval Academy, despite the uniforms, she focused on my becoming an engineer. Veteran's Day, she finally acknowledged that I'm a Naval Officer. She doesn't want to know about the SEAL stuff. You're going to have more trouble with her. You realize that there are physical requirements for Annapolis?"

"Like I'm a marshmallow?"

"I didn't say that, but yeah, despite your running and backyard stuff."

"I know, and I've started on more physical stuff. Jeez, most girls don't know that the best place to meet football players is in the weight room."

"Yeah, well, be careful around all that testosterone. Pregnancy's another good way to get yourself bounced from the Academy or any Navy program."

"I know."

Kimberly could get Meredith an American flight leaving Portland about 1700 and arriving in Norfolk just before 2100. Their Dad would be able to get Meredith to Portland.

Kimberly was at sea for the next two weeks patrolling along the coast of the Carolinas. It was quiet, allowing Kimberly to focus her team on additional training.

"Montana became a very different person after she went to the Academy," Janie Ewing told Kimberly one evening after Kimberly mentioned Meredith's impending visit and plans.

"Good or bad."

"Oh my God, all good," replied Janie, "It started plebe summer, but she became disciplined, physically fit, and got better grades than ever, in courses that were more difficult than she had ever taken." Montana was due to graduate from the Academy that spring.

"Meredith's a long way from being there."

"We should get her out on a cruise."

"With restrictions, Mann okayed her coming onboard. Cruise would not be possible."

"Why not," Janie asked. "Mids do cruises."

"Well, she only has the weekend, and she's a civilian."

"So maybe when she is a Mid."

"Not even then, they need to be on a cruiser or at the least a destroyer."

The Norfolk International Airport is just east of the base, so a quick hop for Kimberly. She decided to take her bike and was halfway there before she wondered what she would do if Meredith were not wearing jeans. When they met in the baggage claim, Meredith was wearing trousers. Kimberly was a bit amused to see that the girl had on store-bought camos that vaguely looked like Navy BDUs. She even had on almost regulation boots. She was also amused by the minimal, compared to the past, makeup. Partially due to her height and under her camo cap, she looked older than seventeen. Kimberly had not even thought about luggage, Meredith only had a backpack.

"How was your flight?" Kimberly asked as they walked to parking.

"Good, except for the part from Washington, where a creep in the next seat had all sorts of questions about my service. I think the guy is like a female military groupie."

"Yeah, well, that's one of the many reasons why we don't wear our uniform off base. What did you tell creepy?"

"Nothing and the less I told him, the more interested he got. I gotta say his special ops scenario was fun."

"So, that's what you told him?"

"Hell no, I just shut up and let him do all the talking and speculating. He didn't even get grunts from me. Men are so easy; they all love to talk. I think he's in baggage claim, let's get out of here." Kimberly's extra motorcycle helmet was only a bit loose on her sister. Kimberly gave Meredith her base pass.

Kimberly thought Meredith might object to the motorcycle, but she loved the trip to the base. By 2230 hours local time, they were at the single officer's quarters. Saturday morning started with a motorcycle tour around the base. Meredith's questions were insightful, even if Kimberly was not allowed to answer several. Kimberly began to see her sister in a whole new light.

"So why all the air stuff here instead of over at the airfield?" Meredith asked in the northwest part of the base.

"Part of the base is a US Naval Air Station. They do training and avionics here."

"Avionics?"

"The electronic systems on the jets, technically any electronics in the air."

They did get aboard a destroyer mid-morning where Kimberly could show her the combat information center. As they were dockside, it was not operating.

As with the destroyer, there should have been only a minimal watch on the USS Detroit. After their limited tour of the ship, they encountered Hans in the wardroom with many of the team, including Janie, Dixie, PO-1 Luis Rodriquez, PO-2 Warren Martinek, and PO-1 Susan Rife.

"So, do I have it correct, there's a core crew under Lieutenant-Commander Shorheim who manage, or I guess in your word's sis, drive the ship, and then a mission group under you?"

"Basically, sometimes Hans lets Lieutenant Ewing, or I drive."

"Okay, so what does a mission package do?"

Kimberly was not sure how to answer that. Dixie saved her the trouble. "Kill bad guys."

"Okay, so what's a possible scenario?" Meredith asked.

Kimberly was starting to think that the whole trip had been a mistake. "Look, this is all classified. You cannot breathe a word of this to anyone, Mom, Dad, Dwaine, a BFF, no one, not even Andria."

"I pretty much figured that out after we passed the guard post," Meredith told her.

Shorheim chuckled. "Ms. Callahan, what your sister says is true," Hans added, "talking about this, about a lot of stuff you might see on base could get a bunch of people killed, including your sister and us, or worse a bunch of civilians."

"I understand, sir, I swear secrecy. I'll take an oath or whatever you want."

"We'll accept that and understand that when you get to the Academy, the Firsties will make you pay dearly for even some perceived breach of security," Lieutenant Ewing told her.

"Okay," Meredith said.

"The correct response is 'ma'am yes ma'am,' learn it now," Janie barked.

"Ma'am, yes, ma'am."

"How do terrorists get to the United States?" Kimberly asked her.

"They fly in. No, wait, terrorists get here any way they can, air, overland or by sea?"

"Correct and different parts of Homeland Security worry about the air and land routes, our job, along with the Coast Guard and Border Patrol, is to keep them from landing by sea," Janie continued.

"There are many routes for terrorists to arrive by sea," Kimberly continued. "Border Patrol manages the passenger ships. The Coast Guard, the Navy, the FBI, and Border Patrol keeps an eye on shipping vessels and their cargo. Our mission is to intercept and close down any terrorist teams looking to land on our shores."

"Close down?" Meredith asked. Kimberly looked at her. "Okay kill?"

"We would like to get them alive as they're a source of information, but yes, kill if needed," Kimberly replied.

Dixie added, "Of course, that is unless they piss off Da Bitch, in which case, they all die." The other Petty Officers snorted.

"Who's Da Bitch? Oh my God, you sis?"

"Yeah, well, that is highly classified, and Chief, you're bucking to get busted."

"Ma'am, yes ma'am," Dixie responded, grinning.

Meredith thought it funny but looked at her sister with new respect. Ashore they walked to the motorcycle.

"So now I gotta be Bitch II."

"God, no."

"God, yes, shit, I had no idea. Sis, you're so fuckin' cool. So, the funky camo and angles, that's all to hide the ship?"

It amused Kimberly that the girl kept the conversation rolling, blocking a comeback about the bitch thing. Kimberly let it go. "Yeah, it's a stealth ship, the angles prevent the radar waves from being reflected, so it's not seen on radar or at least seen poorly, particularly when we're close to shore."

They went to an officer's mess where Meredith chattered through supper. Kimberly was still unsure if the trip had been a good idea, but if it gave her sister some focus, that would be fine. She was a long way from Annapolis and an even longer way from the special ops that Kimberly and her team were doing. Suddenly a civilian sat down at their table.

"No, no, fuckin' no," Kimberly said. The civilian was Malcolm Greene.

"Commander, you have somewhere else to be," Greene told her.

"Crap Malcolm no, she's barely interested. This trip is only about her seeing if she is interested, and I don't want her in your shit."

"Commander, that was an order."

"Meredith this is Malcolm Greene, the Deputy Director of Homeland Security. Do not listen to a word he says." Kimberly saw the look between the two and Greene's nod.

"Kim, we've already met. He was in Augusta and met with Dad and me before he cleared me to be here. He has a program."

"He always has a damn program. I don't want you mixed up in this shit."

"I can see that coming from Mom but not you," Meredith told her sister. "Do I tell you that you can't do the SEAL stuff?" The cocky little "you see" look from her sister pissed Kimberly off.

"That's different; you're my baby sister."

"Lieutenant Commander, I think the Deputy Director gave you a direct order. I can think for myself," Meredith told her.

Shit, she was not going to win this one. Her sister and Greene left, leaving Kimberly staring at her dessert. "Mom and Dad are going to damn kill me," she told her dessert.

Meredith did not show up at the single officers' quarters that night nor the next morning. Kimberly decided she should go to the ship and see if she could learn anything there besides, she rationalized, they were due at sea the following morning, and she needed to check on some things. None of her mission team was there. There was a standard port watch under the command of one of Hans' Lieutenant JG's.

Much of her team's gear was missing; something was going on about which she was not being told. She did not like that, but Greene had pulled stuff like this before. She was even more unhappy when Meredith did not show up for supper and missed her plane home. She was, after all, a high school junior, and her primary responsibility was her schoolwork. Kimberly's cell rang about ten; it was Meredith.

"Hey, sis, I just got to Pease, and Dad is here to take me home."

"What happened?"

"Oh, it was great we had one hell of a party, but I doubt I should tell Mom and Dad about it."

Shit, at seventeen, she had learned to speak code. Likely she had been doing it for years. Okay, Kimberly would have to wait or get it out of some of her team while at sea.

"Okay, hon, glad you had a good weekend. Sleep well and work hard at school," Kimberly told her.

"Oh, I will, both, no sleep at the party. Whoops here's Dad with the car now."

Kimberly wondered if their father had any idea of what his youngest daughter was doing. Hell, unless Greene had divulged more, he only had a limited idea of what his eldest daughter did.

While at sea over the next weeks, Kimberly pieced together some of it, including that the first evening Meredith had been given a truncated weapons course by Luis Rodriquez. Following that was a simulated night patrol, from the sounds of it likely at Camp Perry. On the human targets exercise, Meredith had done well virtually killing the bad guys, and none of the women and children or good guys until one of the women who was carrying a baby kept advancing toward them, despite Anthony Carlos yelling at her in Arabic to stop. Meredith had been positioned the closest to her and killed her. Dixie told her that part during the last couple of days of the cruise.

"... so, Greene starts to dump all over your sister," Dixie tells her, "for killing this woman and the kid. Meredith approaches 'the body' and used her weapon to push the burqa aside, revealing a body bomb. So, Greene changes tactics. He dumps on her for risking a booby trap and that the bomb might've gone off. Meredith growls at him, saying that she shielded the others with her body, which she had. Jeez, Kim, you would have been so proud of her. She was so fuckin' cold. I think Greene thought she would start to bawl. Damn if she isn't a knockoff of you – Da Junior Bitch, although she kinda growled at that one as well."

"What the hell time was this?"

"Around 0800 Zulu."

"What happened then?"

"With all due respect, ma'am, I've likely told you too much."

"Shit, suddenly we're back to ma'am?"

"Yes, ma'am."

She did get some confirmation and later learned a bit more from Janie. Greene had them tromping through swamps as the sun came up. They were all wet and cold, but Meredith kept going. There were a variety of exercises, and they got no rest or food until supper time after which they all cleaned up, and Greene flew Meredith to Pease on a CIA jet. Kimberly was not sure if she was delighted about a great weekend or angry at how it had gone. She did get a check from Watsoo Financial Group that reimbursed her for purchasing Meredith's tickets. That was another bad sign as Kimberly was sure they were CIA.

A week later, Greene appeared at the officer's mess and sat down with Kimberly. "Your sister is crazier than you."

"With all due respect, Sir," said Kim as she stood, "stay the fuck away from me for a while."

"And why should I do that?"

"So, I don't succeed in my temptation to feed you your balls through your nose."

Greene roared with laughter as Kim stomped out of the mess.

Chapter Fourteen – Dropping Through Air

Kimberly had little time to be upset. New orders came for the SEAL component of her team, Lt. Ewing, CPO Dixie Phillips, PO-1 Luis Rodriquez, PO-2 Warren Martinek, and PO-3 Anthony Carlos. SEALs from their original training team would augment them. A party of engineers captured by Congolese rebels and held in a village in the southern area of the Democratic Republic of the Congo needed rescuing. Fortunately, it was a savanna; a parachute drop was possible, and extraction by a helicopter also possible.

"Why the hell don't we just chopper in," Martinek asked.

"Analysis isn't sure of the number of rebels guarding the compound and are concerned about giving us away. We're dropping silently from the sky," was Kimberly's reply.

"Any of these guys disabled in any way?"

"They're not sure," Kimberly told them.

"How many are there," Carlos asked.

"They believe eight," Kimberly told them.

"Do we even know they're there?" Rodriquez asked.

"High probability," was Kimberly's best response.

"So," Lieutenant Ewing summed up, "we're going after hostages that we don't know are there or are all disabled, and with no clue of the force defending the village."

"Basically, and due to the political turmoil in the DRC, no one knows we're coming," Kimberly replied.

"Really, we're doing a clandestine invasion of a sovereign nation?" CPO Phillips, Dixie, asked.

"They're holding our citizens," Kimberly replied.

"Let's go," Dixie replied.

Kimberly thought it was amazing that she was so relaxed as the plane flying them on the final leg into the DRC cut through the night sky. There was no moon; she hoped the starlight would not give them away.

The analysts reported that the DRC air force had six fighter planes. Thus far, there was no indication that the team's plane had been seen on radar, and the fighters scrambled. The flight deck warned them they were near the drop zone.

Night drops are dangerous, but, in training, Kimberly and her team had done so many that a real one into a sovereign nation had the danger of being regarded as routine.   She liked dropping through the air.   Watching her altimeter, Kimberly deployed her chute at the last minute, so there was a short ride to the ground.   She hid her parachute and started for the rendezvous point. The whole team dropped without a problem. Thus far, they had not encountered any hostiles. They started the hike to the village two kilometers away. The entire team was using night vision goggles.

The village was quiet, in Kimberly's estimation too quiet, not even a dog barking. Moving carefully at the perimeter, they identified the building where the hostages reportedly were. She wished she had more personnel as she deployed Martinek and one of the other SEALs to a point where there was a clear view of the village compound. He would provide cover and information.

The buildings between the edge of the compound and the hostage's structure were not guarded nor, on checking, were they occupied.   A building immediately east of the hostage building had an antenna beside it and power from a generator. A temptation for Kimberly was to knock it out, but that would result in an alarm and bring in other troops. The analysts had had no idea how far away those troops might be.

She, Rodriquez, and Carlos approached the front of the hostage building.   There was a guard asleep in a chair at the door. Carlos was able to check the front of the building with the antenna. The guard there was sitting and awake, though hardly alert. Two other SEALs moved up behind Carlos. Simultaneously Carlos and Rodriquez silently cut the two guard's throats, then Carlos, with the other SEALs, entered the building with antennae.   Kimberly heard an exclamation followed immediately by two shots.   Silencers are helpful but don't completely silence a weapon. A dog barked at a building on the other side of the compound as Kimberly and Rodriquez breeched the hostage building.   There were no guards inside. The hostages were waking up. Carlos and the two other SEALs joined them with Carlos reporting that two males in the radio building were dead. They were able to keep the hostages from any loud exclamations. Likely while hostages, they had learned not to make any loud noises.

"We're US Navy,' Kimberly and the other SEALS told each hostage, "we're here to get you home."

All eight were there. The hostages confirmed that they were not aware of any others. They also confirmed that there was no significant group guarding them. They thought about twenty. All eight hostages were weak but would be able to move on their own.

"Hostile coming across the compound toward you," Martinek reported.

To that point, the extraction mission had been too easy. Allowing the hostile to discover them would be bad. "Do you have a shot?" Kimberly asked.

"Clear shot for another fifteen seconds or so," Martinek responded.

"Take it," Kimberly replied. Immediately she heard a single shot; the dog barked a few times. Kimberly checked the compound; there was a body in the middle of it but no further response.

"Come on, let's move, around this building to the east, your left as you exit, then go to the back," Kimberly ordered. Two of the hostages were ex-military and knew the drill.

"Do I blow this generator or the radio building?" Dixie asked.

"It's a risk to leave it, but we'll attract more attention if they suddenly go off the air," Kimberly told her.

It took a minute to clear the building and get between the other buildings to the compound's periphery. Dixie, with Anthony Carlos and his team, were covering their rear.

"Eight hostiles coming across the compound," Martinek reported.

They would be a problem if left to follow Kimberly's team and the hostages. "Engage when you can," she told them. The burst of automatic weapon fire was brief.

"Compound clear," Dixie reported, "permission to sweep the other buildings."

They were missing a few hostiles if the hostage's number of twenty had been correct. "Go," Kimberly told them. It was tempting to add, "but don't take too long, or you're going to miss your flight," but they all knew that, and the less they were on their radios, even as secure as they were, the better.

As Kimberly and Rodriquez with two other SEALs escorted the hostages away from the compound, they heard two additional bursts of automatic rifle fire. The dog was barking and continued to bark when Dixie and Carlos' team, as well as Martinek's team, caught up with them. The dog went silent shortly after. Kimberly was not sure if that was a good sign or not. The extraction helicopter's landing zone was a kilometer away. They made it there without incident, and Kimberly radioed the Blackhawk helicopter crew to come in. They were five minutes out.

The next five minutes were five of the most extended minutes Kimberly had ever experienced. They needed to be on the Blackhawk and out of there as soon as possible before someone in the DRC military figured out what was going on. The politics were confused between rebel groups and the legitimate government of the country. A rebel group had held the hostages, something the engineer hostages confirmed.

"The people guarding us were not terribly well-disciplined, "one of the ex-military engineers told Kimberly. "At times, we considered just walking away."

That did not lessen the risk as the legitimate government of the DRC did not know they were there. The risk of information sharing had been judged too high. Soon they were aboard the Blackhawk and in the air. Kimberly saw the two other helicopters, Apache gunships flying escort. Kimberly suspected that there was an AWACS, the E-3 Sentry airborne warning and control system aircraft, flying high above them. They were flying southeast into Angola's Lunda Norte province. The intelligence analyst had told Kimberly that the closest DRC air force unit to the site the hostages where was at Kinshasa, two hundred knots to their east. It was one hundred and thirty-two knots to Dundo in Angola. The analysts believed flying this corridor between two DRC airports, Kahemba and Tshikapa, was, while longer than some direct routes, the safest. If it worked, they would be safe in Angola in forty-five minutes.

That they were flying slightly above the treetops invited occasional automatic weapon fire from the ground that did not seem too dangerous or very accurate. Even the gunships escorting them did not bother. Kimberly's team's biggest challenge was the anxiety of the hostages. Kimberly had one of her people sit with each hostage.

"You're SEALs?" the guy that Kimberly was with asked. She had adjudged him to be the unofficial leader of the group.

"You're ex-military, aren't you?"

"Yes, ma'am, ten years, Air Force."

"Then you know not to ask that question, and, as will be explained at the debriefing, you have no idea who rescued you."

"Understood, ma'am. I'm sorry, I guess we, and our company, should have paid attention when State told us not to go into the DRC." Kimberly chose not to reply. "I understand why you guys are clandestine, but it's too bad as the public has no idea of how much assistance and lifesaving you guys do."

"Thank you," Kimberly replied.

Other than the occasional ground fire, they landed in Dundo without incident. There they transferred to an unmarked Gulfstream and flew to Germany. The hostages departed the plane to go to their debriefing. Kimberly's team flew to Norfolk, where they would debrief. Rescuing the hostages had been gratifying, and she had not lost anyone doing it, but she still wished she could get at the leadership and money of the people who pervert Islam and terrorize free nations. And their people, Kimberly thought as an addendum.

Shortly after that mission, Kimberly made right her promise to get home more frequently. She was at her parent's place shortly after two in the afternoon. Everyone was at work or school. She still had a key. Her parents arrived soon after five. Meredith got there about five-thirty, having run from the school. Kimberly followed her up to her room and closed the door.

"What the hell happened in Norfolk after Greene absconded with you?"

"They were just tuning me up for plebe summer." Meredith was trying too hard to look matter of fact.

"Like a fuckin' night patrol exercise at Camp Perry."

"Where's Camp Perry?"

"Where Greene had you guys tromping around all night and then the day in a damn swamp."

"Yeah, we weren't always in the swamp," Meredith told her.

"So how much do Mom and Dad know?"

"Nothing except what Greene told them, and you're not supposed to know anything either."

"Yeah, well, I have people loyal to me."

"Security breach. I think Dad suspects something is up. He knows that I'm applying to the Naval Academy."

"Yeah, well, you need the grades."

"Have them, plus I'm training."

"What did Greene tell you?"

"Nothing I can tell you, Commander."

"Crap. You do know that Greene's Homeland Security and not Navy."

"Yes."

"Girls, supper is ready," their Mom called from downstairs.

"We've not finished with this conversation," Kimberly told her sister.

At five-thirty the next morning. Kimberly was awake and thinking about getting up when her sister knocked on her door.

"Come on, Sis, come run with me," Meredith called into her room. Her sister running early in the morning was news to Kimberly. The narcissistic mall shopper was very past tense.

The next hour was a revelation. Kimberly always prided herself on keeping in shape but had to work to keep up. In Meredith's program, the thirty-five-minute, five-mile run, wearing heavy boots, was followed by climbing ropes hung from a massive American elm in the backyard and pull-ups on a home-built apparatus.

"Dad build this for you?" Kimberly asked her sister.

"Dad helped me build it."

After a quick breakfast, Meredith left on the run for school, literally running.

She's going to smell like hell when she gets to school," Kimberly observed.

"She showers there and has what she wears to class in her locker," their Mom said.

"Really, for a girl who used to attempt to get Dad to drive her because she didn't like going on the bus, this is a huge change."

"She's still not on the bus," their Dad wryly noted.

After breakfast, her Dad asked Kimberly to sit with him in the living room.

"What's happening with Meredith?" her dad asked.

"I have no clue." It was a partial fib that Kimberly did not like. The reality was that her bigger lie was, of necessity, not telling her Dad what she did.

"She changed after Veteran's Day when she realized you were a Naval Officer. She changed more after returning from Norfolk."

"In what ways?" Kimberly asked, trying not to dismiss the conversation.

"She became more focused; the whole Naval Academy thing has become an obsession. She seemed to distance herself from friends and focus on her schoolwork plus this obsession with physical fitness."

"Okay, let me ask you, do you have a problem with two daughters being Naval Officers?"

There was a long pause as her father considered his answer. "No, if I thought that they were really Surface Warfare Officers."

Their father was not stupid; he had seen the Bud pin; they had even talked about it. She looked him right in the eye. "What any Naval Officer does is, to a large extent, classified, speculating on what that might be, can be very dangerous."

Their father held her eyes. "I think I have been just told by my daughter to shut up and stop asking questions."

"Or speculating, yes." Their father nodded, and that ended the conversation.

The physical fitness went on through the summer and fall. Meredith found a summer job at a veteran's home. The word was that she incessantly quizzed the veterans, most of whom were pleased to tell her their story.

"God sis, do you have any idea of the shit the Vietnam guys put up with?"

"Getting cold feet?" Kimberly asked.

"Hell no, but civilians can be unappreciative, and I say that thinking of worse adjectives."

No one at the veteran's home was aware that she wanted to get into the Naval Academy. That was looking increasingly possible as she had top grades in her junior year and thus far in her senior year. Boys were not on her agenda.

"What are you doing for senior prom?" Kimberly asked her on one visit home. The reply was a shrug.

The big family event that summer had been Dwaine and Andria's wedding. Andria did ask Kimberly to be a bridesmaid, and despite possible deployment issues, Kimberly accepted. It was fun except for her Mom harping about Kimberly getting married. She struggled with that. Few guys would accept a wife who routinely deployed on dangerous missions. The guy would have to be exceptional. Perhaps, Kimberly thought that to be a wife and mother was not in her destiny. That thought gave her pangs of remorse, but she understood her chosen profession. Her biological clock was running; she couldn't just shrug off the lack of a prom date. Guys managed a military career, even SEALs, why couldn't women? Guys' spouses were more tolerant. Maybe that was unfair. It was a new world compared to her mother's.

At work, terrorism intelligence was hard to come by. It appeared that the terrorist's cells were regrouping. It was too quiet; Kimberly suspected that there was bad stuff coming.

Chapter Fifteen – Shore Leave

She and her team were not going to get Christmas, but they did have ten days off at Thanksgiving. Kimberly headed home to Augusta. Despite Meredith's plans, her family was still talking to Kimberly. They had, over the almost year, become accustomed to the new Meredith.

The flights to Augusta all had two stops. Kimberly booked an American Airlines flight that left Norfolk about nine in the morning. After a stop in Philadelphia, she would arrive in Portland, Maine, at about one-thirty. That would work, except that at noon in the middle of the week, her Dad would not be able to come and get her. She decided to splurge and rent a vehicle for ten days.

She owned almost no civilian clothes, on the base or anywhere else. Those that she did own were mostly jeans and sweats. One day on a whim, she went to downtown Norfolk. At the MacArthur Center, she found a Michael Kors store. The clothing was beautiful. She rarely splurged, but she needed more than jeans and sweats for Thanksgiving dinner. She knew that Macy's had cute stuff, but this stuff was beautiful. She purchased separates and a couple of dresses, one even a Michael Kors designer dress that was ridiculously priced, but she liked. On a roll, Kimberly bought a woman's business suit at Taylor's. It would be what she wore on the plane.

"Jeez, you're going to clean up," was Janie's comment as she looked over Kimberly's purchases.

During the flight to Philadelphia, she thought about Meredith, her family's possible reactions to what had occurred, or she slept. The woman in the seat by her read. The layover was only forty minutes. The flight to Portsmouth from Philadelphia was an hour and twenty minutes.

A male sat down beside her for the flight to Portland. She had not socially been around a man for ages. The guys in her team did not count, that was all work, and they were subordinate to her. A glance told her that the guy was very handsome. He smelled magnificent. Somehow, he had achieved the perfect balance of testosterone and cologne. Kimberly guessed that he was in his early thirties and tall, likely about six-three. As he settled into his seat, she decided that there was something significant happening outside. Not only that, but she tried to meld into the fuselage. Her plan had to been to continue her fretting about Meredith. She needed to be absorbed in a book; she had none, and her long-suppressed libido was acting up. She did not get caught when she snuck another look. The real problem, she rationalized was being at sea too long. That sounded better than just male deprived. She should admit that she was a sailor ashore and seduce him.

"... and there are four exits, two in front and two over the wings."

Kimberly used the excuse of looking for the nearest emergency exit to look at him. Damn, he was gorgeous. Well, no, but very handsome, in a rugged sort of way.

"On your way home?"

Oh, God, he had spoken. No, he had spoken with a deep baritone. Oh, God. Girl, you must reply. You could ignore him. You do not want to. "Yes." Oh God, that was so monosyllabic.

"Portland?"

"No, Augusta. You?"

"We have an office in Portland, so I'm on my way there from here."

"Thus, work?"

"Yes. I work for a business consulting firm that specializes in health care. We have a client in Portland. What do you do?"

"Engineer."

"Really, what kind?"

"Mechanical."

"Wow."

"Why because women are not supposed to do serious stuff like mechanical engineering?"

He chuckled. "Busted, even as I said it, I knew I was so wrong. I'm not even sure why I sounded surprised; we've got a lot of brilliant women in my company. When I was at school, there were females in the engineering school but none as pretty as you."

"Nice try guy, but they do say that flattery goes a long way."

"Yeah, I knew that even trying to dig myself out, I sounded awful, Warren Bradshaw."

He put out a hand that Kimberly shook, while still looking at his eyes. The touch felt electric and did not help her hormones. "Kimberly Callahan."

"So, tell me about Kimberly Callahan mechanical engineer from Augusta, Maine."

"Grew up in Augusta, my father's a pharmacist and mom a para-legal. I do have an older brother who is a business type with a B.S. working at a bank and a younger sister who's in high school. Your turn."

He laughed. "Let's see. Grew up in Scranton, Dad's a tool and die operator, and Mom works as an Admin Assistant at Johnson College. My sister, a couple of years younger, is married, has two children, and works as a CPA. You don't work in Augusta?"

"No, Norfolk, Virginia. There are no direct flights to Portland, so today, I changed planes in Philadelphia."

"I would guess that there's lots of need for engineers in Norfolk." Kimberly was not sure how to answer that and was unaware that she had pursed her lips. "Okay, proprietary, sorry. Let's get to safer ground. What do you do when you're not engineering?"

Undoubtedly that was safer ground for Kimberly. "I like to run, and work out, do taekwondo and read. In high school, I swam, did track plus played basketball, how about you when you're not business-man-ing?" Kimberly was upset with herself; there had been no reason to list her high school stuff.

He chuckled. "Okay, we're both runners, played football in high school, sort of a history buff if I read or I guess when I read, and SCUBA."

Okay, she had left SCUBA and skydiving off her list. "Any particular area of history?"

"Europe, I guess, I'm fascinated by the development of western civilization."

"Heady stuff."

"Not really," Warren told her, "if you read enough, it all starts to come together. The turning point was about 1750 when the conditions were right for capitalism to start in the Low Countries first and then the United Kingdom."

"Really wealth creation, capitalism is just a term for using private or state monies to build entities like mercantile outlets or factories."

"Wow, okay, you cut to the chase quickly."

The remainder of the flight was a discussion of Western Europe from the mid-eighteenth century to today. It was fun and kept him from prying into her life. Kimberly understood a lot of what he was talking about, even if most of it had a business slant. Too soon, they were on final approach to Portland.

"Look, I've enjoyed this, and I'd like to stay in touch. Could I have your phone number?" Warren asked as he offered his card on the back of which he wrote his cell number and a private e-mail address.

"You're married?" Kimberly asked.

"No."

"Really, how did a good-looking guy like you remain on the loose?"

"Just never was in a situation that I wanted to be in a forever relationship. How about you?"

"Single, same argument, I guess, plus too busy." Kimberly found a piece of paper in her bag and wrote out her name, cell number, and an e-mail address that had nothing to do with the U.S. Navy. The cell number was the one she had had since high school, so it had a Maine area code.

Leading up to Christmas, everyone in the family was at work or school. Alone one day, Kimberly decided to drive. She was uncomfortable in Augusta. Kimberly had nothing against Augusta; her problem was the terrorist attack in junior high and her high school experience, much of which she may have brought on herself. Though Annapolis had been an idea before, she concluded that the junior high incident focused her on national defense and pushed her to the Navy. It also made Greene's stuff appealing.

At Capitol Park, she relaxed and continued thinking. The Capitol reminded her of the government and their way of life. It made her feel good that she defended that. She had to stop worrying about Meredith. The girl was seventeen. While seventeen-year-olds were not fully wired, legally, she was almost an adult. It was a long and challenging process through the Academy to where Kimberly was. Meredith might not even make it into the Academy. If she graduated, she might have an excellent career as a ship or even a boat officer. If she made it all the way, Kimberly had to apply her argument; their training to do what they did was excellent, and that made them safer than a lesser qualified person, she hoped.

At noon she drove back across the river to Bangor Street and Whipper's Pizza. The place was mobbed, but there was an open booth where Kimberly could sit. Being one person using a four-person booth made her a bit self-conscious. A woman came in with two children.

"Oh my gosh, Kimberly Callahan, hi!"

Kimberly vaguely recalled her from their days at Cony High. The woman had not been one of the bullies in high school. "Hi, how are you. Please have a seat. I'm embarrassed to be occupying a whole booth."

"Thanks, Donna Eckert, if you don't remember; well, Coleman now, and this is Matt and Marcie. Oh my gosh, you're a Naval Officer. How come you don't have your uniform on?"

Kimberly chuckled. "We don't wear our uniforms off base unless on official business, plus I'm on leave, so the last thing I want to do is wander around in my work clothes."

"We went to the Veteran's Day thing when you were speaking a year ago, Cory's Dad is a Vet, and we saw you there."

"Yeah, I guess I was a substitute."

"Really, 'cause the program said you?" Matt began pushing at Marcie. Without a pause, Donna said, "Matt stop bugging your sister."

"Yeah, I saw that. I guess they weren't printed until last minute."

"Matt was messing around as usual, and I remember that Marcie was fussing, but I listened to what you said about people who choose to defend our country. You could always explain stuff well. In high school, I use to love listening to you. Often, I didn't understand things, but you explained the basics."

"I didn't think anyone was listening."

"Yeah, a lot of kids weren't, and the popular ones used to pick on you a lot. I think they saw you as a threat. God, Brandy George 'Miss Popular' works in her mother's beauty salon, or, sorry, 'cosmetology salon.' She and Mike Jelinski got married, they had to, then a few years ago they were divorced. He works for a cleaning service. God, talk about going nowhere."

"They're useful. People like their hair to look nice and have their property cleaned up after a disaster or something."

"I guess. I got a mechatronics associate and work at one of the factories. My husband came to Augusta about eight years ago, and we got married just over six years ago. You married?"

Kimberly laughed. "No, pretty difficult when you're a sailor. Few guys would put up with their wife being gone weeks and months on end."

"I guess."

Their pizza came. Donna continued to bring Kimberly up to date on classmates and town gossip. At five and three, Kimberly doubted the kids understood, but Donna did try to explain that Kimberly was one of the people who protected them. It was an enjoyable lunch hour.

After lunch, she drove out to Silver Lake, an area she always liked. Many people, perhaps most, were like Donna, quiet, and remained in the background. However, from what she said, now thirteen plus years later, Kimberly had had an impact on her. Donna had seen the bullying that Kimberly endured. Her inference that she and Kimberly were doing things much more meaningful than Brandy George, now Jelinski or maybe George again, was clear. Kimberly was not sure how she felt about that.

Wednesday, while helping her mother prepare for the Thanksgiving feast the following day, her cell went off. Looking at the screen, she was surprised and immediately stepped out onto the back porch.

"Hi."

"It's Warren Bradshaw."

"Yes, I know, hi, Warren."

"Say, I have to be in Portland again after Thanksgiving. I was hoping you would still be in the area Monday evening, and I could take you to dinner."

"Oh, okay, sure, I'd like that."

"Have you heard of the Five-Fifty-Five restaurant in Portland?"

"I've heard of it, yes."

"I estimate that I need to pick you up about six."

"Well, Augusta is about an hour from Portland, so probably better if I meet you there."

"Okay, it's on Congress Street, and the street number is five fifty-five so likely about six-thirty?"

"Sure, thank you. Are you going to be with family tomorrow?" Kimberly asked Warren.

"Yes, I'm driving up to Scranton tonight. I'm going to stop by West Chester and pick up my sister and her family, so we'll all be home."

"Have a good Thanksgiving."

"Same to you and your family."

In Augusta, Thanksgiving went well. The Callahan's got Andria and Dwaine for Thanksgiving; they would be at Andria's for Christmas. The morning was the Macy's parade on television and then family time and cooking the dinner served at about four. Through the meal, the conversation was mostly about the food and previous family events. The cleanup was almost complete when Dwaine took Kimberly's elbow and led her outside. It was twenty degrees Fahrenheit, too cold for Thanksgiving in Augusta. There was frost and a little snow on the ground.

"What is going on with Meredith?" Dwaine asked Kimberly.

"She's our younger sister."

"Don't give me that crap. Now she's an academic, and a fitness nut, and totally focused?"

"Yeah, kinda cool, which reminds me its cold out here; can we go back inside?"

"Not until I get some answers."

"Look, Dwaine, I know you want to watch out for her, but she's seventeen, and I think she's making good choices. I'm sure you're talking about her applying to the Academy, but there is a long way from deciding to apply, getting in, staying in, and what happens afterward, should she graduate."

"She's getting special attention, and somehow you're involved."

"Actually, I'm not, and the less speculating you and Dad do, the better. Even idle comments at work could be very dangerous. Even a Mid has a security clearance and gets aboard ships, so let her alone and don't chatter. Now can I get my chattering teeth inside?" She did not wait for an answer.

Friday, Meredith was amused as she toured her sister around the women's clothing stores in Augusta. They did not have a lot of choices; at The Gap, Kimberly found a cable knit sweater dress that she liked. She knew little about accessories. Fortunately, Meredith did.

"You don't have any clothes, do you?" Meredith teased her big sister.

"I got some just before coming here but, yeah, I pretty much wear my BDUs all the time."

"Yeah, I know. So, who's this guy?"

"No clue really, just a nice guy that I met on the plane. Business type, he's from Philadelphia, or at least that's where he works now, grew up in Scranton, PA. Dad and Dwaine are asking all kinds of questions about you."

"Yeah, I know. What did you tell them?"

"That you are seventeen and the less speculating they did, the better. I don't think it's so much about Annapolis but goes back to when you arrived back at Pease exhausted, and stuff that has happened since. They don't understand that suddenly you're a scholar. They know something's up."

"Yeah, I know. As I said last summer, the CIA plane may have been a mistake, but I was bitching to Greene about having to get back for class. As to being a scholar, they need to make up their minds; even Dwaine was bitching at me when I was a freshman and a sophomore."

Kimberly laughed. "Well, just avoid discussion and cut off speculation."

"I know."

Kimberly did find Congress Street and Five Fifty-Five. She even found a place to park and walked in just after six-thirty. Warren was waiting for her. Her stomach did a flip-flop, and her heart rate went up. She had forgotten how damn good-looking Warren was. Damn, she was not thinking straight. Running crossed her mind. He waved. Damn.

Her recurrent thought as she approached the table was that this was such a mistake. Warren stood to greet her. Damn, she had also forgotten what a nice guy he was. He was asking questions with his greeting.

"Hi, yes, the drive was fine, and I did find a close-by parking spot."

The server was there, almost immediately inquiring about drinks. Kimberly's thought was that this was a suave guy, and beer probably was not a good idea, so ordered a Margarita. Her next thought was that her reaction had been stupid; if she had wanted a beer, she should have ordered one. This guy had her discombobulated. He ordered something neat.

"Okay, what is that?" Kimberly asked.

"The drink?"

"And the term neat."

"Let's start with the drink. Macallan is a single malt Scotch from the northeast of Scotland. Single malt because it is from one distillery and not blended like most Scotch of your acquaintance. Neat as one drinks it straight with no ice, much like wine."

She wished he would stop looking at her so admiringly, so she buried her head in the menu. The menu was not complicated, and it all sounded good. She decided on the pumpkin soup and the house-cured salmon. All the savory plates looked delicious. Luckily there were not too many of them. The truffled lobster mac and cheese sounded interesting. The server brought their drinks and took their orders. They served his Scotch in what looked like a brandy glass.

"Would you like to try a sip?" He swirled the amber liquid around in the glass and had her smell it, talking about the various fragrances. Kimberly was not sure she smelled anything but a sharp odor. She took a sip. It burned, causing her to wrinkle her nose. Warren laughed. "It's very much an acquired taste." Slowly Kimberly relaxed and enjoyed the conversation and food.

He asked about her Thanksgiving and told of his. "Jennifer's kids are eight and five and growing up faster than I can keep up with."

"It gets faster and faster as they get older," Kimberly allowed.

"Your younger sister?"

"Yes, growing up a way to quickly."

"How old is your sister?"

"Seventeen."

"That's a difficult age. What is she planning on doing?"

"Heavy on math and science in high school so likely engineering."

"Where is she applying?"

"A bunch of schools." That was technically correct. If she said the Naval Academy, it might invite questions she did not yet want to answer. "So, look, I have a question, Mr. Business Guy, my brother has a B.S. in Business Management and works at a bank. I've never understood what he does. Wouldn't they hire economics graduates?"

"Some maybe, the larger banks. Likely he manages commercial loans or the bank itself, something like that."

"Okay, that sounds about right. I have heard Dwaine talking about business loans, not specific ones, but in a generic sense. I guess some businesses need loans to operate, not just for building projects."

"Most businesses have an operating line of credit that they use to keep their cash flow smooth, or at least that's how they should use it, and not as a capital expansion loan. The latter should be a separate deal. Particularly in healthcare, there are lags in payments, so sometimes they need to dip into their line of credit, and other times they are putting excess cash into money market instruments."

She had him away from engineering and engineering schools, and onto something that he was both an expert at, and about which he enjoyed talking. If anything, he appeared to be making a conscious effort to avoid her engineering stuff and related questions. He was also anything but boring and explained things in a way that answered many of Kimberly's items.

Her decision about dessert was between the bourbon pecan bread pudding or the apple pie. The latter won along with some coffee.

Once they finished, Warren walked her to the car, extending a crooked arm that she could hug. Her heart was racing again. Arriving at her rental, he thanked her for a great evening, and they agreed they would like to do it again. He held the door for her. Soon she was on the road to Augusta.

"Damn, damn, damn," she was miffed that he had not kissed her good night. "Good grief Kimberly, you're acting as though you're in high school."

Too soon, she was on the return trip through Philadelphia to Norfolk. Her single officer quarters were comfortable. Warren was not there. That was good. No, it was not. She snuggled into her bed, unaware of the problems coming.

Chapter Sixteen – Congress

Immediately after Thanksgiving, they were back at sea. The patrolling was cold but routine excepting that the waters were rough. They were going into winter when the sea tended to get snotty. That probably diminished the likelihood of attempts to land terrorists by sea, but they still needed to be vigilant and watch for patterns.

They were on short cruises, every couple of weeks they were back at Norfolk for a couple of days. The cruise patterns overlapped, so when a ship was in port, others covered their area. Warren discovered that he could text her and she would get it at any time. Whatever he thought, or assumed, Kimberly thought it meant that any ideas he might get that she was out of the country for these periods would not happen. The problem was not only that he found her attractive, but that she thought him fascinating; well, more than that. SEALs were not to talk about what they did or even that they were SEALs. The work Kimberly was doing was highly classified. She had been and was a surface warfare officer but did not like keeping up that camouflage. It would be a way to admit she was a naval officer and then cut off the discussion.

Kimberly had a weekend free. Warren was able to get tickets to Disney's "Beauty and the Beast" at Philadelphia's Kimmel Center. An American Eagle flight got her to Philadelphia.

"Hey, hi," Warren greeted her outside the secure area.

"Hi."

"Here, let me take that; you look tired. Tough week?" Kimberly nodded as he took her cabin luggage, she had just finished a three-week patrol that morning. "Anything checked?"

"No."

"Okay, you're at the Downtown Marriott?" he confirmed.

"Yes."

"Okay, look, I've nothing planned for the evening. Let's just relax."

"That sounds like a plan."

"There's a place called The Circ on top of the hotel. We could get a bite to eat."

She could also try a Macallan neat, given how tired she was, possibly not a good idea. She decided to try it anyway.

"You're correct," she told Warren, "Scotch is an acquired taste."

She enjoyed just sitting and talking with, listening to, this man. A male outside of her work bubble was unique, and the paradigm very different. Nothing more than talk occurred that evening. She was not sure if she liked that or not, assuring herself that she was tired.

Warren arrived back at the Marriott in the morning in time for breakfast. "How did you sleep?" he asked her.

"Very well, I am so sorry about last evening."

"No need to apologize, you were tired."

"I hope you've nothing we need to be at immediately, as I plan to enjoy, not gobble breakfast and run."

Warren laughed, "We all have that problem. Relax and enjoy."

His plan was a walkabout in downtown Philadelphia. Walking a mile and a half or so, up the Benjamin Franklin Parkway, got them to the iconic Rocky steps and, more importantly, to Kimberly, the collections inside the museum. She had been interested in art class in high school but had little knowledge beyond that. Warren's parents had books at home about the world's major museums. Both enjoyed the seventeenth-century European painter's collections the most.

"My engineering sense of proportion is too strong for me to get very excited about much of the contemporary art," Kimberly told him.

"You don't want to rebel from straight lines."

"Really, Rembrandt is all straight lines? His use of light is fantastic."

Dinner was at the Ristorante Pesto. "Oh my God, if I hang around you much more, I'm going to get fat."

Warren laughed. It was a quick ride north along Broad Street to the Kimmel Center to see the musical "Beauty and the Beast".

"The story is well known, and Disney's musical adaptation for the stage is a lot of fun," Kimberly told Warren at intermission. "Of all the characters, I like Lumière best." Warren was exposing Kimberly to things she had heard about but not experienced.

The cab ride back to the hotel was not long. What Kimberly hoped would happen was also what she was afraid of happening. Being with and conversing with this gorgeous man, watching envious females around them, and hanging onto him was fun. It was time for the next level. Kimberly's hormones were ready, and her brain was ninety percent ready. The more she thought about it, the more she was transported off the littoral to the exciting confines of Warren. He had been a gentleman. Disgustingly so. He was in no hurry to dig his vehicle out of the parking garage and head home. They went up to the Circ.

She was starting to like Macallan, but that was the least of her problems. He was. No, she was. She needed to tell him she was a naval officer. Hell no, that could put a wet rag on what was happening. Her heart was racing again, and her stomach was doing flips. Her brain was the problem, her brain, and her hormones. And his clothes. She wanted them off; this fancy bar was likely not the place. She had precious little experience flirting; they were flirting. Maybe she was too civilized; she should just let out the horny sailor girl. How to get him to her room? He was making moves that she interpreted as him wanting to go. Jeez, civilians had all this secret body language.

Pressing the side of her body to him as they left worked to slow them a bit. She knew she did not want him to go. Damn girl, you take on terrorists, stop being so chicken shit!

"Would you like to stay here tonight?" she asked.

"Yes."

God, that was easy! Heading for her room, they embraced and kissed in the elevator. At her room, her hands were shaking, but she got her key card out and opened the door.

Conscious thought ceased as the door closed behind them. It was all sensation, and emotions, and physical, and hormones, and instinct. Kimberly lost her anxiety so she could enjoy the feelings, as they kissed, touched, and slowly, well not all that slowly, disrobed each other.

They were on the bed doing what Kimberly had to admit she had imagined many times since meeting him, wrestling nude. He was fit and solid and tasty. The foreplay had been all evening, hell the past months. Warren was trying to hold back and go slow. It was time for a horny sailor girl to attack.

She did, rolling him onto his back and positioning herself over him before she descended on his shaft. He felt terrific in her. If she had ever been dainty and poised and controlled, that all disappeared as she moved rapidly on his shaft, delighting in the sensations. Someone was moaning, and there were grunting noises that increased as she further lost control. Everything focused between her legs. God, no, her brain was exploding. She could not see. Everything was black with starbursts as she drove down on him. Someone launched a Tomahawk missile. Her world exploded. She was bucking on him and screaming as she pitched forward and lost consciousness.

Kimberly was gasping for air. Her pelvis was still screaming with sensation as her hips reflexively moved on Warren's shaft. Oh God, he had not climaxed. Thank God, he had not, as more sensations built in her. She had never been this out of control. Damn, he thought she was this sweet engineering chick. That brief thought disappeared.

Her hips were still moving on him now more demandingly as her muscles tightened on him. Without warning, she grunted a mini-climax, and then another followed by a series and then a peak where she just stayed in overdrive with her brain exploding. Her brain tired. He was grunting and pushing back harder. He was going to climax.

"Come on, baby, come in your hot chick." Nice girls do not talk like that.

He roared and flooded her. She rolled off him, and he moved over her to the other side to avoid the wet spot. They held each other, trying to catch their breath.

"You know I love you," he told her.

She was still breathing hard. She nodded and moved in closer. "A girl still likes to hear it. God, I fell in love with you on the plane." He laughed, so she defended her assertion, "really, I did too, or at the least, I fell in lust with you. You're a good-looking dude."

"I definitely fell in lust with you, damn what's not to. Beautiful, intelligent, hot body, I fell in love with you in Portland but was still in lust," Warren laughed.

"Yeah well, you'd better stay in lust, babe, what took you so long?" she asked.

"Oh God, I have fought myself over this. I didn't want to do something testosterone and lose you."

"Yeah, well, I like your testosterone," Kimberly told him. They had a great weekend, and too soon, Kimberly was back in Norfolk.

Somewhere someone in Congress discovered that Navy units were going ashore, allegedly to enforce the law. That was not true, but late that January, a particularly vehement anti-Pentagon Representative from the east coast was yelling Posse Comitatus in an appropriations subcommittee dealing with the defense budget. The representative would not allow the discussion to move into a secure oversight committee, so the Chairman adjourned the committee. The representative sounded off to the media.

The Posse Comitatus law was initially passed in 1878 when the Union Army was used in the South after the Civil War to do police work as the South had no infrastructure left. The South did not like the Union Army being there. Apparently, in modern terms, that meant that the local Sheriff should empower a posse of citizens to deal with terrorist threats. It became more complicated as most western countries had designated terrorists as criminals so that they were tried in the civilian courts. The Representative's interpretation was the terrorists were thus criminals. Thus, the naval units were enforcing the criminal law, and that was police work, and under Posse Comitatus was illegal, though the Posse Comitatus law does not mention the Navy. It was mid-February; Kimberly had read and watched news reports, most of it background on the hearings.

"Have you seen this shit out of Congress?" Janie Ewing asked her one morning.

"Yeah, the news reports.   Above our pay grade," she told Lieutenant Ewing.

"It's bullshit, you and I are FBI," Ewing argued.

"Fine line Janie. I understand your angst, but the Navy will still have lots for us to do."

"You've had no special briefing?   Sorry, dumb question. You couldn't tell me if you had."

An FBI guy, who Kimberly had never seen before, did brief them. Everything he told them was already in the newspapers. The real message was that they were to keep doing what they had been doing.

Patrols were arduous, not due to Congress or weather. For the first time since before the Academy, Kimberly was diverted, wanting to be ashore and in Philadelphia, not in Norfolk. The USS Detroit did get back to base early on a Friday. As airfares to Philadelphia were adding up, Kimberly decided to introduce Warren to the biker girl.

Cruising up US-13 through Dover to I-95 into Philadelphia and then to West Mayfair, where Warren's townhouse was, amounted to five hours of foreplay on her vibrating machine. Along the way, she wondered if that and not the risk riding had been her curiosity about motorcycles. Warren was at home; he had not been expecting her.

"Hey, babe, you'd better not have some other chick in there. Please show me where I can put my bike."

He looked at the black leather covering Kimberly's body and grinned. "Damn, my intuition is good! I knew you weren't a mild-mannered New England girl." Warren reached out for her. She kissed him and then moved back.

"What'd ya mean, I'm from Maine. No, no, with the nooky, bike first, then sex, then food, then sex, those are the priorities."

He showed her where she could secure her bike behind his place. Once inside, he was intent on sex as fast as possible. That was okay; after the time at sea and the bike ride, she was ready. She did not need the hog. Just looking at him did it for her. She peeled down her Dakota studded chaps and her jeans. Kicking off her boots and quickly getting a leg free was a trick, but soon, they were having sex up against the wall. Her jacket was open, and she was able to get her sweater and t-shirt up, so her nipples were against his chest. She had to wear a bra on duty, biking she liked being free.

"You like doing your biker chick against a wall, don't you babe? Come on, drive it at me." The imagery and the time at sea were getting to her. She came screaming her arms wrapped around his neck, her legs around his. He grunted and came.

He pulled on a pair of jeans and a top while she got her jeans and boots back on.

"Put your chaps on; you look good with them on."

"I don't need them off the bike. Showing off your biker chick to the neighbors?"

"Of course."

"May get you thrown out of the neighborhood."

"God, not in Mayfair."

There was a Hoagies deli just down the street that he thought would still be open. It was, and the food was delicious, not only because she was hungry. People looked her over very carefully. It might be a prominently Irish American neighborhood, but bikers had a reputation, generally not deserved.

Saturday morning was a slow start after waking and having sex and then breakfast. She grabbed his yellow phone book.

"What are you looking for?"

"Harley dealership, you need gear if we're going riding."

"We can go in my SUV. Wait, I'll shave."

"Hell no, I like the look. And the feel."

They got him fitted with a helmet, and she insisted that he get boots, chaps and a leather jacket for protection in case she had to put the bike down.

Touring around Mayfair and the north end of Philadelphia, Kimberly discovered that, like many people, Warren only knew parts of his neighborhood. There were several parks, some quite beautiful. She liked Lardner's Point Park by the river. The city had recently fixed up the area, and they put in a little patio area as well as refurbished the pier. She loved when they sat on the end of the dock watching the Delaware River go by, heading downstream to the Delaware Bay and the Atlantic. She loved the water and the sea. She thought about coming clean to Warren, but other than to admit she was a naval officer, she felt she did not have the clearance to say more.

The fight continued in Congress through the spring. Due to the politicians' inflated rhetoric, people on both coasts become concerned that military units might come storming into their homes. The supporters of Homeland Security argued, to no avail, that most of the units and their commanders were Coast Guard and, or, that was never very clear, Federal Bureau people so law enforcement and thus exempt from Posse Comitatus. None of that flew with the members opposed who ridiculed the idea that a person could be both Navy and FBI. To them, it was an effort to get around the law, by people who wanted to rule the country through the Pentagon or dispense with the Pentagon altogether and have the Generals rule. To Kimberly, it all sounded ridiculous, but then, to her, political arguments often did.

A concern of Kimberly's was that no one in Congress had learned of the program through her or her team. The information had, inadvertently, come through a unit patrolling the Gulf. Congress acted, and the stand-down order came. The Coast Guard was left patrolling the coast with no added assets. The problem for the Navy and Homeland Security was what to do with the littoral teams. All the members of the Norfolk teams were in a large room when Malcolm Greene and Admiral Mike Mann entered.

Mann spoke, "The Pentagon and the Administration still see you as valuable assets. We're going to try to keep you together. It's an opportunity for the ships to undergo maintenance and for you to train, both to keep fit and to develop new skills. You can also patrol beyond the twelve-mile limit. POTUS has a legal opinion that you can do that without fear of backlash from Congress." Greene shook his head, questioning Mann's statement. "Malcolm?" Mann said.

"I'm am not so sure," Greene told them. "While you will be in international waters, the people in Congress who were opposed want you disbanded and might pretend not to understand that."

Mann and Greene answered some questions that were routine and, in most cases, above the pay grade of any of the team members. They were finished.

Admiral Mann stepped up. "Lieutenant Commander Callahan front and center."

Shit, Kimberly thought, they were up to something with her.

Mann was talking. "Callahan, you are being sent to the Naval War College in Newport. You will complete your training there and return here as a Commander to take charge of all of the mission units and their training." Now they were done.

Kimberly understood why they wanted to announce to the whole group. Once again, she was ahead on the promotion scale. Technically she would be reporting to a Captain on the West Coast who oversaw all the mission units, but de facto she would have control over the east coast units. That might be meaningful if Congress had not just shut them down. She guessed that training for overseas combat was something they could do.

Kimberly caught up with Greene. "Sir, can we talk?"

"As long as it's not that you're turning down the promotion."

"No, sir." She explained what she knew of Warren Bradshaw.

Greene was amused. "Do you think we'd allow you to hang around this guy and not vet him? He's who he says he is. He and his family are clean. You can swear him to secrecy and, in person, tell him all the details about you. Don't do it on the phone." She just gave Greene a look. "Okay, I deserved that, of course, you know not to discuss anything sensitive on your phone. I understand that he doesn't even know you're Navy."

"Correct, Sir."

Greene appeared amused. "You don't have to, but would you explain why you're so averse even to admitting to being a naval officer?"

"I'm not sure, Sir. It started in high school because I didn't want to be teased if I didn't make it into the Academy. I did tell one of the football players that I lifted with, and he didn't spread it. It just stops a lot of questions."

She called Warren. "Hey, we cleaned up our current work. I have to go to New England for a short while, and then I'll be back here with more weekends free than I now have."

"That sounds great," Warren told her, "can you come here on your way home?"

"I'm not going home. New England's a work matter, and I need to be there on Monday. I'll barely have time to get there."

"You're going on your bike?"

"Yeah."

"Is that a good idea?"

"Babe, I've biked all over the country. Don't worry." Despite her comment, it pleased Kimberly that he was worried.

There were two classes she needed to complete and be successful, the rank training and a new terrorism class. The rank training was straightforward.

"Hey babe, I'm half done here." It was Friday night, and Kimberly had the weekend free.

"Can you come to Philadelphia?"

"I'd have to fly in the morning if I can get a flight from Providence and be back here Sunday night."

Delta had a flight in the morning, but she would have to leave at supper time on Sunday. She took it. She needed to tell Warren what she did. She had no idea how he would receive that information. That scared her.

No one bothered her on the morning flight. She would have to remember to wear her biker leathers when she did not want to be bothered. Warren was in the baggage claim wearing a business suit.

"Really babe, you wear a business suit to pick up your biker chick?"

"Yeah, halfway to the airport, I realized I was overdressed."

"I can't imagine what the other passengers are thinking."

"That I own a strip club, and I'm picking up a dancer?"

"Oh God, I could so go with that."

The drive to Warren's townhouse was too long. Since the phone conversation the evening before, she had let her libido loose. Being in his presence was foreplay. The stripper idea appealed to her.

"Tell me about your club."

"Gentleman's Club downtown, three stages, safe environment."

"Table dances, lap dances?"

"Yes, and a VIP area."

Kimberly's head was in the fantasy. At the townhouse, she pushed Warren into a sofa and danced away. Her jacket came off quickly, her boots and the leather pants not so. She liked Warren watching her as she danced in her t-shirt and bikini panties. Her nipples were evident under the t-shirt. She turned her back on Warren, looked back, and removed her t-shirt before turning and dancing to him. He had a twenty in his hand that he put under the string of her bikini panties.

After dancing a bit more, she took the bill in her hand and peeled her panties off.

"Want a lap dance, baby?"

Warren was breathing hard, Kimberly liked that. "Yes."

Placing a knee on either side of his thighs, she climbed on him. She could feel his erection. Reaching down, she unzipped him and brought his erection out, mounting him. She was becoming needy. Before Warren, she could go months without sex; now, she needed him.

"Oh God, oh baby, you feel great," Warren told her.

"Like fucking your sexy, biker chick, stripper?"

"God, yes."

Kimberly drove down hard and fast on him. Her brain was a swirling mix of light and small explosions until she screamed and climaxed. Warren was still hard. Moaning, she continued to move on him, climaxing again as he came. She collapsed into him.

"Oh God, baby, I needed that." Kimberly got up. "Whoops, your trousers need cleaning."

They did little else that weekend, and Kimberly slept on both legs of the flight back to Providence. Driving her bike from T. F. Green Airport to Newport in the middle of the night gave her time to think about her not telling Warren anything more, not even that she was a naval officer. "Chicken shit," she said to herself.

The terrorism class was scary. Even the civilian instructors did not bother to hide their contempt for the members of Congress who had shut down the littoral program. Courses completed, a detour to Philadelphia, was possible. Warren expected her. Late in the evening, she wheeled her bike behind Warren's townhouse. The next morning it was bright, sunny, and hot. Kimberly knew where she wanted to go, Lardner's Point Park. Warren asked no questions. Once seated on the pier staring at the water, Kimberly formulated her thoughts.

"Nothing I've told you is a lie; I just haven't told you the whole truth." That Warren was listening attentively with no visible reaction was good. "First, much of what I'm going to tell you, you can't tell anyone. You can't even infer that you know this stuff, even if our relationship goes south."

"Okay."

"I'll flag when we get to the sensitive stuff."

"Alright."

"You've been smart enough not to push me on where I went to engineering school. That was perceptive. As advertised, I'm a mechanical engineer. I graduated with that degree from the Naval Academy, so I am a Naval Officer. They just promoted me to an O-5, a full Commander. I originally qualified as a Surface Warfare Officer but stopped doing that many years ago, when I was a Lieutenant. I'd been on destroyers working in the fire control, mostly plotting. They sent me to SEAL training, where I qualified. The less said around SEALs, the better, as protection for you and your family. Here is where it gets tricky, and from here in, it's very secret. A while ago, Homeland Security formed anti-terrorism teams, some members, like I am, are SEALs, some with other skills. I was sent to Quantico and qualified as an FBI Agent and then to a camp that does not exist and qualified as CIA. While we are Navy and we have an Admiral commanding the naval part of the program, the whole program is under Homeland Security or was. At this point, I really don't know. I directly report to a Homeland Security guy."

"This is what all the stuff in Congress has been about?"

"Yes, but that's political, and I can't comment on it."

"I can; it seems to be stupid grandstanding."

"Anyway, that's my story. I headed up one of the teams, and as you now know, we were the mission packages on littorals that formed a line of defense to assist the Coast Guard."

"What's a mission package if I may ask?"

"Two different crews. For example, on an aircraft carrier, they have a core package, the Captain, and crew that drive the ship. Then they have the air wing. The people who maintain, load, and fly the planes. Of course, an aircraft carrier could have more than one mission package with Marine units aboard and others."

"A littoral's a type of ship?"

"Yes, basically a modern corvette about one and a half football fields long."

"What does a mission package on a littoral do?"

"In this program, we went after terrorists. We developed intelligence on the ships that are out there, and if someone tried to land a terrorist group, we interceded."

"At sea?"

"Sometimes, more commonly on land, which is where Congress has its problem. Apparently, according to the law, the local Sherriff is supposed to deputize some citizens as a posse, and go after them, not the military."

"A sheriff and untrained citizens, even trained deputies, don't have the capability."

"Not my problem and a way above my pay grade."

"Damn, so what happens to you guys now?"

"I have no clue, again way above my pay grade. What we were told is that the Navy is keeping us together, for now, and we're to train. I'm currently in command of all the mission packages on the littorals on the east coast. I'm at the Norfolk Naval Station. Most of the individual units are commanded by a Lieutenant-Commander an O-4. They are training their teams at Norfolk, and a Lieutenant has been drilling the unit I commanded. When I get back, I will be meeting with them, and who knows who else, to plan more intensive training. For the public, worst-case scenario, they break us up, and the SEALs go back to regular SEAL teams functioning off-shore."

"So, the message this morning is that I am in love with a brilliant engineer, who is an awesome, pretty, biker chick, a fairly senior Naval Officer, and a SEAL, and dangerous as hell."

"Yes."

"Combat boots, and assault rifles, and all that."

"Yes."

"Damn."

"And in case you don't know it, you were vetted by the FBI so that we can have this conversation."

"I heard they were snooping around; I assumed it was about some defense stuff we're bidding on. Navy never crossed my mind."

"Okay, it may have been two birds with one stone. They told me that you were vetted, and we could have this conversation." Warren stared at her for several moments. "What?" Kimberly asked.

"It's just that … well, wow, and this really needs to be processed." Kimberly's heart sunk; it was what scared her. She liked this guy. "What … no, no, I'm not going negative on you, God, if anything this has, in a weird way, made you even more appealing."

"Being the significant other of someone in the military is difficult, in the Navy's case, we can be at sea for months. Likely that has been some of my reluctance to share this with you."

"Plus, I am sure the terrorists don't just throw up their hands, likely they shoot at you. May I ask if you have had an incident or incidents?"

Kimberly as not sure how much she could say, she trusted Warren, and no one had put boundaries on the conversation. "Suffice it to say yes."

"What happened?"

Maybe business guys do not know the word suffice, but she thought she knew what his concern was. "The terrorists all died, or we captured them; once my two IC got a flesh wound."

"Two IC?"

"Second, in command."

"Okay, I guess I have to learn not to ask questions." Kimberly smiled at him; he was still processing. "And enjoy the rewards."

"Rewards?" asked Kimberly.

"Are you kidding, having sex with this beautiful, sexy, SEAL, Naval Commander who kicks ass."

Kimberly punched him on his shoulder. "Hopefully, some of that is also making love," she asserted.

"Yeah, well, it depends on her mood. Some days she is into slow, beautiful lovemaking; other days, she assaults me." Kimberly reflected that that was about right. "Damn, I can't even tell people."

"What, that you're doing a sailor girl sex maniac? You can say that much, nothing more." That got her a return punch on the shoulder.

The main news of the summer was Meredith's acceptance at the Naval Academy. Janie Ewing's daughter, Montana, completed Basic Surface Warfare School and was an Ensign on a light cruiser.

Chapter Seventeen – Action

Being in limbo professionally was difficult. Both Admiral Mann and Deputy Director Greene were intent on keeping the teams together.

"Commander," Admiral Mann told her during a video conference, "there are lots of enemy coastal areas where the littorals could be reassigned. The same goes for you and the other SEALs. You are to remain in top physical condition and repeatedly train different scenarios, including ones that might occur given your original mission."

"What are we at this point, Navy, FBI, CIA, Homeland Security?" Kimberly asked.

"Yes," Mann told her. The units remained affiliated with Homeland Security, a detail that Congress missed as they moved on to other things.

The weeks and months went by as they created different scenarios taking on Marine units or other units mimicking the bad guys. They did more training onboard ships. However, it was more like being back with the surface Navy, weeks at sea beyond the twelve-mile limit. They were able to scan ships and call suspicious information to the Coast Guard.

"Commander, you realize that the personnel are all bored," now Lieutenant-Commander Ewing told Kimberly. "They're going to get stale."

"I know. Would you assemble the unit commanders, please? I have something interesting from the west coast."

She explained at the meeting that a Captain, her alternate on the West Coast, did get to take a couple of littorals to the Philippine islands. "As you are aware, the Philippines are a group of islands, big and small. They have a problem with some terrorists, guerrillas, freedom fighters, whatever one wishes to call them. A militant group, Jemaah Islamiyah, captured some Americans and were holding them hostage. Our teams, landing from blacked-out littorals, rescued them. It was executed very well, mostly without fanfare, and with no allied casualties. As a result, the brass is rethinking our mission so that we may be roaming wider than the east coast."

"Why didn't they just send in a SEAL team?" one of the unit commanders asked.

"In a sense, they did. You're a SEAL, as were most, if not all of that landing party. Given the geography and the circumstances, it was better to bring in more assets than a sub-based landing party, or choppers could, in addition to SEALs. The littorals did that."

The moral of the unit members improved, and they worked well for a few weeks. Kimberly did get all the unit members together for a pep talk, pointing out that they could not schedule incidents, but that the crews needed to be ready should one occur. That helped, a little.

"Commander, we have a problem." Kimberly was on a video conference with Miranda Davidson. "We know little about this group, but we've been aware that they have camps on one of the islands in the Los Roques archipelago. They've grabbed several tourists, many of them American and Dutch."

Kimberly needed orientation, "that's an archipelago off Venezuela?"

"Yes, under Venezuelan control. That's part of the problem; we don't know Venezuela's relation to the group. They've denied the group's existence. We're working on a rescue mission with the Dutch. With you in command, I want four of our littorals at sea. After Puerto Rico, each ship will go a different route to meet ASAP with the Dutch north of Venezuela. I'll contact you aboard as we work out details with the Dutch and get more intelligence."

Being back at sea again was fun. Having the potential for action was fun. Janie gave up her sea cabin, so Kimberly had a secure area to work. Due to the unrest in Venezuela, the U.S. State Department had warned against travel there. KLM had direct flights that the Americans had used to get there, intent on having their planned beach vacation, unrest, or not.

At twenty-two knots per hour, they were pushing it, but their little flotilla made San Juan in two and a half days where they refueled. Each of the littorals then left on different courses to the archipelago. They met a Netherlander frigate and two of the Netherlands' Holland-class patrol boats, with Dutch Marines aboard. The patrol boats are similar in capability to the littorals but without the stealth configuration and paint.

"The intelligence information each of our countries has developed agrees. We have a tabletop mockup of the compound. We believe there are six Americans and fifteen Netherlanders," Kimberly told the Netherlander commander and his second in command.

"Yes, and our information agrees with the numbers and your model of the compound."

"We've worked out an approach," Kimberly explained their plan.

"Who is the U.S. Marine commander?" the Netherlander second in command asked.

Kimberly had the thought that someone had been too vague to the Netherland's unit. "We won't be using Marines. Our rescue team will be SEALs, and I am the commander."

"Women are SEALs?" the surprised 2IC asked.

"Hou je mond," the Netherlander commander said sharply. Kimberly did not know Dutch but suspected the second in command had been told to shut up. The Netherlanders were very co-operative as they reviewed the details.

"We are not going to use our weapons?" the Netherlands commander asked.

"Not our assault rifles," Kimberly told them. "We prefer silence." The Dutch nodded when she explained that they liked to use knives.

"Onze marine-commando's kunnen dat doen," the second in command said.

"In English," his commander ordered.

"Our Marine Commandos can do that."

"Yes, of course, and we have sufficient personnel," the Netherlander commander agreed.

"Some of our team are not SEALs," Kimberly disclosed. "They are good and will be covering us. We'll determine firelines, as I suspect you will wish rifles covering you."

"Yes."

Kimberly had three small boats in the water. The Dutch launched five off one of Kimberly's littorals. The Dutch frigate and patrol boats were off the coast over the horizon and would simulate sailing by until the radar was disabled.

The Dutch Marines went into the compound first, killing the guards at the radar and disabling it. Other Dutch Marines were killing guards, as were the SEALs, in the rest of the compound. It was eerily quiet.

"Gaan," Kimberly radioed once the compound was secure. They had taught her the Dutch word for go.

"Gaan," the Dutch Commander repeated.

As they entered from the rear, there were screams then a short burst of automatic rifle fire that sounded like a Kalashnikov in the front area of the building immediately followed by a single shot. "Guard inside neutralized," the Dutch commander reported. Except for crying, there was silence. Kimberly turned on her hooded flashlight. Silence continued. The others lit their lights.

"We're American and Dutch special forces. Keep quiet, and we'll get you out of here," Kimberly said. The statement as immediately repeated in Dutch by one of the Netherlanders.

The six Americans turned out to be seven. There was a ten-year-old boy with one family. His mother was crying, scared out of her mind. The boy who had been staring wide-eyed at the rescuers moved to hug his mother.

"Quiet Mom, it's okay. We've been rescued."

Kimberly hoped like hell that the boy was correct. The gunfire could be a huge problem. They needed to quickly get off the island and get the ships into international waters. Though weak, the American hostages were in reasonable condition and could make their way to the beach. When they were halfway to the beach, someone in the compound woke up. Both the Marines and the U.S team had a rearguard, both of whom returned fire. With the hostages out of the way, there were no restrictions on the rules of engagement. The continuous sound of automatic rifle fire went on as they loaded the hostages on boats, and they started for the littorals. The compound went silent again.

"Status," Kimberly asked the rear-guard teams still at the compound.

"No further firing from the compound. We are coming to the beach," the Netherlander officer commanding replied.

"Good, casualties?"

"None with your guys or with us," the Netherlander officer replied.

In the boat going back to the littoral, the Dutch commander explained that the guard inside the building had fired wildly at the door. The SEALs were out of the fire zone waiting with other Dutch Marines to see if there would be fire. The Dutch point Marine was crouched low and had reached around the door to kill the guard.

The seas were calm, and twenty-five miles out, the littoral, with the Dutch Marines and hostages, joined the Dutch frigate. A Dutch patrol boat was secured to the littoral to transfer the Dutch.

Chapter Eighteen – Crisis

Kimberly did get to Philadelphia frequently. The relationship with Warren grew as summer become fall.

"What are we doing for Thanksgiving and Christmas?" Warren asked.

Turkey and turkey would be flip. "As in visiting families?"

"Yes."

"I've never told my family that our relationship has progressed. They only know about you from when we were first dating," Kimberly told him.

"That's one up on me. I'm in trouble."

"How so?"

"How do you dump a serious relationship with a Navy officer who's a SEAL on them, when I haven't even admitted to a serious relationship with any woman?"

"So, I'm an engineer. We should visit one family on Thanksgiving and the other at Christmas."

"You could get leave both holidays?" Warren asked.

"Not sure, what about you?"

"No problem." They let it drop for the moment.

Back at the base, Kimberly was able to get time off for both holidays. She called home. Her parents were delighted that her relationship with Warren had continued. Kimberly called Warren. Thanksgiving would be in Augusta while Christmas would be in Scranton.

Aside from Warren having to try to discern how much her family knew, Thanksgiving in Augusta went well.

"Warren, for a good reason, Kimberly keeps her cards tight. I don't know what you know, and you don't know what I know. Let's leave it all alone," Kimberly's Dad told Warren. Kimberly smiled.

Warren did not meet Meredith as she was at the Academy and would only be home for a few days over Christmas. Kimberly had neglected to tell Warren that her flaky sister was now a Midshipman Fourth Class. Not only was she a Mid but one who had done very well during plebe summer and was continuing to do well.

Dwaine and Andria were with her family. They would be in Augusta for Christmas. As he had never seen her in uniform, Warren was intrigued by the photographs of Kimberly and Andria at the Veteran's Day ceremonies two years before.

Once he stopped worrying about who knew what, Warren got along famously with her father. He delighted her mother. Kimberly's view was that it was because there was a marriageable male in her daughter's life. Kimberly hoped that she would do as well with his family at Christmas.

Back at Norfolk, Kimberly briefly considered scaling back training for the holiday period and then decided that they all needed to work the turkey off. The usual problems were scheduling conflicts with other units for the various facilities. The solutions were negotiating. She discovered that after a problematic prolonged exercise, they did best if they had a couple of days off. Thus, the plan was that during the week before Christmas, they would be off the Thursday and Friday, then do another exercise over the weekend, debrief, and most of them leave for Christmas on the twenty-third.

Saturday morning, she had all the teams in a shed doing a tabletop exercise, a simulation of a scenario with a model of the target, as a prelude to a live-fire exercise planned for that afternoon. Her iPhone went off.

It was Malcolm Greene. "Call me on a secure line."

Kimberly immediately went to her office and called back.

"There's a huge problem ongoing near Philadelphia. It's a highly sophisticated multi-pronged attack at a large shopping mall southwest of Philadelphia. The perpetrators, we believe foreign terrorists, are still shooting. In addition to the mall, they took out the two nearest State Police barracks and the government center at the nearby county seat that included the city police, the dispatch center, and the Sheriff's office. There are hundreds of hostages at the shopping mall; no one has an accurate account. POTUS has done an emergency order activating you. The mall is your assignment. Move fast."

"Really, shit, that's miles away. All the hostages will be dead before we get there. Likely the State Police could get a negotiator there faster."

"They aren't negotiating," Malcolm told her. "The 305th Military Airlift will be ready shortly to move you from Naval Air Station Norfolk to Philadelphia. Drive your vehicles onto the planes and bring your communications and anything else you might need. We're scrambling everyone to help you load. Operational orders and copies of the building plans should be on your fax. You're going to have to prepare in the air."

Kimberly's mind was racing as she returned to the shed. Calling the unit commanders together, she briefed them on the situation.

"It doesn't sound as though the armored vehicles will be useful. The mission is an assault on a huge shopping mall," Kimberly concluded.

"Can we get on the roof?" one of the Lieutenant Commanders asked.

"Good idea, we'll see en route, but I'll ask for a Blackhawk," Kimberly said.

"And an Apache," Lieutenant Commander Ewing added. "The roof may need clearing."

"Good," Kimberly said, "we need to pull equipment quickly. Each unit will use its trucks. Dixie see me about the layout of the building. We'll need explosives."

"Can we re-visit the armored question?" an officer asked.

"Of course."

"We may need to drive through entrances or otherwise be under armor."

"Good point. We'll take four over to the field and see how many the 3-0-5 can take," Kimberly told him.

A quick call back to Greene secured a promise of the Blackhawk and an Apache. Green thought that the Pennsylvania National Guard would be able to provide them.

They did not have to waste time assembling units. Shortly the trucks were rolling the minimal distance within the base to the air station field. The timing was perfect; the C-17 Globemaster III's were landing.

An incredible number of people were mobilized to load each of the C-17's. Very shortly, they were in the air with all of their equipment, including the four armored vehicles. Kimberly used the time in the air to plan the approach with the commanders of each of the units.

"This is a huge mall," Kimberly told them, going over the diagrams of the mall, "with three levels, counting a garage. There are multiple entrances, and likely each one is booby-trapped. Master Chief Phillips, let's plan to blow them with C-4." Dixie and the other ordnance people agreed and pulled away to begin planning.

"I want full teams assaulting at each of the big doors and through the garage. I have confirmation of the choppers, so once the Apache gives the clear, I want Charlie team on the roof using the Blackhawk. Let's do communications checks."

In Philadelphia, they would have priority onto Runway 9R and to offload at the UPS terminal. They would be there shortly, the airspace was cleared for them, and over the two hundred and forty miles, they were on a direct route to the end of a runway.

They landed, and with assistance from the Pennsylvania National Guard, they quickly unloaded. The Guard had flatbeds, so the Norfolk teams could swiftly move their armored vehicles. The Pennsylvania Highway patrol escorted them the short distance to the mall. Despite the briefings, what they encountered at the mall was entirely unexpected.

Kimberly jumped out of her command vehicle when they stopped at the perimeter set up by a mix of State, County, and City police.

"Jesus are we pleased to see you," a State Police Lieutenant crouched down behind a squad car greeted her.

"You in charge?"

"For now, I was out on patrol when the barracks blew up. Our resources are improving as people get here from the rest of the state. The Governor also has National Guard coming from all over the state, which will allow us a full perimeter."

Kimberly could hear occasional shooting. "Anyone inside except the terrorists and the hostages?"

"No."

Using binoculars, Kimberly surveyed the area outside the mall. There were vehicles burning in the vast parking lot and people lying on the pavement. None of the people were moving. A group had on police uniforms.

"What happened to the police?" A Blackhawk and an Apache, taking fire from the mall roof, landed behind her.

"The snipers on the roof killed them when they tried to rush the mall."

No one there had thought about the roof. "Communications with inside?"

"The 911 Center was destroyed. Currently, they are trying to switch, allowing another dispatch center to manage the calls. If you're asking about the perpetrators, no, no one has attempted to make contact either way. We have no number to call them. We've tried some mall numbers without success. They seem to be systematically killing hostages every few minutes, no rhyme or reason."

Kimberly moved back to talk to her commanders. "Charlie team to the Blackhawk and the other teams deploy to your positions. Keep your heads down; you heard the snipers on the roof try to hit the choppers." She started for the Apache.

"Whoa, whoa not so fast. Who the hell are you?"

"Commander Callahan, Homeland Security Anti-terrorism; the unit that the President dispatched. Who are you?"

"I'm Congressman Mitis; I'm the civil authority on the scene. I'm in charge, and you'll do nothing until I say so."

"I'm sorry, sir, but our orders are from the President of the United States. You guys can argue about all this later, but our job is to rescue the hostages."

"We're negotiating with the perpetrators, we'll get them out," the Congressman told her.

"Who is doing the negotiating? I am not aware that any contact has been made."

In the distance, coming from the mall complex, she could hear automatic weapon fire. She could see her teams moving into place; she needed to get the Apache in the air.

"You guys were disbanded, what are you doing here?" Kimberly imputed that no contact had been made with the people attacking the mall.

"Really, the local Sheriff is going to form a citizen posse and go after these guys. Hell, they'll all be as dead as the police in the parking lot."

"Everyone is not a bunch of warmongers like you guys."

"Congressman, so far, we're not the guys shooting. The mission is a defense and hostage rescue, and I don't believe you have any training on how to do this." She noticed an FBI agent standing aside. "My orders from the President and Homeland Security are clear. We are to rescue the hostages and secure the complex then turn the scene over to the FBI," she told the Congressman.

"Special Agent in Charge Alan Wearing, my orders are the same Commander," the FBI Agent stated.

"How many FBI are here now?" she asked him.

"About twenty with many more on the way," the FBI agent said.

"What the hell is going on here?" Malcolm Greene had arrived.

"Good afternoon Sir," Kimberly greeted him. "Congressman Mitis says he is the civilian authority and is going to direct the operation. If I'm reading the gunfire correctly, hostages are dying as he wastes time."

"Commander get the hell out of here and direct your team to rescue those hostages. Good afternoon Congressman, I am Malcolm Greene, the Deputy Director of Homeland Security in charge of the Anti-terrorism teams. I am here by order of the President, as are the teams. You are not, I repeat, not in charge."

Kimberly signaled Wearing to follow her as she headed for the helicopters. She provided him with communications gear, so he was in the loop. Charlie team was on the Blackhawk.

"The pilot tied into your comms?" Kimberly asked the Charlie team commander.

"Yes, ma'am."

The Apache pilot looked as though he should be in high school. He also appeared severe and focused. "You locked and loaded, Warrant Officer?" Kimberly asked him.

"Yes, ma'am."

"Your comms networked with ours?"

"Yes, ma'am."

"Two missions." She showed him the drawing of the roof of the complex and all the places people might hide. "I need all the snipers dead before my people land. Try to stay away from those huge glass windows because there are people below. Mission two will be Intel for Charlie team, who will be on the Blackhawk, and for me. You set?"

"Damn right, ma'am. I doubt I need FAA clearance to take off." Kimberly grinned at the pilot's joke and returned to her command vehicle.

"This complex is huge. Are your guys SWAT with automatic weapons and body armor?" Kimberly asked the FBI agent.

"A few," Wearing replied. Kimberly grimaced. "I know, I'll have more shortly, but they have to be assembled. We only had a small ready squad, insufficient for this."

"Understood, do you have building diagrams or need a copy of ours?" The agent's diagrams appeared identical. "Okay," Kimberly told him, "I may run out of personnel so when it's safe for you guys to enter, I want FBI teams in the garage and around the periphery of both levels to secure the entrances and more as my people move deeper into the complex."

"Understood, we may need Guard and Troopers to help with the periphery," Wearing told her.

"Yes, of course, no problem but under your control," Kimberly told him. Wearing agreed. "We need Guard with weapons, ammo, and flak jackets; FBI's agent in command," she radioed to Greene.

The Apache was in the air approaching the complex to cross east to west about the middle of it. Automatic weapons fire started from the roof, so the Apache immediately opened up with its guns.

"Okay, move to takeoff position now," Kimberly ordered.

The teams positioned to move just outside the doors and walls as soon as the Apache neutralized the snipers. If they were not dead, the snipers were busy. The Apache crossed twice more to be sure and then gave the clear for the Blackhawk that moments later was hovering a few feet from the roof with the personnel from Charlie team rappelling to the rooftop.

The roof was clear. The ground teams moved in, close to the mall wall. Charlie team positioned at the known roof doors, and was clearing all the crevices on the roof, and checked for undocumented roof entry points. Kimberly discovered that they had unwanted guests, a squad of police officers.

"Who the hell are you?" she asked a police officer with Sergeant stripes.

"Police Chief told us we were the lawful authority, so had to affect the rescue."

"No, you don't, you have no armor, minimal weapons, no communications, and you're going to get in the way. The last police to try that are dead in the parking lot."

The Sergeant nodded, "The Chief is going to be bullshit."

"You're going to be alive. I'll deal with your Chief."

The Sergeant nodded, "can we help?"

"Over there," Kimberly pointed at Wearing, who was with the State Troop lieutenant. "The FBI are running the perimeter and the backup. Talk to them, and for Christ's sake, get flak jackets on. If you don't have any, the Guard or Staties may."

Charlie reported all roof doors covered and the roof clear. The Blackhawk moved out.

"Shit," came over Kimberly's headset as she and her unit ran for their assigned door.

"What?"

"Sorry, ma'am," one of the Blackhawk pilots said, "we almost ran into a news chopper we did not know was here."

"Damn, Malcolm got that?" Kimberly asked.

"On it," came Malcolm's reply. The information at the airport had been clear, excepting military aircraft; there was a wide no-fly zone over southwest Philadelphia.

All the units confirmed to be in position. "Doors are armed with C-4," Master Chief Phillips reported.

"Blow them," Kimberly ordered, "Breach, breach, breach."

She heard the other entrances blowing. Moments later, all the teams were inside. Just inside one of the doors were the bodies of a Salvation Army bell ringer and a young boy. She could see bodies all over the floor of the food court. Nothing was moving. They fired a small flare that provoked nothing. She signaled Rodriquez, who started to move in; that started some nonautomatic fire. Sniper style the terrorists were aiming for him. He dove back into cover and gave a thumb up. The terrorists at this entrance were lousy shots, but she wasn't going to plan on her excellent luck holding.

"Charlie team drop a flash near the Burger King in the food court," Kimberly ordered.

She heard glass break just before the flash grenade went off. They moved fast from pillar to pillar firing while the Foxtrot team breached the food court from the opposite end. The Sierra team reported that many kids were dead in the play area.

"Move back, don't start clearing the halls yet. Damn it, move systematically. You can't have cleared that department store yet."

"Just looking into the cracks," came the reply from Sierra's commander.

"Same here," reported the Bravo team leader. They were clearing the department store in the southwest corner.

"You have a second level Bravo,"

"We cleared it. It appears they just killed everyone and moved on. We found some hostages locked in a storage area."

"Slow down everybody. Go back over that second level Bravo and hold it," Kimberly ordered. Understandably everyone's adrenaline was high. They knew better, but the layoff had dulled them.

"Both levels on the southeast are clear. No bodies, but a bunch of civilians hid here. We're processing them now," reported the Juliet team leader. "This store was empty, closed; no one was here."

"Okay, everyone, be sure nothing is behind you. Once you're sure there are no terrorists embedded in there, leave some people to secure the area and move to the hall. Pat them down but full process later," Kimberly instructed the Juliet team leader.

"There's weapons fire in that center store," India team leader reported.

"I know I can hear it. The terrorists that are left may have withdrawn back to there. Okay, move into the square hall. India and Echo be careful of those escalators," Kimberly replied.

Small bands of terrorists were in some of the little shops along the way, some with hostages, making securing the halls dangerous and slow. In some stores, there were only scared shoppers. It took a lot of time, but systematically they checked each store tossing in a stun grenade wherever they got fire. They were then able to enter and secure the store in most cases. In other cases, they had to kill the terrorists or, in some cases, seize the weapons and secure the terrorist. They started moving searched hostages to the empty store the Juliet team found. It bothered Kimberly that it was on two levels, but she was assured that both levels were secure. They had blown the mall doors three hours earlier.

At a confluence of halls, they encountered a dead Santa Claus, his elves, and many children and parents who had been awaiting a photo op. The carnage was awful throughout the mall.

As large as her force was, Kimberly started to worry about running out of personnel. The automatic fire continued in the large central department store. It took too long, but they finally had the halls and small shops safe. It had been four hours since they blew the doors.

Kimberly brought half of the Charlie team down from the roof, and half of the garage Golf team came up so they could conduct the final assault on the big central store.

"FBI, do you copy?"

"Roger that," Wearing answered.

"Can you move in to secure the periphery inside now? My guys will hold the halls for a little while longer. The garage is clear; please secure it. We need to mass to assault the big department store in the center."

"Roger that."

On the roof, Charlie team found a point where they could observe most of the broader upper level of the store from the roof. The Charlie leader reported that the terrorists were so intent on the room that they were paying scant attention to the ceiling.

"Pick targets for each of your members, when I say, start shooting."

Moments later, her teams were in place. "Take your shots, Charlie." Kimberly heard the multiple individual shots of several weapons. There were screams in the store. "Go all teams," she ordered.

Coming from the four points of the compass, the teams stormed the vast store. This part was the most dangerous of the tasks that day, but Charlie team had done their job. Only a few terrorists were still alive, and they were immediately killed or captured. A call to Wearing brought FBI personnel into the store. He told Kimberly that the Guard was holding the external perimeter.

It took another hour to recheck everything, to clear people, and to move hostages out the south door of the big central store and down the hall into the big unused retail area. Her teams could now move more freely. FBI was taking over the full processing of the hostages massed in the big empty store space.

More FBI personnel arrived, and Kimberly was advised that even more National Guard were at the perimeter. She asked Wearing to move the FBI people in deeper to secure the hall around the big store as her people checked every closet.

She was with CPO Rife when they secured a closet. Several people were hiding there. Kimberly was bothered by the image before her of a terrified young mother and her two kids. She had not had time to think about it, but this was terrible for anyone, including her hardened troops. Likely that was magnified several times for the kids. A couple of Rife's people started to move the rescued hostages to the collection point. They covered the children's eyes before moving them. Greene and Wearing showed up.

"Team leads any casualties?" Kimberly asked. Aside from a couple of graze flesh wounds, there were none. The mall was secure; the carnage was over. Kimberly had no idea of the civilian casualty numbers, dead and injured.

"Don't worry about that," Greene told her. "Wearing's people will mop up. Get your people back on the trucks and to the airport. Debrief back at Norfolk. Nothing between now and the twenty-third except debrief and mandatory counseling."

"Yes, Sir."

"Special Agent Callahan, Commander, you guys do nice work," Wearing told her. She looked at him a bit perplexed; he was grinning. "Yeah, I know you, and many of your people are trained, sworn FBI. They told me that before I came here. I like having you guys on our team."

"Thanks. What's going on out there?"

"There's sufficient personnel to mop up. A Guard mortuary team just arrived. They will work with the State crime lab people. As you can see, the EMS teams are in here for the wounded. More are coming from the other end of the state. The Pennsylvania National Guard has formed a perimeter around the mall; no unauthorized people get inside that. Beyond the Guard, it is a zoo of terrified civilians and media. It's dark outside, so you guys just got done with the roof on time. You'll love that Mr. Greene arrested the crazy Congressman."

"On what charge?" Kimberly asked Greene.

"Obstruction, not sure it will stick, but at least it got him out of the way. The local Police Chief shut up when he saw the dead police in the parking lot."

"Can we bring the trucks in tight and load my people from the garage?" They would need to pass the least amount of carnage going that way. Even with that, Kimberly thought they would have many drops from the teams. The degree of slaughter was terrible. Everyone, including from her teams, the FBI, police, Guard, and EMS personnel, were going to have nightmares.

"Yes," Greene told her.

Kimberly heard that air traffic control had given the news chopper a heading to immediately get out of the restricted air zone or get shot

down. Even later, the FAA fined the helicopter operators and the
pilot.

It was just after twenty-two hundred hours Zulu, seventeen
hundred hours local time. It had been a terrible six hours, more if one
counted from their departure from Norfolk. The adrenaline started
to fade from her body. She was exhausted as she climbed into the
command vehicle, and they pulled away from the mall heading for
the International Airport, again with Highway Patrol escort.

Back at Norfolk, someone had placed tables in a shed, so they
could all be fed, after which everyone showered and changed into
fresh BDUs.

"Each team find a spot. I want you to talk about the day. At each
table, there'll be someone you do not know, psychologists who are
there to help. Please do not shut up. Commanders listen to your
personnel and lieutenants listen to your commanders. Everyone, I
mean everyone, myself included, is damaged from today. We want
you better. We need you better. Those severely stressed will be
pulled out and begin individual counseling immediately. Don't resist.
I don't give a shit if you don't like talking, talk, that's an order."
Kimberly's little almost a joke got a laugh. She hoped they followed
through.

After the initial counseling, Kimberly slept for two hours, tossing
and turning. Then she was wide awake with images of the previous
day playing in her head, terrible images. Breakfast was served in their
shed. Most of her commanders joined her. On the surface, everyone
appeared relaxed. Once again, she hoped that she did not lose
anyone over this.

A mess steward approached. "Officers, there is stuff on the news
that you may want to see."

"Why the hell would we want to watch the news," growled one
of her male Lieutenant-Commanders.

"Sorry, Sir, I wasn't sure, but someone had a long-distance mic."

They all looked at each other. "Guess we'd better see what he's
talking about," Janie said. Others nodded. The steward turned on the

wall-mounted set nearest them and tuned into the station he was referencing.

Indeed, one of the news outlets at the scene had had a long-range shotgun microphone that picked up, quite clearly despite voice-altering masking, the exchange, after they first arrived, between Kimberly, and the FBI guy with the Congressman. Their producers refused to play any of it until after the crisis was over. Now they were praising the Navy team and dumping all over the Congressman. More broadly, they were dumping all over Congress and the suspension of the Navy Anti-terrorist teams. Retired Admiral talking heads opined that these teams had been great intelligence gatherers and a wall of protection that had assisted the Coast Guard.

"Ten hut." Admiral Mike Mann was entering the shed with Malcolm Greene.

"At ease," he told the assembled people. "Let's start with that you people did an amazing job yesterday. POTUS has asked that I convey his thanks. Here is what we have learned thus far. We found the rafts that the terrorists came ashore. They sailed into Delaware Bay and up the Delaware River. There are even satellite images of them hugging the east shore of the river, including south of Chester Island. That allowed them to make the relatively short overland trip to the shopping mall. They had help as vehicles were awaiting them once they came ashore. In my opinion, shared by others, the Naval Anti-Terrorist Teams off the littorals would have stopped the attack before it started. As it is, not counting the terrorists, there are three hundred and sixty dead at the shopping mall, with two hundred and twenty-five injured one hundred and nine of those are critical. The estimate is that there were over twelve hundred in the mall when the attack started. Many escaped immediately. Additionally, there are the dead J Barracks Troopers and people at the Government Center. Authorities are still trying to get the police communications systems back up."

Watching the news, Kimberly learned that the Admiral's opinion that the littoral teams would have prevented the attacks was shared by other experts, many if not most journalists, and a large segment of the shocked and horrified public.

Kimberly walked away from the televisions. She did not want to watch any more news. Mann had told them what they needed to know. She required her motorcycle to get her to the old Norfolk Medical Center Portsmouth, where she had a meeting that morning with a psychologist. The psychologist just wanted her to talk.

"What the hell can I talk about? Damn, the whole thing was a SNAFU; I assume you know what that acronym is." The psychologist did. "Damn, if we'd been left alone, it would never have happened. As it turns out, the fuckers just paddled up the river. It was fuckin' horrible in there. How the hell do children have Christmas when they've just seen Santa Claus dead. God, I hope that only a few kids saw that."

The psychologist let her ramble on before dropping his bomb, "You were in a terrorist attack before."

"Really? Doesn't my record show I'm a SEAL. We deal with terrorists all the damn time."

"Before the Navy."

That shut Kimberly up for a minute. "In junior high?"

"Yes."

"What bearing does that have?"

"I'm asking you."

"To be honest," Kimberly told him, "I'm not sure. It pushed me to Annapolis and the SEAL program, but I've never had nightmares or anything like that. Do you think that will start to bother me?"

"At the moment we don't know. The psychologist that evaluated you pre-Annapolis wrote that you were a cool cucumber, to use his words. Your pre-SEAL evaluation is about the same. I'll need to see you weekly. Here's my card, if you have any nightmares or similar problems I need to know."

"What would similar look like?"

"Well,' the psychologist said, "minimally provoked temper tantrums."

"More than my normal as a Commander?"

The psychologist laughed. "Your evaluations are that such behavior is rare to nonexistent."

"I can be a badass."

"You can, but that's not what we're talking about."

Chapter Nineteen – Christmas

"Hey," Kimberly said when Warren answered.

"Hi, you okay?"

She had wanted to hear his voice. "Why?"

"Just worried, you sound tired."

"Oh, yeah, I'm okay."

"Will you be able to come for Christmas?" he asked.

"Yes, no change there."

"Good, why don't you fly?"

"Damn, I know you like the biker chick image, but, strangely, then you don't like me on my bike."

"Yeah, not so strangely. Those things are dangerous; besides, you're too shaken to drive safely.

That set Kimberly back. How much did he know? Maybe he had a point about driving. The weather also could get nasty over the holidays. "If I can get tickets," she told him.

If the forecasts held, it would be nice, just a bit cold but not enough for snow. Kimberly decided that she liked that at this late date, there was no seat available on any airline by any circuitous route.

"Screw it; I'm taking the bike."

The five-hour drive to Philadelphia was relaxing. Warren left work early and was at the townhouse to greet her. For all the PTSD debriefing, Kimberly decided that being in bed with Warren, making love, was the best therapy. Except for a short time needed to eat a pizza during the evening, they remained in bed until morning. Kimberly was relaxed as they drove to Scranton using Warren's vehicle.

Warren was avoiding any talk of her work. She was not sure if she liked that or not. His security clearance was good so that she could dump on him. Warren had been talking. Kimberly wondered what about; she had not been paying attention. He had said something about his mother being excited that he was dating an engineer. She knew that his mother worked as an Administrative Assistant at a Christian Academy in Scranton. Her mobile phone buzzed that a text had arrived.

"Nice job." Meredith had seen the news and was messaging.

"Thanks," Kimberly texted back

There were no more texts. Her sister was learning, had learned.

Kimberly called her, "Where are you?"

"In Philadelphia waiting for the plane to Portland."

"How are classes?"

"Great, God, I'm so happy there, even with the youngster bullshit. The assholes busted my footlocker the other morning at oh-dark-eight-hundred Zulu." Kimberly laughed, that would be three in the morning, typical sophomore stunt.

"You passed?" Kimberly laughingly asked her.

"Of course, I've learned to sleep in my BDUs."

"The youngsters are going to want them pressed."

"I know, I do that every night."

"Calculus okay?" Kimberly asked.

"Math has always come easily to me, and calculus fits right in. It all makes sense." That was a good sign. They chatted a while longer and then disconnected.

"Meredith?" Warren asked.

"Yeah, it seems weird that she's Midshipman Fourth Class Meredith Callahan. That sounds so weird for a girl who was a flake."

"She grew up," Warren laughed.

"Growing up."

"Talked about courses?"

His question gave Kimberly an opportunity. "Studiously avoided the news, politics, or what her big sister has been doing. She's learning. God, in high school, she was the antithesis of me, very friendly. Now she can work hard, and keep her mouth shut. She'll do well in the Navy." Warren ignored her lead.

The Bradshaws lived in a working-class neighborhood of Scranton in a generic modest but very well cared for house. There was not a lot of space. She and Warren would be at a nearby Fairfield Inn. They checked in, refreshed themselves, and then head for the house.

His sister Jennifer was sitting at the kitchen table; her two children were in the room. Jennifer did a slow double take on seeing Kimberly, and then her eyes widened. Kimberly glanced at the two children.

She was the woman with the children that had been in the closet at the mall that Susan Rife and Kimberly cleared. Despite the combat gear and face paint, Jennifer thought she recognized her. Kimberly shook her head at Jennifer as she acknowledged Warren's introductions.

June, his mother, was small and quite pretty. She welcomed Kimberly effusively. Warren had warned her that his mother was anxious that her son marry, anyone. They had laughed as Kimberly had a similar problem with her mother.

"Can I speak to you outside?" she asked Warren when she had an opportunity. He was perplexed but went along with her. As they stepped out, she heard Jennifer speak.

"It's okay, Mom."

"Were you aware that Jennifer and the kids were at the mall that the terrorists attacked?" Kimberly asked Warren.

"God, no."

"Okay, likely she has her reasons for not saying anything, but she and the kids, with a bunch of other people, were hiding in a closet."

"Damn, so I was correct that you were the Commander who got into the argument with the Congressman."

"Yeah."

Television news played the tape after the incident. They obscured her face, and the faces of her team, and others, except the Congressman, as well as disguise her voice. With the masked shotgun microphone, identifying speakers was difficult, as intended. Warren knew her too well.

"Okay, what now?"

"Your family has been vetted. I'm not sure how we keep the kids quiet if they recognize me, but we'll have to try." They returned to the kitchen.

"Mom, could you take the kids somewhere for a few minutes, please?" Warren asked.

"What's wrong?" his Mom asked.

"Nothing, we'll talk later."

Warren's mother looked at him for a moment and then rounded up the kids to play in the living room. Jennifer was still staring at Kimberly.

"Hello Jennifer, I didn't realize that we've met before," Kimberly said after Warren's mother and the kids left.

"We did, didn't we? I wasn't sure, but you're an officer, a Commander, in that Anti-Terrorism Task Force that rescued us."

Kimberly recalled that Susan Rife had addressed her by rank.

"Yes, it's a Navy task force, and I am a Commander in the Navy."

"She is in command of that operation for the east coast." She had told Warren that after her promotion, but now, it was unnecessary detail.

"How are you and the children doing?" Kimberly asked.

Jennifer started to cry. "I don't know. I'm still terrified, and both the kids are. Madison keeps talking about all the dead people. Nicholas listens to her but isn't saying much of anything."

"Are you getting professional help?"

"That was difficult as everyone in the area wants to see a shrink. Allan got us in with a friend of his, Dick Wallan, who is seeing all of us even though he's an adult psychiatrist."

"Does he have experience with PTSD?" Kimberly realized, too late, that she should not be using the acronym. It did not matter. Jennifer understood.

"He got his degree through the Army and spent time in Afghanistan, plus many of his patients are veterans."

"Good, that sounds very good."

"He says it'll take a long time."

"Yes, it will."

"I hope the kids will be okay, the psychiatrist says they are resilient, and Alan agrees. He keeps telling me the same thing; he makes me talk about it."

"That's known to help."

"God, I was so scared and so relieved to see you guys. That one you called Chief is female also."

"Yes, there are several women in the unit."

"You're all scary, but I guess that happens when you're carrying weapons. They smelled."

Kimberly managed not to laugh. "Yes, of gunpowder."

"You'd been firing them?"

"Yes."

"I thought that it was only guys that do that?"

"That used to be true."

"Kimberly's a SEAL," Warren added. Kimberly shrugged and hoped Warren got the message.

Jennifer's eyes widened again. "God, I was happy to see you guys, and so scared, and scared some more when they moved us to the empty store. You guys were nice, and the FBI people were nice."

"Thank you. Your mother knows something's up, so we're going to have to explain to your parents what happened."

"Yes, and you to my husband. He's the one who's forbidden us to talk to anyone except the psychiatrist about what happened. My God, you're Warren's girlfriend?"

"Yes."

She looked back and forth between the two of them, finally focusing on Warren. "How do you keep up with her?"

"I don't even try."

"Jennifer, there's one other thing," Kimberly added. "Outside of the family, the less said, preferably nothing, about me and my unit, the better."

"I know. Alan has even said we cannot talk about being in that attack as it could make us targets because we survived."

"Possible but unlikely, the greater risk is that Warren and I are in a relationship."

"Yes, I would imagine they want to find you."

For more than one reason, Kimberly thought. Her biological clock was ticking, or something; she had dumped Harrison because she did not want to bring her shit down on him. "Your mother is concerned as to what's going on. We're going to have to tell her something about me, but it's secret."

"Yes, likely, my Dad also."

"Yes," Kimberly agreed. "Would you go get Madison, please, Jennifer?"

"Why?"

"I want to know if they recognize me, and we should do it one at a time, starting with the eldest." She nodded and went to the living room, bringing Madison back in a couple of minutes.

Kimberly squatted down to be at Madison's eyeball level.

"Hi Madison, you're eight, correct?"

"Yes." The girl was a bit timid.

"Have you ever seen me before?" The girl bit her lower lip and looked at her Mom.

"It's okay, Madison."

"Daddy says we can't talk about it."

"Remember, he said that you could talk to Dr. Wallan, well you can talk to Kimberly too." The girl's gaze shifted to Kimberly, who already knew the answer.

"Yes."

"Yes, what, honey?" Kimberly asked.

"Yes, I've seen you before."

"Where?"

"You're one of the soldiers who rescued us at the mall that day, but you have different clothes now, and you had black stuff all over your face, and a soldier hat."

"Okay, good, but your Dad is correct that other than with your Mom and Dad, Dr. Wallan, and I and Uncle Warren, you cannot talk about that afternoon. But you must talk to your Mom and Dad, and Dr. Wallan about it, but also to me if you want to. Now your Mom is going to get Nicholas."

"He likes to be called Nick."

"Okay, but if he doesn't recognize me, you can't tell him who I am except that I'm your Uncle Warren's girlfriend."

"Okay"

"Hi, Nick, have you seen me before?" The five-year-old was shy and hid behind his mother.

"Nick, it's important that you answer ... ah Ms. Callahan's question," Jennifer gently told him. The boy shook his head no.

"Sure?" He nodded, yes. Kimberly had him go back with his grandparents.

"Talking about it with you helps us?" Madison asked.

"Yes, it does," Kimberly replied. The girl nodded.

"You're going to have to tell my parents, aren't you?" Jennifer fretted again.

"Yes," Kimberly replied.

"Allan did not want me to, which made it easy. They're going to be so angry that I had the kids there."

"That's unlikely Jennifer, and it's not you that they should be angry with, it's the idiots in Congress," Warren told her.

Jennifer took the children to the backyard to play. Warren's dad, Harry, had arrived home from work and was sitting talking to his wife. Kimberly knew that he worked as a tool and die machinist. Harry was a slightly stockier, older version of his son. Both he and June looked up when the pair entered the living room.

"What in the world is all the secrecy about?" June asked.

"I know, and I apologize," Warren told his parents. "We've got a lot of catching up to do, and that may answer your questions. Let's start with that Kimberly is a significant person in my life, and I'm very much hoping she will become even more important. Hell, let's jump right in. The mall attack? Kim commanded the response to that."

"What?!" his parents chorused.

"Yeah. Kim's a mechanical engineer, but also a Naval officer," Warren explained. "She has the rank of Commander."

"Why would the Navy be called in?" his dad asked.

Kimberly thought she had better speak up. "Because we have specialized anti-terrorism units that are both Navy and FBI, working through Homeland Security. I'm a Navy SEAL, as well as an FBI agent."

"That Posse Comitatus bullshit on the news? As if a civilian posse could fight terrorists!" his father exploded.

"The idea of these units was that civilians, even trained police officers, do not have the training. It was due to the Posse Comitatus law that many of us went to and graduated from the FBI Academy, in addition to our naval training," Kimberly explained.

Warren interjected, "she commands all the east coast anti-terrorism teams that Congress shut down."

"They'd better fix that damn fast," his father stated.

"But what does that have to do with Jennifer and the children," his mother asked.

"For good reason, Jennifer and Alan have kept it from everybody, but Jennifer and the children were there," Warren explained. "Alan is correct that no one can talk about it. Dad, when you get worked up with your buddies, you can't say anything about your grandkids being there or Kimberly for that matter."

"Why not," his father demanded.

"The terrorists are dangerous and frequently know a lot about us. It's unlikely, but they might come after us," Warren answered.

Kimberly thought she had better speak up. "I'd better say this before Warren and I get in deeper. More likely than Warren's scenario is that they come after me or you to get at me. I do a lot of terrorist interdiction. They don't like me." She saw Warren's face fall.

"That's why the Mexican Marines wear face-covering around the drug cartels," Warren's father responded. "If we worry about you and Warren's relationship, the terrorists are winning," he argued.

"But what about Jennifer and the children?" his mother asked.

"Jennifer recognized me as soon as I walked in the door. Madison also recognizes me. We'll work with them, and they're getting psychiatric care," Kimberly answered.

"Were any of your people killed, Commander" Warren's Dad, Henry, wanted to know.

"No, a couple of flesh wounds, none serious. Please drop the rank; I'm Kimberly."

"There were police killed," Warren's mother said. Warren saw Kimberly grimace.

"Yes,' Kimberly responded, "the first police units to respond. As well trained as the police might be, they were no match for the terrorists. They didn't realize that the terrorists had snipers on the roof, and the police were out in the open."

Henry looked at Kimberly. "Congress should've left it to the experts, you guys." Kimberly shrugged. "Your people are all okay? I mean, it must have been intense?"

"Yes, we're all undergoing PTSD counseling as well as the routine debriefing. What we saw in there was horrific. As much as possible, we routed the hostages away from the carnage and covered their eyes, particularly the children. I am hoping we won't lose any of the team members as they are highly trained and outstanding warriors."

"Well, if they had only flesh wounds, you won't lose them," June offered.

"No, not that way, but the PTSD can be bad, and people resign."

"Oh."

Jennifer came into the room. "Alan's here and with the kids, may I join this conversation?" Jennifer asked. Kimberly waved her in.

"When did you discover you were dating a Naval Officer, son?" Harry asked jokingly.

Warren laughed. "About the time that Congress shut down their program, and she was promoted to full Commander, so several months ago. Up to then, I knew I was in over my head with this badass biker chick, a mechanical engineer. The Navy sent her to Newport, Rhode Island, for training, so she felt she had to explain why she would be away for a while. She sat me down on a pier at Lardner's Point Park in Philadelphia and dropped the whole story, or as much as she can talk about, on me."

"Warren, that's not a nice way to talk about Kimberly," his mother admonished, still mentally much earlier in the conversation.

"What the badass comment, Mom?" asked Jennifer. "Oh, my God, you've never seen her in battle dress with weapons and commanding troops in an assault. She's totally a badass and scary as crap. I was so damn pleased to see her and her Chief, another scary female sailor. Warren's in way over his head." His father thought the comment funny; Kimberly just looked a bit nonplused.

They had to explain it all over again to Jennifer's husband, Dr. Alan McGovern, a family physician. June and Harry sat in and asked more questions. Kimberly talked about her early career as a surface warfare officer on the destroyers. Fortunately, Warren's family was

very admiring of her. She was able to persuade Alan that the kids
should talk about their bad experiences with the family.

"Allow them to explore and find some answers," Kimberly
suggested. "But you also need to reinforce what they have been told
about not talking about it outside of the family. Even if another child
talks about the incident at school, they say nothing, not even to
remind the other child that they're not to talk."

Christmas Day was enjoyable. Kimberly did get to call home to talk
to her parents, as well as Meredith, Dwaine, and Andria. She sensed
that her mother did not mind that she was not there for Christmas if
a son-in-law was possible.

The afternoon of December Twenty-Sixth was bright and about
fifty degrees. Madison had her coat on and announced that she
wanted to go for a walk with Kimberly. Kimberly laughed at Jennifer's
concern, found a jacket, and went with the girl.

"It's probably safest to talk outside where no one can hear us,"
the child stated. Kimberly's immediate thought was that it was not a
good sign that even children were learning to be covert.

"Probably," she wondered what Madison's agenda was.

"Are there a lot of lady soldiers?"

"There are Madison, but most people don't know that."

"Daddy says you're not a soldier."

"Oh?"

"Yes, he says you're a sailor, and I shouldn't get the two
confused."

"Well, yes, but we do similar things and can look a lot alike so that
it can be confusing."

"Yes." There was a pause as they walked, and the child formulated
her thoughts. "Were you scared?"

"Yes, of course, a person should always be scared dealing with bad
guys, but you have to control that and not make noise or do things
that could reveal your hiding place. In my case, I can be scared, but I
must control that so I can give the correct directions to the people
working with me."

The child nodded. "Are you still scared?"

"Yes, and that is why, like you, I go to counseling so that I can deal with those fears."

There was another nod. "Can I tell Dr. Wallen about you?"

"Who's that?"

"The psychiatrist we all go to."

"Oh, sure, yes, you can."

"Would you teach me how to shoot?"

"Maybe, in about ten years."

"Daddy said the same thing."

Kimberly grinned. The girl grinned up at her and then appeared perplexed again. They continued to walk. "What?" Kimberly asked.

Being perplexed turned into a frown. "I wish you could talk about what you do."

"Why?"

"I'd like to bring you to school."

"Like 'show and tell'?"

"Yes."

"We couldn't talk about the mall."

"I know."

Now it was Kimberly's turn to think. "Madison, I have done stuff like that, just talking about being a Naval Officer in general. I would need to get permission, but maybe it could be done."

That satisfied the girl. "Billy Scales will be so upset."

"Who's Billy Scales?"

"A Neanderthal."

Okay, Grade Three students are not even supposed to know that word. Madison had a lot more questions about ships and being at sea.

Back at Norfolk, Kimberly finished a meeting with Greene. The purpose was to let her know that there was some political action on the anti-terrorism task force. "You never told me that Warren's sister and her kids were hostages," she stated.

"What are you talking about?"

"Oh my God, do you mean there is something that the amazing Malcolm Greene doesn't know? Chief Rife and I found hostages in a closet just before you and Wearing showed up inside the mall. In particular, I noticed a woman with two kids. It turns out, it was Warren's sister, whom I'd never met."

Greene insisted on knowing the details of how Kimberly had handled the situation. He approved. He also supported, if the Navy was okay, her going to Madison's class as a generic Naval Officer, even a SEAL. The Navy agreed, again insisting on service dress whites. She called Jennifer, who would talk to the teacher.

Congress could not skate backward fast enough, completely rewriting the Posse Comitatus law. Some of the most anti-military before the mall incident now flip-flopped completely and wanted the law canceled. The more thoughtful, carefully revised it so that citizens were protected from the unwarranted threat from the military. The new law allowed the military to act in the nation's interests under the civilian control of the President, on United States soil, and in United States waters. The new law spelled out that the local legislative people had no authority. Allegedly that was to prevent muddy waters, but it was a slap at Congressman Mitis' television performance.

Kimberly learned that she sincerely disliked the responsibilities of her rank. She had to oversee the mission crews administratively. The higher the rank, the more that was office work. She had good young officers and non-coms who manage the logistics and paper. She tried to focus on the training, but also be aware of what was happening, being sure the technology was as good as possible, and that the training was sufficient and appropriate. The unit commanders tolerated her oversight of the training, maybe. She much preferred to be in the field or at sea. On all of the U.S. coastline, the littorals were back patrolling, supplementing the Coast Guard.

Late in April, she was in the Philadelphia area on Navy business. That made her trip to Madison's class easy. Jennifer and Madison met her in the Principal's office. The District Superintendent had just caught up with what was happening and tagged along.

Using notes that she and her mother made, Madison introduced Kimberly to the class. "My uncle's girlfriend is amazing. She is a United States Naval officer, a Commander. I met her at Christmas time. I asked her to come to talk to us about it."

Kimberly talked about how important school was and how, after high school, she had gone to the Naval Academy and became both a mechanical engineer and a naval officer. She stressed the math and science involved. Kimberly then said that had she trained as a surface warfare officer. She talked about the destroyers and being at sea.

"After some time on two different types of destroyer, I was accepted at the Special Warfare School and trained as a SEAL. Does anyone know what that means?" One of the kids had human SEALs confused with the animal variety. One of the boys had the meaning of the acronym partially correct. During questions, some of the kids thought she was a Captain, so she explained the difference between three wide bars and the four.

"But you can't be at war."

The question, really a statement, came from a big chubby kid at the back. Kimberly glanced down at Madison, who was staring at the boy with undisguised contempt. Kimberly guessed that this was the Neanderthal.

"It is what Surface Warfare officers and submarine officers do," she put a slight emphasis on the word "warfare."

The kid frowned. "You're a girl; you can't be a SEAL; they're tough guys."

"Your information is out of date. Women can train as SEALs, and many do extremely well."

Madison had told her this was part of what she wanted her class to hear, for her classmates to know that women did this stuff. Kimberly walked down the aisle to the boy's desk.

"I am a SEAL, and that's what this pin says. SEAL means 'Sea, Air, and Land.'" She explained as she walked to a board and wrote it out underlining the SE and the A and the L. "We are Special Operations Naval forces trained to attack by parachuting from the air or swimming in underwater in SCUBA gear, or overland. A few years ago, the law was changed so that women can qualify as SEALs. Without changing the qualifying standards, every job in the Navy can now legally be carried out by either men or women. That is true throughout the military and, for that matter, the civilian world. The world is changing."

By his facial expression and body language, the kid did not believe her or did not want to believe her. The rest of the class got it.

Going back to the office, Kimberly got Madison to hang back.

"That was the Neanderthal?"

"Yeah."

"He's going to irritate you, bully you. If you argue with him, you cannot say anything at all about seeing me in battle dress."

"Oh my God, I know, no, I would never do that." Kimberly had thought that one had to be a teenager to use the 'Oh My God' expression, apparently not.

Chapter Twenty – Reinstatement

Despite the renewed patrols and new legal authority for them, the next several months were quiet for all the anti-terrorist services. Having pulled off their sophisticated attack at the mall, the terrorist organizations were again retrenching. There were some problems in the Middle East and Central Asia and a few incidents in Europe but nothing more in North America.

The littoral program became stronger. With the law changes, they no longer needed redundant multi-service training. The Navy, in cooperation with the Coast Guard, began to develop a single specific training for the littoral anti-terrorism mission. The best of the candidates went to the SEAL program as it was still useful to have about half of each team be SEALs. As a component of the littoral program, the Navy and Coast Guard taught some of the criminology-law training that they had received at the FBI Academy. More than anyone in the military, the mission crews for the littoral program needed to understand the new Posse Comitatus law. They learned some of the spook stuff. Both the Navy and Coast Guard were developing a different warrior, specific to antiterrorism.

The following Christmas, Kimberly and Warren, were expected at her parents. Their relationship was still developing. Kimberly allowed herself to be a bit upset that Warren had not proposed, but she was more upset that he had never started a possibility of marriage discussion.

Her reaction to Meredith's successes was still an enigma to Kimberly. Kimberly was proud of her as a Midshipman Class Three. The problem was that Kimberly had not entirely internalized that the young teenaged flake was developing into an excellent naval officer. Meredith was demonstrating some of Kimberly's love of danger.

"I'm not sure the Navy is ready for the both of you," Warren voiced during their Christmas visit. That got both of his shoulders hit as he had one of the women sitting on each side of him.

Early in February, Kimberly received orders to go to the White House. As a rule, Kimberly disliked politics and Washington, D.C., avoiding the area as much as possible. She could not ignore the Commander-in-Chief. The call had come from the Oval Office, not the

West Wing. Besides herself and the President, the only others in the Oval Office were William A. Sanburg and Miranda Davidson.

POTUS smiled and returned her salute then put his hand out to shake.

"I have heard a lot about you, Commander Callahan, and thank you for your excellent work a year or so ago at that mall. The people at DoD tell me that you're exceptional. After going over the after-action reports where you were involved, I must say that I agree. Department of Defense has recommended you for a new situation, a recommendation with which I wholeheartedly agree. You know Miranda Davidson from the CIA. Miranda, would you please fill in the Commander.

"Yes, Sir. A terrorist leader, Abd al-Karim Bakr, has initiated some successful attacks in Europe. In the estimation of the FBI, he is also very successfully enabling the self-radicalization of young Americans, particularly males, with little education and little opportunity. He is very charismatic, and that brings us to our new threat. He and his followers have overrun the Gulf State of Zahrat, throwing out the legitimate government. With good intelligence, a CIA team can normally find such people and order a drone strike that kills them. The problem is that we have failed several attempts to get this guy. We now think that there is an opportunity to get this guy on the ground. The population is opposed to his band and want their government back. The government was aligned with the United States and, properly managed, the whole country could be flipped back to be an ally."

"Okay, and the lecture on geopolitics is because?" Kimberly asked.

Sanburg took over the discussion. "Our sources deep within the legitimate government believes that if someone removed Abd al-Karim Bakr, his henchmen would fold, and the legitimate government could take back their country. Most of Bakr's men are not from Zahrat, so likely both premises are correct. We get involved because they want the backing of the U.S both militarily and economically, and they want a clear U.S. signal of that backing."

"So, send in a Marine unit and hand them their country," Kimberly said.

"Too blunt. There are too many allies of Abd al-Karim Bakr, or countries that have to talk like they are allied to him, that would cause us trouble in the UN," Sanburg said. "We need a very modest but successful surgical action."

"What are you suggesting?"

"We aren't, it's a plan from the Zahraties. A sniper team infiltrates the country and, assisted by the Zahraties, takes out Abd al-Karim Bakr."

"I don't like it," Kimberly assessed. "Huge problems. It smacks of regime change even if the existing regime is illegitimate. Too many people are read in. Anyone in that rebel team on the ground could sell out the whole idea. Why has the CIA missed him, was that due to faulty intelligence? If that is so, a ground team could walk into an ambush used to embarrass the United States."

"Do you have a solution?" Davidson asked.

"No.' Kimberly admitted. "Flipping a country is never as easy as it looks on paper. Usually, amongst our allies on the ground, there are multiple competing groups, some secretly aligned with the opposition. It's never clean. Additionally, if this guy is so charismatic, why do the locals want to overthrow him. Likely some of the so-called rebels of the legitimate government do not."

"Bill, the Commander has the same arguments that I had," the President told Sanburg, "the plan tries to do too much."

"Let's start working on it; my people on the ground will continue to develop intelligence. If we can get him with a drone, we will. Flipping the country will be phase two."

"I'm sorry," Kimberly said, "but what is the 'it'?"

Commander Callahan," the President said, "the CIA plan is to send in two snipers to work with the locals, and by killing this guy signal the start of an uprising. I've been told and believe that you are one of the best. However, I agree with your objections to the plan. The idea needs more thought." The meeting was over. Kimberly hoped that she had heard the last of it.

Three weeks after her visit to the White House, Kim was working on a pile of logistics reports, when there was a tap on her office door. She looked up to see an unfamiliar lieutenant. He saluted.

"‫تحية قائد، وأتمنى أن جمعيتنا سوف تكون مثمرة‬ ."

The name on his badge looked Italian. Kimberly returned the salute and nodded to a chair, all the time trying to process what this could be about yet concerned that likely she knew.

"What the hell was that?"

"A greeting to the Commander in Arabic and a wish that our association will be fruitful." Kimberly held his eye. The Lieutenant looked back. He was wearing Navy service khakis, had a trident insignia, and there was a large brown manila envelope tucked under his arm.

"Wearing that uniform, you're likely not Arab."

"No ma'am United States citizen by birth, born in Baltimore. Lieutenant Hamza Malvestuto, I go by Hamilton or more frequently, just Ham."

"Of Arabic parents."

"Mother from the United Arab Emirates, father of Italian heritage."

"When did you learn Arabic?"

"Shortly after I was born, my parents thought it important that I speak several languages. I do speak Italian, but that won't help us here."

"Damn, they still think that fuzzy plan will work?"

"Permission to speak candidly, Commander."

"Of course."

"The intelligence is good."

She stared at the Lieutenant. "And you were told to say that as well as deliver that packet of orders to me. If it's so damn good, why doesn't the CIA do it themselves?"

"No ma'am on the intelligence, I'll explain that in a minute. Not the CIA, due to me and another Navy SEAL. Yes, Ma'am, about the orders, and I'm to stay close. If anything happens to you, I'd better not return."

"Someone said that to you? Greene?"

"Not quite in those words, but the implication was clear."

Kimberly noticed that he said nothing about Greene; it was unnecessary.

"What happens as you're staying close?"

"I and others teach you Arabic, we infiltrate and assassinate Abd al-Karim Bakr and then either get the hell outta Dodge or lead a victory parade as the real government takes over."

"You're a language teacher?"

"No, like a good Arab woman of the old-fashioned tribal culture, you're going to keep your mouth shut, ma'am, sorry ma'am. We'll teach you some Arabic, but if you speak too much, it'll give us away." The Lieutenant returned her stare.

"This is effing screwy."

"That's what I told them ma'am, but it's also just audacious enough to work."

"They tell you a timeline?"

"Careful not to; they want the team on track and comfortable. You have the authority to abort at any moment."

"Once started, I don't tend to do that."

"That's what they told me."

"How big is this team?"

"You, me, and another male SEAL of Arabic heritage, Petty Officer First Class Mash'al Naji. He goes by Marshal.

"We just waltz in?"

"I get us to the rebels through my family. That's why the intelligence is believed good. The CIA doesn't have the family connections."

"Really? God, this is screwball."

"Not quite. The current plan is that we'll be left in the desert where we'll join my family. We wander around the desert for a while and, when the time comes, go into town. We find a position that we can fire from, do it, and escape. The currently recommended position is an apartment across from a principal government building. When Abd al-Karim Bakr shows up, we kill him, and the populace revolts while we escape."

"All this time, we're lugging weapons?"

"No, ma'am, the family will hide and move them."

"Your family."

"Yes, ma'am."

"Why the hell haven't the drones been able to get Abd al-Karim Bakr?"

"I wondered the same thing, ma'am. They told me that you should explore that with somebody named Sanburg."

That would not get Kimberly anywhere. In a sense, Hamilton's, the Lieutenant's characterization of just audacious enough to work, was correct. She could abort at any time.

Two weeks later, she was on a desert in California with the Lieutenant. He introduced PO-1 Mash'al Naji. The men went by un-Arabic names of Ham, short for Hamilton, and Marshal. The names made sense; Ham was Hamza or Lion, and Marshal Mash'al or Torch. She never did learn if the names were their real given names or were operational.

Despite many of the population of Zahrat knowing the plan, or so it seemed to Kimberly, the CIA buried the mission. There was another Commander at her desk in Norfolk. Warren was told that she would be away for a while. Both families had been told not even to look. To Kimberly, that was yet another strike against the project. She should have been allowed to tell Warren personally. To the CIA, this was exceedingly black; it did not exist, so she could not communicate anything about it. She did not exist. The plan scared Kimberly, based, as it was, on an unknown number of people in Zahrat knowing the program and not delivering it to Abd al-Karim Bakr's people.

The mockup sites Kimberly had been at during SEAL training were excellent. Much better was this allegedly Arab village in the California desert; it was amazingly real. No one explained the place. Kimberly's dog tags and her cell phone were confiscated; she was not sure which loss was the scariest. No one had uniforms; the site was total immersion. She was learning how to manage an abaya, a burqa, and a niqab. Fully immersed in Arabic and the Koran, she spoke no English. No one did. There were language, culture, and religious teachers. The Koran was easy; despite some differences, it is much the same as the Old Testament. Kneeling and bowing to the east, she prayed five times a day.

Kimberly and the two other SEALs worked together on a day to day basis. They helped her with language so she could eat. Outside the tent, it was hot and dry with blowing sand. Other people were training in the village for different missions; various branches of the military used it. Possibly they were all CIA. The others were all males, so she could not speak to them or even be in their presence without her alleged brother, Hamza. Though the two male SEALs spoke Arabic, both the men needed brushing up and cultural training. They were too American. Based on tribal culture, and as fascinating as it all was, she was pleased that she would be Arab only for a while.

Kimberly took Spanish in high school. While she had done alright, Kimberly was never very serious about it. Now it turned out that she had an aptitude for language, at least for Arabic. The Semitic alphabet was challenging, but even that she began to understand. Over the weeks, their conversation was increasingly in Arabic. A bit over three months into it, she realized that she was thinking in Arabic.

The situation on the ground did not change, and there were two more failed drone attacks. Hamza and Mash'al were her contacts to the outside world. The conversation in Arabic was in private in a tent between her brother and his friend. Usually, she just listened.

"Why are the drones missing him?"

"The delay time," Mash'al reported, "between when he's spotted and when we can get a drone on him is a bit long, but not outside of operational norms. He disappears before the drone gets to the target."

"Family members report that he never stays in one spot for long," Hamza said. "That may be the reason, but we still can't prove that Abd al-Karim Bakr isn't being tipped off, somehow." If that were true, the whole operation would be compromised.

"How can we learn that for sure?" Kimberly asked.

"Don't think in terms of U.S. families, I have many cousins," Hamza told her.

"You trust them all?" She asked.

Hamza shrugged, "are all the Princes loyal to the Saudi King?"

"Damn, how many in your family know about this mission?" she asked Hamilton, Hamza.

"My uncle and me."

"So how is the populace going to be prepared to rebel after the assassination."

"Two issues. The so-called rebels, who belong to the legitimate government, know that a revolt is coming. They are being told several scenarios about the U.S involvement and how that will signal the start. A best-case scenario is a drone gets Abd al-Karim Bakr, that's a signal, and we'll go back to our home bases. Should our mission go forward, only my uncle and I will know of it. Again, with several scenarios, the legitimate government rebels will be alert."

Her CIA training had taught her about strange worlds where nothing is obvious, and there are no rules. That had been theoretical. Now it was three SEALs and likely a bunch of Hamza's family who had their asses on the line. The idea of legitimate government rebels seemed an oxymoron. That was the least of Kimberly's problems.

Kimberly learned how to ride a camel. They all learned as neither of the guys could. No one in the village thought it odd when they left on their camels, away for hours at a time. They had to leave the camp and go further out on the desert to practice with weapons. The sniper rifles they would use were Steyr SSG 69 weapons from Austria. Of outstanding quality, Kimberly did wonder about the five-round magazine. She'd better need only one round.

She awakened suddenly. The desert was quiet, not even a dog barking. She had been dreaming in Arabic. Everything happened in Arabic; she had to think to be in English. As immersed as she was in the language, culture, and religion, the many unknowns of the mission still bothered her. She wanted to talk to Greene. He was out of the loop, and she had no means of making contact.

A few days later, Miranda Davidson showed up on the desert in a Land Rover. "You look good in a burqa, hell you always look good," Davidson greeted her.

"This is such bullshit. Why couldn't I tell Warren I wouldn't be around for a while."

"Who?"

"Warren Bradshaw," Kimberly exploded.

That got her a long stare. It occurred to Kimberly that Davidson likely was trying to assess her state of mind. Kimberly could have told her, pissed. "Why would he be of any consequence to an Arab woman in Zahrat?"

"Chelb, I should cut your throat, American."

She had just called Davidson a dog, a great Arabic insult. The insult and threat to kill Davidson fit Kimberly's mood.

"Okay, that's more of what I expected," Davidson told her.

"Fuck you. I still don't understand this damn operation," Kimberly told her. "If this guy is going to be so visible, why the hell do the rebels need a US Navy Seal team to assassinate him?"

"They don't, but the rebels, really the legitimate government, are afraid of being left hanging by US politics. They want the US directly involved in starting this thing. For the record none of you are Navy, you're all CIA," Davidson told her.

"But Ham and Marshal are SEALs?"

"Yes, both. They've also had covert training," Davidson said.

Kimberly sighed deeply. "Damn, I guess based on our history, that makes sense. Shit, even this doesn't guarantee that they won't get left hanging by US politics. Okay, my larger concern. Every drone attack, including recent ones, has failed. I guess that somehow, he's being tipped off. Why wouldn't he learn that a CIA team was in-country? This whole operation has little but loose ends."

"Both Naval intelligence and CIA have looked carefully at the drones missing the target question. The guy is wily, he moves constantly, and quickly, with no schedule or pattern, at least none that the locals know. We believe that the time lag of information and his never staying in one place for long is why we've missed, and not his having specific knowledge of our targets and timing. Thus, the need for the boots on the ground."

"'You believe,' dammit spook lady, this thing has a whole lot of reasons why it'll go south," Kimberly told Davidson.

"I know, that's why you have the authority to abort at any time."

"You know damn well that's the last option with me," Kimberly told her.

"Yes. By the way, you look good on a camel."

"Fuck you."

"I'll take that as a polite goodbye for now," Davidson laughed.

Kimberly had not thought much about the insertion process. Her concerns were more about what happened once they were in the Zahrat desert.   Speaking Arabic and wearing an Abaya, Kimberly could feel the distrust of her team by the American sailors on the submarine and even the SEAL team members who paddled them ashore. To those sailors, they were three Arabs. Once ashore, they were alone with nothing to identify them as United States Navy or anything other than desert nomads, except their communications gear, a significant danger.

The following morning a few of Hamza's family caught up with them. With all the profuse greetings done, the three Americans mounted their camels. Soon they were incorporated into the whole group. It did not surprise Kimberly that only her closest alleged sisters greeted her, even hugged her. More than the uncle knew what was happening. Hamza's uncle ignored Kimberly, talking only to the two men. The nomadic caravan of about sixty camels started moving. Kimberly's senses were all on high alert.

Kimberly was amazed that she understood much of what they were saying. The language immersion had worked. It took a while before she realized that Hamza's uncle only spoke to the men, but, if the information was mission-critical, always in her presence. About then, she realized that a female cousin of Hamza's, the alleged sister that she was to hang with, knew that she was American.

"You are good; I would not know except that uncle told me. May I correct your pronunciation?" the woman asked her in Arabic.

"Please," Kimberly told her.

"We are concerned that you speak very little. While good, your speech might give us away."

"Hamza told me. I'll be careful."

There were a few word corrections. The incorrect pronunciations were more about tribal differences than a westerner speaking Arabic. Though she settled into the nomad band quickly, Kimberly was very uncomfortable being in potentially hostile territory without a weapon. Her usual paradigm was to go ashore or drop through the air, complete a mission, and evacuate, all within hours. The weeks seemly wandering about the desert or camped on the desert, were unnerving. Kimberly needed to remain vigilant and listen to what was going on but could not maintain a constant high alert. Doing the cooking, washing up, and cleaning clothes with the other women kept Kimberly busy.

Two men arrived in the camp several weeks after the three SEALS joined the family. Standing around the edge of the meeting with the other women, Kimberly could hear the conversation. Both visitors claimed to know where Abd al-Karim Bakr was and stated that the rebels were ready to overthrow the government. Two of Hamza's older male cousins and Hamza's uncle asked excellent questions.

"We have spoken with Fahd Irfan Rababi, and he assured us that the people in the south are ready," one of the men asserted.

"When was that?" Hamza's uncle asked pleasantly.

"Eight days ago."

"Where?"

"In Madinat al'Adwa'," they told him.

"You spoke to Fahd Irfan Rababi in Madinat al'Adwa' eight days ago?" the uncle asked, still with a pleasant tone of voice.

"Yes." For all their assertions, the visiting men were suddenly ill at ease.

Nothing more was said. Hamza's uncle looked up at two men in their caravan and almost imperceptibly moved his head. The two members of the family picked up the two visitors who started screaming. They were dragged out onto the desert, still crying. The screaming stopped.

"I spoke to Fahd Irfan Rababi in Qiada eight days ago," Hamza's uncle told Hamza and Mash'al. That meant that the messengers were lying and, likely, informants. Kimberly was frustrated. All the intelligence she was trying to process was bogus, possibly even a trap. Killing the informants might alert Abd al-Karim Bakr's people. Allowing them to go definitely would.

"We will go to Qiada now, that will be the safest," Hamza's uncle decreed.

Camels are not helicopters. Three days later, they camped outside the city. Kimberly, with the two male SEALs, accompanied a group of men and women from the caravan into the city. In the bazaar, there was an excitement in the air about the impending revolt, too much excitement, in Kimberly's estimation, as the secret police would quickly pick up on it. Hamza voiced the question to his uncle that evening.

"There is always talk of revolt; in a way, it's a cover. The secret police will ignore it unless they have other information. No one was interested in us today," the uncle asserted.

Over subsequent days Kimberly got eyes on Abd al-Karim Bakr twice, neither time was he where people thought he would be. That might explain the faulty intelligence and that this plan might work. Hamza's uncle and the other rebels wanted Abd al-Karim dead as much as the U.S. did. Kimberly still did not fully understand why three U.S. sailors had to start it; any one of the rebels could assassinate him. Possibly that would be even easier to accomplish. Davidson had told her that the question was above her pay grade. The plan always had been to time the revolt with an assassination.

Some of the female family members with Kimberly and the men moved to an apartment adjacent to a plaza. The site choice had two principal factors; it belonged to a distant family member who they knew to be away, so their presence there would not arouse suspicion. There was also a clear view out onto the plaza and across to the broad steps of a government building that was one hundred and eighty meters away. It was hot. Air conditioning was rare, even in Qiada, so that windows were always open was in no way suspicious.

Abd al-Karim Bakr was seen in Qiada twice more, moving around rapidly while he was in the city. The family moved the Austrian sniper rifles into the apartment. One afternoon Mash'al went to the encampment outside the city. He was back the next morning.

"Done?" Hamza asked. Mash'al nodded. It meant that a two-word message. "Be praised" had been sent, and a single word, "Allah" came back. The CIA knew something was about to happen and had positioned to extract the team. Kimberly hoped like hell that was true.

No one saw Abd al-Karim for the next two days. They were warned of his imminent arrival twice and unpacked their weapons, only to have to hide them again. To Kimberly, that was a sign of poor intelligence, and aborting the mission occurred to her. The family believed that the information that Abd al-Karim was still in the city was accurate. Once again, the problem was that he moved fast. They also thought he changed his plans frequently, as he did not trust his deputies. The action had to go down soon as each day increased the hazard of discovery.

One morning one of Hamza's many cousins came in to say that Abd al-Karim had been sighted and that everything was in place. Intelligence was that he was coming to the government building across the plaza. Men suddenly put in place a bank of microphones with speakers directed out over the square. Kimberly's team unpacked their weapons, but, other than assembling the tripods, kept them hidden. The floor-based tripods allowed them to keep everything back from the open windows.

There was sudden activity on the stairs of the building across the plaza. A Mercedes-Benz drove in with several other vehicles.

"That confirms the vehicle intelligence, that thing is all armored plate," Kimberly told Hamza and Mash'al. Mash'al was watching closely with binoculars. Kimberly and Hamza attached the calibrated sniper weapons to the tripods.

Other than a bunch of men running around, nothing happened for a minute or two. Advantage our side Kimberly thought; it allowed the rebels to move forward, appearing to be curious onlookers. Surrounded by people in khaki uniforms, a person exited the government building side of the vehicle. That he wore a dark green keffiyeh on his head was controversial in the Arab world, many disagreeing that he was descendant from the Prophet. The keffiyeh was held in place by a gold circlet of rope.

"The dark green keffiyeh and gold agal fit," Mash'al noted. They knew of the headdress and the controversy it had provoked.

The person mounted the few steps. Any of his speeches were always brief, so Kimberly and Hamza had only minutes to confirm and act. Through his binoculars Mash'al, and through their scopes Kimberly and Hamza, each confirmed that it was Abd al-Karim. His security people kept moving around him to block shots from the plaza. Those people moving did not obstruct Kimberly or Hamza. The opportunity that would last only moments was too good to abort the mission. Kimberly confirmed that they both had acquired the target. She gave the shoot order; both weapons barked almost simultaneously. Abd al-Karim went straight down. Through her scope, Kimberly confirmed two headshots.

Immediately there was a lot of gunfire around the plaza. The men in khaki were dropping. Some people tried to get Abd al-Karim's body to the Mercedes, but people in the square killed them. The rebel elements were to follow this attack plan partially to confuse where the original shots came from and to start the revolution. Kimberly was not so confident of the latter. The question was how many weapons the rebels had been able to smuggle into the plaza.

Another problem was if, outside the plaza and outside of Qiada, the rebels were being equally as successful. Two young men arrived and took the Austrian weapons away. It was get out of Dodge time.

The women, with Hamza and Mash'al, and another young man Kimberly had never met, made their way down the stairs and slowly out the back entrance. The young man wanted to run, but Hamza spoke sharply to him, and at a leisurely pace, the group walked away from the apartment and the plaza. Four blocks away, a vehicle picked them up, and soon, they were on the outskirts of Qiada, an hour from the sea.

There was one city, Hadiqat Khadira', between them and the sea. There were no problems at the checkpoints entering the town or departing the other side, but about three kilometers outside the town, they encountered a tank and a Land Rover.

"The question." Hamza muttered, "is whose tank is it, as both sides have tanks. A few military units are loyal to Abd al-Karim, but most are loyal to the legitimate government."

"It's flying the Zahrat flag, but that could mean anything," Mash'al said. "The legitimate government military is also supposed to have green flags."

An officer was standing in the Land Rover yelling and gesturing at them, Kimberly could not make out what they were saying. The guy in the tank's turret appeared very nervous, jittery.

The cousin driving the SUV yelled back, "We're going to the family compound a few kilometers toward the sea."

That might have worked except that the officer was scared, jumpy, and kept yelling at them and waving his arms. Then he dropped dead. The shot came from their left, where there was a berm. The tank began to execute a turn toward the berm. The tank machine gunner on the left was likely over-excited. He began to fire as the tank started turning long before his sights were on the berm.

Kimberly heard the woman beside her grunt and then felt something hammering her back. She grabbed at her abdomen and felt liquid; her hands had blood on them. The tank blew up. The world began to swim in front of her. The tank was burning, and dead people were in the Land Rover. It was burning. Kimberly could not focus. Hamza was putting pressure on her abdomen. It hurt like hell. Kimberly blacked out.

The lights came back on. Many people were talking in some language; she thought Arabic. She was not sure. Everything went black again.

Consciousness returned. A woman called, and a man came to her. The woman spoke English, the man Arabic. She felt consciousness slip from her again.

Chapter Twenty-One Grounded

Kimberly tried to wake up. She felt as though she was swimming. Her brain was not working. There were voices around her. Gradually she could hear them better. The people were speaking English. Someone left. She felt the cotton sheet over her body. Her belly hurt. Slowly she opened her eyes. There was a window to her right where daylight was streaming in. She was alive and, in a hospital, somewhere. She looked left. Someone was sitting in a chair watching her. She tried to focus. Slowly a face came into focus, a male, Warren. Shit, Warren was there. No, it was good that Warren was there. She was hallucinating. No, it was Warren.

"Hi, where am I?"

"Bethesda Naval Hospital."

"In the States, oh, how'd you get here?"

"You have pull, or your friends do."

"Really? How'd I get here?"

"A Blackhawk covered by four Apache's to the U.S.S. Abe Lincoln, from there to a hospital in Germany where you were for several long agonizing days, and then you were evac'd here a few days ago."

"I was dying in the fuckin' desert. A Blackhawk just swooped in and saved me?"

"Yeah, from what they've told me, you were dying. Lieutenant Malvestuto kept pressure on your wound, and they got you inside a city, let's see if I get this right, Hadiqat Khadira', where, they tell me, a rebel surgeon saved your life and then the Blackhawk came for you. I think Hamilton or Marshal had called someone."

"They're both okay?"

"Hamilton was hit but is up and around on crutches. Marshal is fine."

"I recall a tank."

"Yeah, they say you demolished it."

"I couldn't have."

"Your friends did."

"Oh."

"You were badly shot up," Warren explained. "The rebel surgeon that operated on you was trained in the U.S." A guy in scrubs and a white coat entered. Warren continued, "Honey, this is Dr. George Martin; he's your surgeon here."

The surgeon saluted, "Lieutenant Commander Martin, Commander. Welcome back to the land of the living."

"Okay, so what's the deal?" Kimberly asked.

"We've just let you out of a medically induced coma, so you're going to be groggy for a few hours. Your liver was shot up. That Lieutenant Malvestuto kept the pressure on it until they got you to the hospital in Hadiqat Khadira' certainly helped. All the surgeon there could do was tie off major bleeders and pack it off with sponges to try to stop the rest of the bleeding. They started transfusing you and then prayed to Allah. Petty Officer Naji had your comm equipment and called the Abe Lincoln, who were expecting to pick you up, only not from a hospital in Hadiqat Khadira'. Aboard the carrier, they wisely did not try anything other than more transfusions. Other than being partially conscious and flailing about, you were stable, so they put you into a medical coma, on a ventilator, and sent you to Germany. In Germany, the surgeons gave you more blood, changed the packs twice, and decided to do no more; and that they could safely get you here. A couple of days ago, we removed the packs and clean things up a bit. You had stopped bleeding. This morning we decided to let you wake up."

"But honey, they don't want you doing any weightlifting," Warren added.

"Fuck you."

"Okay, you're better, but the doctors say that'll be a while," Warren laughed. She grinned at him and thanked the Lieutenant Commander as he left.

"I," Warren told her, "have to call parents, a sister, some guy named Greene and the U.S. Naval Academy, and a Lieutenant JG Howle." Kimberly groaned, Warren got his mobile phone out and pushed at the screen.

"Hi, Mr. Callahan. She's awake and doing fine. The Doctors say she's going to be okay."

"Yeah, well, we've not had that discussion yet."

"Haven't had that one either."

"No, Meredith has it set up so I can call the Academy and leave a message."

"Okay, I'll keep you posted." He disconnected and called his parents. Following that call, he had a bit of trouble convincing a school office to transfer his call to his sister's classroom. Kimberly was having trouble keeping the focus on all the calls.

"This is Warren Bradshaw calling about Commander Callahan; I believe you were expecting the call."

"Yes, she's awake and doing fine, the doctors say she's going to make it."

"Yes, Midshipman Two Callahan"

"Thank you, ma'am." Kimberly slipped into sleep for a moment. She awoke again as he called Malcolm Greene, said something then set his mobile phone aside for a moment.

"You still awake? Malcolm Greene is on his way over. The hospital already called him. One more call." He dialed.

"Warren Bradshaw for Lieutenant JG Montana Howle, please." Damn, Janie would never let her live this down. This pause was longer; then Warren continued with the message that Kimberly was okay and said goodbye.

"You still awake? Okay, all the people who've threatened to kill me if I didn't keep them updated are updated," Warren told Kimberly.

"I'm tired."

"Of course, the doctors say you'll be a while before you're back on your feet."

"Oh, God, Admiral Mann's going to kill me."

Even in her partially drugged state, she heard someone enter the room. "No possible way, Commander, welcome back from the dead. I told your boyfriend that you were too tough for a fifty-caliber round," it was Malcolm Greene with Admiral Mann

"Oh God, hello Admiral Mann, hello Malcolm."

"We had to see for ourselves that you were okay," Mann said.

"What the hell happened? I recall a tank."

"Yes, Greene replied, "it was turning to face the rebels who were shooting at it and who almost immediately blew it up. The machine gunner was trigger happy and started shooting before they fully turned. The two women in the back of the car with you, as well as the driver, were KIA. Fortunately, you were seated in back, on the left and outboard. A fifty-caliber slug clipped your right flank and shot off a part of your liver. They say you don't need that part anyway. Had it been fired a fraction of a second later, the round would have taken out your whole liver and likely your aorta. You wouldn't have made it. Hamilton and Marshal are okay. Hamilton was shot up a bit but not as bad as you. He'll be fine. You guys got Abd al-Karim, and the rebels were successful in getting the legitimate government back in place. Then they went after Abd al-Karim's followers with a vengeance." Kimberly nodded.

"For the record Commander Callahan," Mann said, "we're going to have to promote you, so you stop doing these crazy missions." Kimberly did not feel like arguing. They chatted some more before Admiral Mann and Malcolm left.

Kimberly fell asleep again, and this time slept naturally for about an hour. On waking, she made Warren go over, again, everything she was told. There was a knock at the door. Hamilton and Marshal were there, Ham on crutches and in hospital garb, Marshal in uniform.

"My uncle says that the best damn things my mother ever did were to marry an Italian American and then make sure I could speak Arabic," Hamilton laughed

"I'm sure your mother was pleased to hear that."

"She was, once she got finished boxing my ears for taking such chances. She has constantly been praying to Allah to look after you."

"Well, thank her, according to the doctors Allah is. This is Warren Bradshaw, my boyfriend, just in case you guys haven't met."

"We introduced ourselves a couple of days ago."

"Ten-hut," came the loud command from the hall. Kimberly had not realized that there were people out there; she had a guard. Several people, including the Commander-in-Chief, entered the room.

"I heard you were awake, Kimberly. I just wanted to be sure that my favorite Navy Commander is alright."

"Too damn stubborn to die, Sir."

"Yes, they told me about you."

"Sir, Lieutenant Malvestuto and Petty Officer First Class Naji were my team on the ground there. They were fully engaged in the mission and likely responsible for getting me out alive, even though the Lieutenant was wounded."

"Yes, I was coming to visit both of you Lieutenant and Petty Officer, please convey the appreciation of the American people to your family for what they have done for us."

"I will, Sir. Thank you, and on their and Zahrat's behalf, may I thank you for assisting them getting rid of Abd al-Karim Bakr and the terrorists with him." The President smiled and nodded then looked at Warren, who was standing.

"Sir, this is my boyfriend, Warren Bradshaw. He's a civilian businessman."

"Pleased to meet you, Warren."

"Thank you, Mr. President."

"I realize that you're drugged up, Commander Callahan," POTUS said, "so I'm not expecting an answer. We'll have this conversation again when you've recovered. I know that Admiral Mann has been here. He and I have the same objectives. Those are that you're grounded and that you have four bars on your sleeve. He's not sure how quickly he can do the latter. I don't care about your rank. Grounded is a poor term. We want you active, but not at sea, and certainly not on dangerous raids. I want you at the White House on my National Security team. I have over a year left in my current term, and polls are saying that there will be four more. I need someone in the Situation Room with me who has your smarts, your experience, and the willingness to argue with me. Thank you for all you have done for this country."

The President and his entourage left. Kimberly heard what he said, but was having trouble processing it. If she had understood correctly, she might be even better able to avenge Layla's death. Kimberly later recalled Hamilton and Marshal saying good-bye. It occurred to her that if she were to be full time ashore and in Washington, Warren would be more accessible. She fell asleep.

Also by Robert T. Chambers and available through Amazon:

Hidden Wounds

Story Summary

Elizabeth Stephenson is a Captain of Canadian combat engineers sent to assist a 25th Marine Infantry Battalion to secure a town in Afghanistan. She is severely injured. After recovery, she goes to reserve status and becomes a civilian engineer. She meets an asocial, non-military, geek, civil engineer, Derrick Norman, with whom she starts a relationship. The story is of her battle with PTSD and her angst over reentry into civilian life. Derrick learns about the military and how to deal with Elizabeth's PTSD. Despite their attraction to each other, neither of them is sure they want the relationship or that it is even possible.

Sample:

Come dawn, at about 0500, they were still loading charges. The colonel was starting to wonder if the Canadians would make the 0800 target. He and the XO went to the Canadian command vehicle where a lieutenant told him that the captain's orders were very specific that the wall would blow at 0800. With radio silence Stephenson was unavailable. Dawson was told that she was up in the tunnel.

"How are you blowing the charges?" he asked the lieutenant.

"We're running measured lengths of fuse back from the charges. Burning a meter takes two minutes. With five-meter fuses, the captain can get back from the end of the fuses in ten minutes so at 0750 Captain Stephenson will light the fuses and come back."

From Harrison's body language Dawson believed that his XO thought the Canadian commander was crazy. For the first-time Dawson was inclined to share his viewpoint. However, if it got the job done, it was better than being stalled here with his men slowly being picked off.

Slowly the sun rose in the sky. They could hear the Taliban moving back up to the wall. The weapons company unleashed a round of mortars high into the air landing inside the wall. It was a pattern that they had developed before the Canadians arrived as they tried to disrupt the Taliban's return to the wall each morning. That morning, between mortar rounds, the sense was that the noise level of the Taliban was greater and different. It sounded as though some tracked vehicles were moving up. That was new, and nothing from intelligence had even suggested such weapons were in the town.

Two minutes before eight a tank came around the north side of the wall and headed for them. That was new. If the Canadian lieutenant had been correct, the fuses were lit. Dawson ordered mortar fire to kill the tank. The distance was too short for the correct deflection. A shot on target was not possible, the round missed. For some reason, the tank stopped. The colonel guessed that the Taliban tank commander had no clue about fighting tanks. It was an old T-62 tank. The Russians had used them during their excursion into Afghanistan in the early eighties. The tank started rather slowly and inaccurately firing its 115-mm big gun at them. More importantly their 7.72 mm machine guns were raking the berm. A second mortar shot also went well over the tank for the same reasons the first missed. With horror, the colonel realized that there was a depression immediately behind the tank. He thought that the depression was near the Canadian tunnel. Their tunnel support system did not support a forty-one-ton tank. Using binoculars, he could see a soldier down in the depression working with a trenching tool on the town side of the tunnel. The soldier was too close to the tank, well within the killing area of the mortars. The colonel ordered the mortars to stop firing and the machine gunners to direct their fire along the top of the wall to keep the Taliban down.

The XO was counting down the seconds to 0800. He reached 0800 and continued to count. The Canadian soldier was free of the depression but receiving fire from the Taliban. It was a short distance from the depression to the back of the tank. The soldier climbed onto the engine compartment. At least twice the colonel thought he saw the soldier get hit. He had no clue what was being attempted then recalled that the tank had an ejection port at the back of the turret that opened to the outside. A Sargent reported that another T-62 had appeared at the south side of the wall. The colonel had the thought that battle plans almost always went awry in some manner. Ten seconds after 0800 the wall blew taking the south tank with it. A couple of seconds later the tank on the north side blew up. He had seen the Canadian soldier get off the engine compartment but get blown back from the tank. Immediately dust obscured everything. The Marines were moving rapidly toward the dust cloud and the town. There was no opposition. These Canadians believed their "Live, Fight and Move." He suspected that the soldier was no longer alive but had fought, and his Marines were moving. He hoped his guess as to the identity of the Canadian was wrong as he yelled to have a corpsman check the Canadian soldier.

Robert T. Chambers is a Trauma Surgeon who is retired and living in west-central Minnesota. His family has many strong women dating back to the Isle of Skye in the nineteenth century and likely before. As he watched the culture change, he became interested in writing about women warriors.